BOUND TO BE

# Tempted

Emergence, Book Four

## BECCA JAMESON

Bound to be Tempted
Copyright © 2017 by Becca Jameson
Print Edition

eBook ISBN: 978-1-946911-23-0
print ISBN: 978-1-946911-24-7

Cover Artist: Scott Carpenter
Editor: Christa Desir

# ACKNOWLEDGEMENTS

As usual, I want to thank my editor Christa for all her hard work on this series! We've come a long way since this project began, and I'm so much more educated on so many subjects thanks to Christa. Who's ever met an editor who cut sex scenes? Is there such a thing as too much sex? Apparently. And I've mastered the notion…

# ABOUT THE BOOK

**_Bound to be Tempted_ is a rerelease of the fourth book in the Emergence series.**

The Emergence series follows the lives of several men as they meet the women of their dreams and forge Dominant/submissive relationships. Each book takes the starring characters down their respective paths of self-awareness and discovery. The first two books feature the same three characters as they form a bond between two men and one woman. The last two books cover the lives of two other submissive women as they acquaint themselves with their true paths and the men who will partner with them for life.

_Bound to be Tempted_ (Emergence, Book Four)

_If they let the past control them...the future will never take hold._

In the six months since Margaret Donovan broke up with her girlfriend, she has prowled Emergence, hoping to find a Dom to help her explore her bisexuality. The only man who's caught her interest in all that time is the bouncer.

He's a firm Dom, and after all, it's just a trial run. An experiment. He doesn't need to know the details of the troubled past that makes her long to get over her aversion to being under anyone's thumb.

Carlton Fisher's keen eye has been tracking Maggie, as well. She looks exactly like the childhood sweetheart who's haunted him for over a decade, but she doesn't need to know that. Two weeks' instruction should get her over her hump, give her the confidence she needs to work with a Dom...and get her out of his system.

Neither is prepared for the floodtide of explosive emotions. It's cathartic and therapeutic, but if they can't purge themselves of the pain of the past, their hearts could suffer irreparable damage.

# Chapter One

"**W**HEN ARE YOU going to talk to her?"

Carlton yanked his gaze from the model-perfect body he'd been ogling and turned toward his boss, Jason Garwood. "Talk to who about what?" He straightened his shoulders and resumed his usual stance as the front-door man Jason could count on.

Jason smirked. "That's how you want to play it?"

"I don't know what you're talking about." Carlton pretended to look around Jason. After all, his job was to ensure everyone in the club played by the rules, safe and consensual.

"Fine. When are you going to talk to Margaret about your feelings for her?"

"Maggie?" Carlton flinched. He hated his reaction, but he couldn't stop it.

"Do you know another Margaret? Yes, Margaret. Margaret Donovan. The only Margaret we know." Jason chuckled now. "Come on, man. You're killing yourself, and frankly you aren't at the top of your game lately. If you don't talk to her soon, I will."

Carlton yanked his gaze back to Jason. "You wouldn't dare. Stay out of it. She's been through a lot. She's hurting. I'm just keeping an eye on her, especially when Lori and Jude are here. I know she says she's fine, but watching them together has to hurt."

"It's been six months since she broke up with Lori. She comes here nearly every week. She's happier than I've ever seen her. The only thing she lacks is a Dom."

Carlton's mouth opened. He closed it to consider his words carefully. Just because he found Maggie attractive and intriguing didn't mean he wanted her to submit to him. He was simply worried about her. "A Dom? Or a Domme?" Carlton crudely grabbed his crotch as he said the word Dom and then rounded his hands in front of his chest as he said the word Domme.

Jason rolled his eyes. "So what if she's been with women in the past. It doesn't mean she's a lesbian. I'm not convinced she doesn't do guys also. If you don't make your move soon, she'll stop waiting and take one of these other guys up on the numerous offers they toss at her feet."

At that pronouncement, Carlton stiffened. He fisted his hands at his sides and glared at Jason, angry with himself for letting his boss and best friend of ten years get to him. "Who's making offers to Maggie?"

"Ah, so you *do* care." Jason chuckled. He slapped Carlton on the shoulder. "Listen, I'm not saying she needs specifically a man or a woman to dominate her. I think she's attracted to both. I'm just suggesting that I've seen changes in her lately. I have no doubt she has baggage neither of us can imagine.

"No matter how you look at it, Margaret is a submissive, and she needs a firm Dom to help her through, a man or a woman. But if you wait much longer to claim her, someone else will. I've seen how you look at her, Carlton."

Carlton lowered his voice and his gaze. "Of course I look at her. Everyone does. She's gorgeous. And she's vulnerable." A small shiver raced down his spine as he pictured her perfect body, her sexy smile, the way she tossed her hair back. Visions of her had haunted him since the first time he'd set his eyes on her over a year ago. Every time he saw her, she brought forth old emotions that had lain dormant in him for over a decade.

That didn't mean he wanted to take her on or become her Dom. He was only reacting to the eerie similarities between her and the first woman he'd ever been in love with. It didn't mean anything. Karen had been the love of his life. He would never love another woman like he had her. He knew he guarded his heart against all other women, but he didn't care. As far as he was concerned, the saying was all wrong: it was indeed better to have simply lost than to have loved and lost.

"Yeah, but no one looks at her the way you do. I'm not talking about leering in her direction in awe of her beauty. I'm talking about that deep, penetrating stare you bore into her until she shivers and glances around, wondering what caused the breeze."

Carlton swallowed. He rolled his eyes and lifted his gaze to Jason. For all that Jason insisted Maggie needed a Dom, Carlton wasn't wholly convinced Maggie went both ways. He'd never seen her with a man. "I don't stare at her." He knew he was lying as the words left his mouth. He couldn't *not* stare at her. And his reasons were far more unsettling than anyone would ever know. But it was an easy secret to keep. No one needed to know that his reasons for nailing her with his gaze had nothing to do with lust for her personally and everything to do with who she reminded him of. She was a looker. He wasn't kidding when he said that everyone stared at her. "I watch everyone in this club. It's my job. I keep an eye on all the women who come to Emergence, not just Maggie, especially the ones who aren't currently with a Dom. They're more vulnerable. I want to make sure they're safe." All of that was true.

Jason grabbed Carlton's biceps and squeezed. "I know you do. That's why you're the best man to work my front door. And I appreciate how astute you are. You can read the patrons like the back of your hand and tell when something's going the wrong direction before it happens. I've mentioned this before, and I'll say it again. Never leave me. I need you.

"However, stop kidding yourself about Margaret. Go for it. If you need my permission, you have it. I don't want to see you silently moping around any longer. What's the worst thing that can happen?"

"I'm not looking for a permanent submissive, boss. And what makes you so sure Maggie is into men?"

Jason rolled his eyes. "Lori told me once months ago that Margaret has always been interested in men."

Carlton stared at his boss, not sure he believed what Jason was telling him. "I've never seen her with a man."

"Neither have I, but that doesn't mean she isn't interested." Jason smirked and walked away as he finished. He didn't turn back toward Carlton. He stuffed his hands in his pockets and ambled through the crowd, making small talk and checking on the customers.

*What's the worst thing that can happen?* The words rang over and over in his head as he watched his boss's retreating back.

The answer was easy. But there was no way he would give voice to it.

Carlton couldn't possibly take on any sub, let alone this one. No matter how attracted he was to her, he wouldn't let himself fall for her. He'd been there, done that. It had been years since he'd let a woman into his heart, but no amount of time would erase the pain. He never wanted to feel that kind of deep hurt again. And to avoid such a thing, he would forever guard his heart against a woman.

Even this one.

Even this sexy, gorgeous submissive who made his cock twitch every time she entered the room. Even though she was no longer with Lori. Even though she was available. Even though he could see through her façade to the dormant hurt that lay deep in her eyes from some unknown pain she harbored. She was still a woman. And Carlton wasn't about to trade one hurt for another. Because that's how it would end if he let himself feel for her.

Carlton groaned. He nodded at the man who came to relieve him of front-door duty so he could take a break. He headed to the door on the back wall that led to the employee area. It would be quieter as soon as the door snicked shut. He could find a place to relax and close his eyes for a few minutes.

At least that's what he intended to do. But then he noticed Maggie leaning her hip against the corner of a wall, watching a scene. He lifted his gaze to find Lori and Jude were the subjects attracting so much attention.

Carlton moaned inwardly and slumped his shoulders. Why did Maggie torture herself by watching her ex with the man who had returned from the dead to re-stake his claim?

Instead of heading to the quiet of the back room, Carlton inched closer to Maggie, watching her reactions as they spread across her face and paying no attention to the scene itself.

God, she was beautiful. The way she stood there, tall and sure, belied several other physical characteristics only a keen eye would notice. Her eyes were wider than necessary, her breaths shallow. Her bottom lip was tucked between her teeth on one side. And she gripped the corner of the wall so hard her knuckles were white.

She stood around the corner enough that Jude wouldn't specifically notice her. Lori was blindfolded, so there was no way she would see Maggie. And besides, all of Jude's attention was directed toward his sub, as it should be.

Lori stood at a St. Andrew's cross with her back to the crowd. She gripped the rope loops above her head with her fists, but she wasn't strapped down for the scene. Jude had already flogged her several times, judging by the number of pink lines across her upper back and ass. Jude set his finger on one of the welts and traced the line across Lori's butt and down to where it met her thigh.

Maggie flinched, drawing Carlton's attention back to her. Did she empathize with the pain Lori was feeling, remembering similar situations she'd been in when the roles had been completely different?

Carlton narrowed his gaze. He stood only feet from Maggie now. But Maggie's attention was so intent on the scene that she didn't notice him. He swore he heard a low moan escape her lips as Jude traced another line.

Perhaps it wasn't Lori whom Maggie was paying attention to…

# Chapter Two

MARGARET WATCHED, MESMERIZED by the way Jude stroked Lori's skin. Her pussy tightened as she imagined what it would be like to have a man pay that level of attention to her own body. As Jude's fingers grew closer to Lori's spread thighs, moisture leaked between Margaret's legs.

She'd been watching scenes like this one with every sort of Dom at Emergence for months now, pondering what it would be like to submit to a man. And she fully intended to do something about that. She just needed to find the right Dom and ask him to do a scene with her.

Suddenly, she flinched when a low voice reached her ear from much closer than she'd realized anyone stood. "Do you miss her?" Carlton's question took her by surprise.

She turned toward him, flattening herself against the wall around the corner from Lori and Jude. She met Carlton's gaze. "No. She's with the right man. She was meant to be with Jude."

"You didn't answer my question." He narrowed his gaze and stepped closer.

Margaret shrugged. "There's no right answer to that question. I'm gonna plead the Fifth." She tried to smile at him, knowing it was forced.

Another man stepped up next to Carlton. She'd seen him several times at Emergence, but she didn't know his name. He was relatively new at the club. At first, she assumed he was about to address Carlton about some issue. After all, Carlton was in charge of all things happening inside Emergence.

But then she realized he was looking directly at her. Only after he reached her side did he glance at Carlton and nod. His gaze returned to Margaret's. "Hey. I'm Steve. I've seen you here almost every time I've been here. You're never with anyone. I'm relatively new to the lifestyle, but I've been working with a sponsor. I was wondering if you'd like to do a scene?"

Margaret flattened herself closer to the wall. *Here's your chance. Take him up on the offer.*

She licked her lips, trying to ignore the glare coming from Carlton, and nodded. "I'd like that. I'm rusty. It would need to be something less intense." She smiled as she angled her chin in a gesture toward Lori and Jude.

Steve smiled. "No problem."

Margaret righted herself from the wall, but Carlton interrupted. "You do men?"

She gave him a sharp look, pursing her lips and narrowing her eyes.

He looked immediately chagrined by the question that must have flown out of his mouth before he could rein it in. "Sorry," he muttered.

She spoke to him pointedly as she stepped around him. "I've been building up my courage to do a scene with a Dom for a while now. You know, someplace where I know I'll be safe." She furrowed her brow at him, emphasizing the word *safe*. Maybe he would take the hint, back off and also keep an eye on her.

She was uncertain about Steve, but at the moment she felt the intense urge to take a leap. What did she have to lose? Steve seemed confident enough. Carlton would be close by. She'd be fine.

Steve lifted a hand and Margaret took it, brushing past a rather immobile Carlton. Was he truly that shocked?

Of course, to be honest, she was a little shocked herself. But she knew it was time. And this particular Dom seemed like the perfect opportunity to give it a try. It wasn't as though she was going to publicly fuck the man. She just wanted to know what it would feel like to have a man's hands on her.

Steve set a hand on the small of her back as he led her to an open alcove where no one was currently doing a scene. He lifted the schedule on the wall and then turned to her. "This space is open. Are you good with this?"

Margaret looked around him at the bench in the center and nodded. She could probably do a spanking scene. Low risk. And she could feel Carlton's eyes boring into her from behind. She was certainly safe.

Margaret lowered her gaze and took a deep breath. She needed to concentrate on remaining calm. *It's just a scene. You've done hundreds.*

Steve led her to the bench, still holding her fingers with

his. He helped her get situated across the top, her knees and elbows on the padded sections below her. She turned her face to one side and inhaled long and slow.

Steve kneeled at her side so his face was level with hers. "What's your name?" He brushed a lock of hair from her cheek, his touch tender and soothing.

"Margaret."

"Good. So, Margaret, do you usually sub for women?"

"Yes." *Shit.* He must have heard Carlton's stupid question.

"But you're okay with this?"

She nodded, as much as she could with her cheek to the side. "Yes, Sir."

"Would you like me to strap you down or keep your hands and legs free?"

"Free, Sir. If you don't mind."

He nodded. "Okay. Red okay for a safe word?"

"Yes, Sir. Red."

"I'll start out gentle." Steve stood and set his palm on her shoulder, kneading the tight muscle there perfectly. He switched to the other shoulder next, carefully stroking his fingers along her upper back so she never experienced a moment without his contact. There were no surprises initially that way. And Margaret was grateful.

Eventually, Steve released the naked skin of her shoulders above the tight bustier she wore and caressed down her back, carefully touching the exposed areas between the laces that held her top on. When he reached her butt, he circled behind her and smoothed both hands up her thighs, lifting her loose, short skirt until he squeezed her cheeks and flipped the material out of the way onto her lower back. She was left with nothing but her thin black thong covering the most intimate of her parts.

The exposure didn't bother Margaret. She'd been nearly naked on many occasions under Lori's command. But Steve's touch was different, firmer, broader. She closed her eyes and concentrated on the feeling.

"I'm going to spank you now, Margaret. Are you still okay?"

"Yes." The word came out on a breath, barely audible. It had been so long since anyone topped her. She needed the release so badly it almost didn't matter at whose hands she was submitting.

The first slap was quick, but not so hard as to make her nervous. It stung. She knew there would be a pink area on her left cheek, but she'd been spanked harder.

Another swat to the other cheek helped her relax into the role. Steve was astute enough to realize she suffered from nerves. He kept one hand on her lower back, grounding her. And he leaned down to her ear to whisper, "Still okay?"

"Yes, Sir."

"Good." He tucked another lock of hair behind her ear and caressed her cheek. "Use the word *yellow* if I go too fast."

"Yes, Sir." He wasn't too fast at all. In fact, she longed for more than he was giving her. But she wouldn't ask for it. The idea shocked her and scared her at the same time.

Steve firmed his hold on her back and spanked her two more times at the juncture of her thighs and ass.

She flinched, a natural reflex, nothing more. Warmth spread up her back and down her thighs. It felt good.

"Your ass is so sexy like this, all pink." Steve rubbed the skin with his palms, his thumbs grazing the undersides of her cheeks, making her stiffen as they got closer to her sex. She wasn't ready for more than the spanking tonight. Sex was the farthest thing from her mind. It would take an entirely different level of subspace for her to submit sexually to a man.

Steve must have read the signs, because he backed off and resumed swatting her just enough to make her fully aware of his contact, but not enough to inflict any real pain.

Perfect.

Just what she needed for her first foray with a man. He wasn't the firmest Dom, but he was educated enough to recognize her needs, especially her hesitation. And for that she was grateful.

Steve stroked her warm skin for several minutes, loosening his touch until he lowered her skirt over her butt and then rounded to face her again. "You okay?"

"I'm good. Thank you, Sir."

"Thank *you*. I enjoyed our time." He helped her off the bench and settled her on her feet, still holding her hand.

She wasn't so deep into subspace that she couldn't manage on her own.

"Perhaps we could do it again sometime?"

"Maybe." She smiled at him, not wanting to commit to anything right then. She nodded toward the bar. "I'm going to get some water. Thanks again."

"No problem." Steve released her fingers as she walked away.

As soon as she stepped out of the alcove, she practically ran right into Carlton.

He grabbed her shoulders to steady her.

"Geez. Did you stand there the entire time?" she asked. Her heart rate accelerated as his enormous presence surrounded her, nothing at all like Steve's gentle, easygoing manner.

"I did." His look was wary, his eyes narrowed. "I wanted to be sure you were safe."

"I'm fine." She smoothed her hands down her skirt, shaking a bit from the endorphins.

Carlton leaned back, still holding her shoulders, and glanced up and down her frame. "You need a firmer Dom."

"Really? And you're an expert on this?" She planted her hands on her hips, trying to keep from shaking and hold her own against Carlton's high-handedness.

He nodded. "Yes. I see what you're doing. You just got your feet wet. Dipped your toes in the water. That guy wasn't strong enough for you."

"I'll keep that in mind." She rolled her eyes and squirmed to get out of his clutches. He was potent and distracting her to the core. She rationalized it was probably because she'd so recently come out of a scene, but she needed some distance from this suddenly overbearing Carlton who'd gotten in her face twice tonight.

She wiggled free and ducked out of his hands to head for the bar, leaving him standing there.

She could feel his stare penetrating her backside, and

she had the urge to smooth her skirt down again and ensure it truly covered her ass. Even though Carlton had seen every inch of her skin in the past, he hadn't ever been the Dom to control it.

Why did it feel like he'd topped her with his gaze alone?

✧   ✧   ✧

CARLTON WIPED HIS PALMS on his jeans as he stepped into the nave of St. Vincent's Cathedral. He made his way to the left side and took a seat on the back row as he'd done so many times over the years.

There were only a half-dozen people inside the church this afternoon. No one paid any attention to him. It was what he preferred. The anonymity was what allowed him to keep coming.

He'd never attended a service. In fact he wasn't even Catholic, but that wasn't why he came.

Karen had been Catholic. She'd gone to church every Saturday night with her parents. She'd insisted it was peaceful.

Carlton had laughed at her at the time. Karen hadn't ever been a peaceful sort of woman. She'd always been running at full speed. The idea that she took an hour a week to relax and reboot had made him chuckle. But it was serious for her. And he'd respected that.

Since her death, he'd felt the urge to come on her behalf, light a candle in her memory, sit and attempt to absorb the peace the church had given her.

Carlton had chosen St. Vincent's for its size. It looked

like the church Karen had attended years ago in their hometown. He'd never been inside that one, but he assumed they were all similar.

The crazy thing was it brought Carlton some level of peace. He felt closer to Karen when he was inside a space she had loved. He sort of spoke to her in his mind.

He closed his eyes and pictured her giant smile, her eyes wide with mirth, her belly laughter. She'd been bigger than life, too much for this world.

What would she think of the choices he'd made since she'd left him alone on this earth, extinguishing the tinkle of her voice for all time? Would she be proud of his decisions? He doubted it. If she could see him now, she would probably admonish him for remaining so aloof for twelve years. She would have wanted him to move on and be happy. She couldn't have known how deeply he felt about her, still did.

He wasn't a hermit. He'd gone out with several women over the years. He'd had many different submissives under him at Emergence. But none had been long-term. None had made his heart pound like the memory of Karen did. And it had been a long time since he'd brought someone to his home.

And now Maggie had stepped into his life.

Carlton didn't trust his feelings for Maggie. She was the spitting image of what he imagined Karen would have looked like had she lived to be twenty-seven. It wasn't Maggie's fault, and she didn't know anything about his demons, but every time Carlton saw her, it gave him pause. He'd known her for a long time, and every time he saw her, he did a double take.

Did he want to Dom for her? Fuck yes, he did. He wanted to bring her to her knees in front of him and watch her eyes glaze over with need while he made her squirm. But he never had relationships that were more than casual with any woman for a reason. He never wanted to hurt like he still did for Karen.

And Carlton knew instinctively if he took Maggie as a submissive, it wouldn't be casual. She made his dick pulse and his heart pulse harder. As much as he wished he could Dom for her, and perhaps in doing so purge himself of his demons, he feared the opposite would occur, and he would instead be lured into her web.

He was chicken. He admitted it, if only to himself. Jason had made him think about something he'd never considered. Did Maggie need him? He couldn't stand the thought of her submitting to another Dom in order to get her feet wet. When he'd watched her submit to Steve the other night, he'd gritted his teeth. It had nothing to do with his feelings toward her. Hell, he cared about her. She was a friend. He'd known her for over a year. If she wanted to experiment with male Doms, he didn't want to see her hurt.

She'd never once come on to him in any way that would make him question her motives. But the woman needed a firm Dom. Not a newbie. Not a dabbler. She needed more, and Carlton knew he could be the man for that job.

But could he guard his heart in the meantime?

Jason had insinuated he was into her. Carlton knew

better. He was into Karen. And Maggie looked like Karen. Was she as wild and risky and carefree as Karen? He didn't know yet. If Jason was right, Carlton was in trouble. What if he couldn't separate his feelings for a long-dead girlfriend from his longing for Maggie? She wasn't a substitute. It would be cruel to use her in that way.

Carlton stared at the ornate, carved depiction of Christ hanging at the front of the church. He took a deep breath and pushed himself to standing as though his body weighed a ton. He made his way to the left wall, staring at the dozen or so candles burning already. Other people had come throughout the day and lit a candle for another loved one. He would join them as he always did, adding his flame to the rows of flickering orange light in hopes that he would feel one-tenth of the peace Karen had always professed.

# Chapter Three

THE NEXT FRIDAY NIGHT, Margaret entered Emergence wearing her favorite outfit, a short black leather skirt that barely covered her ass and a red bustier that laced up in the back, leaving plenty of pale skin visible. It was her favorite because it made her feel sexy. The compliments she received when she wore it, and the sideways glances from both men and women, never hurt either.

The clothes gave her confidence that warred with her emotions. She had thought about last Friday repeatedly during the week, both the scene with Steve and her reaction to Carlton. The doorman had undoubtedly just been looking out for her safety, like he'd said, but what if it was more?

It was late when she arrived. The club was full. She barely nodded at Carlton as she passed him in the entrance. He was busy helping a couple of women fill out release forms. Did his gaze land on her longer than usual? She shivered. Surely she was imagining things.

She wove through the throng of people and made her way to the bar, where she grabbed a bottle of water and turned around to survey the landscape. This section of the club near the bar was the only section where the noise level was so high. In the rooms lining the hall, people were respectfully quiet as scenes played out.

A tap on her shoulder had her spinning to the left.

A man she'd seen a few times in the past let his gaze roam up and down her body before coming to rest on her face. "Are you topping or bottoming tonight?"

She smiled. "Neither." She knew she appeared neutral in tonight's outfit. She could go either way. But this man didn't know her well enough to realize she was never a top.

"Care to dance?" He either misunderstood her answer or chose to ignore it.

"No. Thanks. I'm just going to mill around for a while." She pasted a fake smile on.

The man nodded and wandered away. Margaret exhaled, unaware she'd been holding her breath. *What did you expect to happen? Just because a man asks you to dance doesn't mean he won't take no for an answer. Geez.*

Margaret gripped the water bottle with both hands. The condensation on the outside dripped onto her fingers, and she lifted first one hand and then the other to wipe her neck, cooling her heated skin marginally.

Even though she'd gotten brave last weekend and allowed a man to top her, it didn't mean she was ready to bottom for just any guy who approached. She knew she wanted to give another man a chance. Steve's touch had been titillating, awakening a longing inside her. And then Carlton's brooding looks had made her shiver.

Was it just her, or was the noise level unusually high?

In her candy-apple red stilettos, she lifted on tiptoe to see over the taller members of the crowd. She glanced around the room, searching for Jason Garwood, the owner. Any time she'd ever gotten freaked out at Emergence, she'd been able to count on him to bail her out, even if all she needed was a trip to the employee area behind the scenes to take a break.

She didn't see him. In fact, she didn't see Carlton anywhere either, and that man was impossible to miss. He was taller than most men she knew and broad enough to fill a doorframe.

Margaret worked her way through the crowd, hoping the area surrounding the dance floor was less busy. When she reached the edge, she found she was out of luck. Her spirits dampened. She felt an irritation creep up her neck.

Week after week she came to Emergence. It was a habit she'd developed as Lori's sub. They came here every Friday. It seemed lately Lori tended to come more often on Saturdays, but Margaret kept her schedule. Why? Before last Friday, she hadn't participated in any scenes in months. The few she'd enacted after breaking up with Lori had been purely cathartic. They kept her from losing herself entirely. And they'd been with women.

Margaret turned to head back to the front, but she ran into someone. "Sorry," she blurted, grabbing the man by the biceps to keep from toppling. It was the guy from earlier. At least it wasn't a total stranger.

"Change your mind?" He lifted one brow, but held on to her biceps with both hands also, not releasing her even though she was no longer in danger of falling on her ass.

"About what?" she asked.

"The dance? You seem to be looking for someone. I hope it's me." He smiled too wide and led her toward the floor as though he'd gotten the consent he needed.

"I…" She wanted to say she wasn't in the mood, that she hadn't been looking for him. But it seemed easier to just dance with him. She could give this man one dance and then beg off.

The second they hit the dance floor, she regretted the decision. Somehow she'd missed the fact that he was drunk when they'd spoken before. Alcohol wasn't permitted at Emergence, which meant he'd either drunk his fill before coming inside, or carried it in his pocket against policy. His breath reeked.

He leaned too close to her, wrapping his arms around her middle and hauling her against him until she couldn't avoid the cock pressed into her belly. When he spoke next, his breath gagged her. Bourbon? Undoubtedly straight. "You smell fantastic." He pressed his nose to her neck and inhaled, reminding her of a wolf.

Ironic he would choose those words when she'd been thinking the opposite about him. He smelled like stale cigarettes and foul body odor from too much sweating.

*One dance. Hold your breath.* Margaret tried to separate her body from the octopus who suddenly had more arms than the two God gave him.

When his hands landed on her ass and squeezed, she'd had enough. "Stop." She pressed against his chest to get him to release her. "You're drunk."

He held her tighter, his fingers kneading her ass, his

tongue landing on her neck.

"I said, *stop*," she shouted louder this time. Maybe he couldn't hear her over the noise and the music. "*Red*." At least if this asshole wouldn't listen, someone standing around would hear her use the universal safe word.

He ignored her. His body swayed, but he was off beat, and she feared he would fall over, taking her down with him.

"Dammit. Let go of me." Margaret pushed harder. When he didn't release her, she slapped him. That was it.

Two large hands reached around the bastard's shoulders and pulled him backward one second after the impact of her palm against his cheek. "I believe the lady asked you to release her." Carlton. Of course. Even though she hadn't been able to find him in the crowd, he was there. Nothing got by him. Thank God.

It took a moment for Carlton to sufficiently extricate Margaret from the drunk's clutches.

"Ah, man. What'd you go and do that for? I was dancing with the lady."

"The lady said no."

"She did?" He had trouble standing without swaying now. How had she not noticed his level of intoxication before? "I didn't hear her. She asked me to dance with her."

Margaret's mouth fell open. "I did no such thing."

Carlton turned the man away from her, keeping a tight grip on the asshole's shoulders and leading him toward the entrance. "Let's go, buddy. Alcohol isn't allowed inside Emergence, and you know it."

"I don't have any alcohol," the man protested.

"Yeah, well, drunks aren't permitted either. Next time come sober or don't come at all. I'll be watching you like a hawk." Carlton reached back with one hand and grasped Margaret's, possessively tugging her along behind.

She followed. He hadn't given her another option. With one strong grip on the drunk guy's shoulder and one tight clench of her small palm with his larger one, he maneuvered the three of them to the front.

When he reached his desk, he turned toward Margaret. "Wait here, Maggie."

She nodded, shivering at the way his nickname for her sounded as it slipped off his tongue. He'd called her Maggie from the first time she'd met him. No one else called her that. Not even her parents. But from Carlton, it just fit.

She watched as he led the drunk guy from the club. It took a few minutes to get him out the door. The man continued to protest his expulsion, arguing belligerently with Carlton as though he might possibly be able to win the larger man over with his slurred speech.

Margaret trembled again. She wasn't sure if it was from relief over her rescue from the clutches of the drunk guy or from watching Carlton in action. The man was solid as a rock, and when he spoke, people did as he said. He didn't take no for an answer. He wasn't one to be pushed over. Reasoning with him was a lost cause. Only a drunk would attempt it.

Margaret wondered how he would use that power behind closed doors. She bit her lip thinking about the intensity in his gaze as he leaned over a woman. She'd seen him in action in the club as a Dom more times than she could count. When he wasn't working and he did a scene with a sub, everyone in the vicinity stopped to watch. He could make any woman's panties wet just standing near him. Even hers.

Finally, Carlton said a few words to the man guarding the door on the outside and turned back to Margaret. He took her hand again. She glanced down at the way he threaded two of his fingers with hers, almost intimate, or perhaps a coincidence. Either way, her heart pounded. He'd never held her hand before. Now twice in one night.

Carlton leaned in to speak discreetly to another employee as he led her away from the front. The other man nodded, stood taller and took up a stance manning the entrance.

Without saying another word, Carlton led Margaret through the crowd until he reached the employees-only door that led to the private areas of the club. He tugged the door open with his free hand and ushered Margaret through in front of him with a nod of his head.

Margaret ducked under Carlton's arm where he held the door.

Still not releasing her hand, Carlton led her to the first office on the left, opened another door, and repeated the gentlemanly gesture until she was safely ensconced in his personal area.

She'd been in his office before, but never alone with him and never holding his hand, and never with her heart pounding so loud she thought he could surely hear it.

"Sit," he commanded in a voice gruffer than usual. He angled her toward a guest chair opposite his desk and didn't let go of her hand until her arm was stretched awkwardly away from her body as she settled in the seat. At that moment, he let go as though she'd burned him, muttering, "Sorry."

Margaret licked her lips. How had she so quickly managed to land herself in his office, the vulgar noises of the club that had grated on her nerves all evening cut off, leaving her with a faint ringing sound?

Carlton leaned his ass on the edge of his desk and crossed his ankles. She was so close to him that he grazed her ankle with his shoe on the way by. He narrowed his gaze as though assessing her for injury. "You okay?"

"Yes." She nodded.

"Why were you with that guy in the first place?"

Margaret gasped. "What? I wasn't with him. He manhandled me onto the dance floor."

Carlton stared hard at her for a second and then ducked his face and rubbed his temples with one hand. "Of course. I'm sorry. Didn't mean to snap at you. And I'm sorry I didn't see him quicker. It's too crowded out there tonight. We really need a limit." His brow remained furrowed when he lifted his head.

"I was fine. You were fast. I'm not sure how you saw me so quickly, actually."

He nodded, his gaze wandering from her face down to her chest, and then lower. Was he looking for bruises? It hadn't been that bad.

"You need a Dom," he stated as though it were the simplest solution to an imaginary problem.

"What?"

Carlton's gaze darted back to hers. So fierce. If she didn't know better, she'd think he was angry with her. "You've been hanging around here for months alone. You're an open target for predators. You're too sexy for your own good. You need a Dom," he emphasized again.

"What?" she repeated. She had no idea what he was getting at.

He rolled his eyes then, the furrow loosening slightly. "Maggie, you're fucking gorgeous." He waved his hand through the air toward her corset and then her skirt. "I know you tend to wear more than most unattached women in the club these days, but, baby, I can almost see your pussy under that skirt. And your breasts..." his hand paused midair in the vicinity of her chest, inches separating his fingers from her nipples, "...God, woman."

Margaret giggled. She couldn't stop herself. Carlton in his overbearing protective mode was almost comical.

"What are you laughing at? This is serious." He narrowed his gaze.

"What's serious, Carlton? The fact that I'm sexy or the fact that you can't control your tongue?"

His gaze snapped to meet hers again. He closed his mouth.

Margaret stood slowly. She stepped closer to him until she could feel his breath on her cheeks. Even leaning against the desk, he towered over her. She watched as his Adam's apple bobbed with his swallow. She had him tongue-tied. Now what was she going to do? "Did you want to volunteer?"

Carlton swallowed again. "Volunteer for what?" His

voice was hoarser than usual, deep, so fucking sexy she wanted him to keep talking.

"To be my Dom. You said I needed a Dom. Are you volunteering?" She lifted an eyebrow, proud of her ability to hold her ground. Inside, she was shaking fiercely. Her pussy was soaking wet from his proximity. She was aroused by everything about him—the way he gripped the edge of the desk on both sides of his body, the way his jaw ticked at her challenge, the way his eyes widened and his mouth opened to utter no response.

How had she never noticed her incredible attraction to him? Or maybe she had simply ignored it or written it off as a coincidence caused by his enormous size and his domineering mannerisms. In any case, she suddenly wanted him to be the first man to really dominate her. She needed the experience in a safe, sane, consensual environment. Carlton was all that and more. She knew him well enough to be sure he would handle her appropriately as she explored this hidden side of her she'd kept barricaded for her entire life.

Seconds ticked by. Margaret could hear his heart beating, or maybe it was hers. Perhaps both in sync. It seemed the temperature in the room rose with each passing moment. Her skin heated as a flush spread across her chest and up her cheeks.

She remained perfectly still, not letting her fingers fold into fists even though she desperately wanted to do just that. She forced herself to stand tall and keep her hands at her sides to avoid crossing them over her chest.

She waited, not letting her gaze fall from his. She waited while he stared at her in shock. She waited longer while he lifted both hands to her shoulders and wrapped his fingers around her bare skin.

"Yes," he stated.

Now it was Margaret's turn to blink in shock. Had he said yes?

# Chapter Four

CARLTON COULDN'T BELIEVE WHAT he was saying. He couldn't fathom how this had transpired so quickly. What was he agreeing to?

Sure, he'd been watching Maggie for months, but only from the side and not with any intention to act on it. After all, his reasons for noticing her in the first place were less than stellar. He knew the only reason he felt so strongly about her was because she so closely resembled Karen.

But Maggie needed him. If she was going to dabble in submitting to a man, she needed a much stronger Dom than any of the ones he'd seen ogling her in the last months. He could do this. Help her over this hump. Help her learn to enjoy a man's touch if she was so determined to experiment in that area. Help her learn to submit more fully in the safe environment he could only trust himself to provide.

And in so doing, she could help him extricate himself from the demon that plagued him every day of his life—Karen. Perhaps if he spent enough time with Maggie, he would heal, or at least stop the endless comparison.

Maggie was a very sexual being. She had always lit up under Lori's command. He'd watched her many times. She needed to learn she could experience the same sexual intensity, if not more so, with a man. And if she intended to experiment in that area, he didn't want her doing so with some random asshole.

Deep brown eyes widened under his stare. He smiled. "No wonder you haven't had a Dom. Do you meet every man's gaze like that?"

Maggie flinched, her eyes blinking a moment before she lowered them.

Carlton chuckled. "That's more like it. I shouldn't have to train you at everything, should I? You've been in this lifestyle for a long time. Hell, you've been coming here for over a year. Even when you've been unattached, you've been here nearly every week witnessing what it means to be submissive."

He released her shoulders reluctantly. What he wanted to do was dip his fingers under the edge of her bustier and graze her nipples. But it was too soon for that. If he didn't break contact with her skin, he would embarrass himself. "Sit."

She hesitated and then resumed her spot on the chair.

"Good girl. Now then. I know you challenged me just now, probably not expecting me to take the bait, but I meant what I said. I'd be honored if you'd let me work with you. Did you mean it, Maggie? I'll give you a moment to think and take it back if you acted in haste, but if you're serious, I need an answer."

"I meant it." Her voice was soft, delicate. She didn't

31

hesitate.

Carlton straddled her knees, the ones she currently had smashed together in a manner he would never ordinarily permit. But the woman was flustered. And it made his cock rock hard. He took her chin in one hand and lifted her face to his. "Come again?" he asked with one brow raised as though he hadn't heard her correctly.

She cleared her throat beneath his firm grip and licked her lips with that sexy tongue that he suddenly wanted wrapped around his cock. "I meant it," she repeated louder.

"I don't think I'm hearing you correctly." He waited.

Finally, her breach of etiquette dawned on her. "Oh. Shit." That tongue swiped her lower lip again, making Carlton fight to keep from moaning. "I meant it, Sir. I would be honored if you would dominate me, Sir. Just to clarify, though, are you referring to a scene for this evening, Sir? Or were you thinking of a longer arrangement?" She held his gaze.

He was proud of her. She was bold, and it humbled him the way she asked for what she wanted. He shook his head, not realizing the implication until he saw her face fall and her gaze lower. "Maggie. Look at me." He waited until her gaze returned to his. "I'm talking about a temporary arrangement that extends beyond one night. Two weeks is a good time frame. You need a safe place to experiment under a firm Dom's touch, and I'm offering that." *I can't offer anything more. I don't have it to give.*

Her mouth opened, but nothing came out.

Carlton smiled. "Is that what you want?"

"Yes, Sir." She shivered beneath his touch.

It took all his strength to release her again. "Stay here. I need to take care of a few things." He stepped back until he flattened himself against the door. "Will you be okay?"

"Yes, Sir." She lowered her gaze.

"I know it's been a while and you're rusty, but think about your position while I'm gone. Everything about your stance screams that either you've forgotten how to submit, you're nervous as all hell, or your previous Domme did a shitty job of instructing you. And I know that last choice isn't true. I'm going to go with number two. And that's a good thing. Nervous I can deal with. I can work with that." He grinned at her and turned to leave the room before he could change his mind, strip her naked and take her on his desk right then and there. This wasn't about fucking her. It was about helping her work through whatever issues she had with submitting to a man. He needed to get control of himself.

Oh, who was he kidding? He wanted to slide between Maggie's legs and make her scream his name. He longed to hear it from her lips. And he prayed he could take her, make her beg for it and still keep his distance from her emotionally. Because this arrangement was temporary. It had to be. To pretend otherwise was ludicrous. Carlton didn't have enough heart left to give Maggie what she needed permanently.

Carlton's entire body shook as he leaned against his office door and sucked in a breath. That woman's scent had already filled his working space to the point that he'd never be able to concentrate in his office again.

*Obsessed* would be the word he would have used to

describe his magnetic pull toward Maggie. The unavoidable memories she brought forth had weighed him down with their uncanny accuracy for more than a year. And here she was coming to him of her own accord, challenging him to dominate her. Risky move on her part. Like Karen. Risky. She took a chance. He accepted the challenge.

It took him several minutes to pull himself together enough to stand straight again and move from his spot. He was glad no one passed him in that time. He had no idea how he would have faced another soul. Even Jason.

Carlton groaned. *Jason.* He needed to hunt the man down. He needed a replacement for the rest of the night. There were plenty of employees around who could fill in for him. It wasn't as though Carlton ever took time off. He never did. That made it all the more easy to ask now. And all the more difficult. Jason wouldn't leave it at that. The man would question Carlton until he had the answers he desired. There was no sense in lying. It would all come out soon anyway.

Maggie was currently sitting in his office, waiting to submit to him. "Fuck me." He had never once expected anything like this to occur. He never would have had the balls to approach her. He didn't trust his reasons for ogling her so closely. *She's not Karen. No matter how similar they may seem. Don't forget Maggie is her own person.* The woman would be fucking pissed if she found out about his strange fetish for her and the reasons behind his desire to dominate her. He never wanted her to know that he likened her to his first love.

Didn't matter. She would never find out. No one knew

about Karen. Not even Jason. And Carlton intended to keep it that way. Carlton needed to compartmentalize his emotions and step up to the plate here. Maggie needed a Dom. He was the man for the job. That was it.

He shook the image of his high school sweetheart from his mind, shoved off the door to his office and trudged down the hall in search of his boss. He could already visualize the "I told you so" look he would get from Jason.

Pushing through the door to the club, he didn't have to search long. He was taller than nearly everyone. It made his job easier. That and he had a good sense about people. Rarely did he misjudge anyone. He could kick himself for not noticing that asshole earlier had been drunk when the guy came in tonight, or maybe Carlton should thank the bastard.

Carlton wound his way through the crowd to get back to the front entrance. He spoke to the man he'd left covering the door and asked him to finish out the night in that capacity. It wasn't unusual. The man nodded his assent and returned to the conversation he was having with someone who'd just entered.

Carlton shook his head. The club was private. Only members and their guests were allowed. Several lists were kept at the front door at all times with the names of members, regular guests of members and guests for this evening only. Anyone else could argue until they were blue in the face. It would do them no good.

"Carlton." Jason's voice came from behind as Carlton spun around to face his boss.

"I was looking for you." He didn't give the owner a

chance to say whatever he'd intended. "I need the rest of the night off."

Jason raised an eyebrow. "Really? Are you okay?" He looked up and down Carlton's frame as though he might spot an open wound or a broken bone. Anything less than that would not give Carlton cause to leave work.

"Of course. I'm fine. I've never been sick a day in my life."

Jason smiled. "True. At least not in the ten years I've known you. So, you're going to do a scene? Who's the lucky lady?"

"You know her well. And she's in my office. And I would appreciate it if you didn't tease her or say anything about this to anyone until we've hashed out an agreement and ensured we're suitable for each other."

Jason narrowed his gaze. "So not just a scene. You have someone you intend to proposition for more than tonight?" His eyes widened. "Margaret?" he whispered. He glanced both ways to make sure no one was listening, took Carlton by the arm and led him to a corner near the entrance. "You asked her?"

Carlton scrunched his face, knowing his expression would cause more questions than answers. "I'm not sure she would see it that way, but in a manner of speaking, yes. And stop looking at me like that. This is purely a business arrangement. She needs a firm Dom to help her relax under the commands of a man, and I don't want to see her get hurt working out whatever issues she has with someone else."

"I'm not even going to go there right now." Jason

chuckled. "Good for you." Straightening his face to a serious expression, he continued, "Be careful. I know you. You're a fantastic Dom. Make sure she's ready. I'm not saying you aren't right for her. I think you're the best man for the job. But please, don't hurt her. She's...vulnerable."

"I know. And I'll do my best to ensure she is safe, sane and consenting, boss. You know I will."

"Of course." Jason nodded. "Well, get out of here. Don't leave the lady waiting." He shoved Carlton away as though unaware Carlton outweighed him by nearly double.

✧   ✧   ✧

MARGARET SAT RIGID in the spot Carlton had left her. She didn't dare move for fear she would either bolt for the door or trip over her own feet and embarrass herself.

What the hell had she consented to? Now that she had exactly what she wanted, she didn't know what to do with it.

She hadn't considered him agreeing when she'd tossed the proposition his way. Sure, she'd love to do a scene or two with him, but submit to him beyond tonight, for two weeks? She wasn't sure why she was so nervous about the concept. Except that Carlton made her panties wet and her sex quiver more than any man ever had.

If she didn't guard her heart against him while he worked with her, she would get hurt. She couldn't fall for the first man she let past her defenses. The last thing she wanted was another broken heart. Breaking up with Lori was still fresh on her mind. Even though it had been months, she needed to take things slowly.

*Be careful what you ask for…*

Margaret gripped her knees with her hands, in part to keep them from bouncing, and in part to ground her. She feared if she let go, she might somehow float off the chair and hover in the room. This evening's events were surreal.

What would Carlton request of her? She breathed heavier as she pondered the options. He might take things slow. After all, she hadn't been with anyone for months. She was rusty. He'd already acknowledged that. She hadn't been with a man ever. And he didn't know that. She certainly had no intention of telling him either. The last thing she wanted was for him to look at her differently. She had plenty of sexual experience—just none involving actual, living human cock.

Not only did she want to submit to Carlton, but she also wanted to take a giant leap of faith and fuck him senseless. She hoped he would do more than dominate her outside the bedroom. She wanted the full experience.

She flinched. *Too late to back out now, girl. Pull up your panties and take whatever the man offers.* The thought of seeing Carlton's length, holding it in her hands, tasting it…all those things gave her the chills. She was both scared and excited at the same time. Part of her felt like a virginal teenager. In a sense, it wasn't far from the truth.

She'd hold on to that little secret for as long as possible.

Her mind returned to this evening's possibilities. Baring herself in public was no challenge. Lori had expected it of her often. She was used to that aspect of the D/s relationship. She was confident about her body and uninhibited to a certain extent.

There was always the chance he would invite her to his house, or demand it. He might even insist she stay with him while he worked with her. Was she ready for that? She'd just moved a few months ago into a smaller apartment after splitting with Lori. It wasn't much, but it was hers.

Maybe Carlton would want to come back to her place. She shook that idea away quickly. It was doubtful. The man was an established Dom. He would have equipment at his place. She had nothing. Would he be a kind, loving Dom? She knew the answer to that before the thought finished forming in her head. She expected firm, but not out of anger.

He wouldn't tolerate half what Lori had permitted. Of that she was confident. Her pussy tightened at the idea. She stifled a moan at the realization she was looking forward to his firm hand.

Margaret's life demanded so much of her that she relished the idea of relinquishing the reins to another person when she wasn't "on".

As an accountant, she worked hard all day with clients. She managed their finances. They relied on her to keep her head in the game and pay close attention to their transactions. The stress was ever-present in her mind. She never wanted to let anyone down.

The added stress of staying strong in light of her past and dealing with her parents weighed heavily also. She wore a mask every day to hide her inner turmoil concerning those two subjects. She'd been through more than any one woman should be forced to handle in her life. It had left her tarnished in ways she knew weren't normal. But she had a deep inner strength and she would prevail.

She exhaled and relaxed marginally when she considered how awesome it would be to let Carlton control her outside of those three life issues. It would keep her sane, or at least steer her toward sanity. A break from the real world.

She trusted him.

Living with Lori had done a fine job of masking her pain for the time they'd been together, but Lori hadn't been a firm Domme. She'd allowed Margaret more freedoms than perhaps Margaret would have preferred in hindsight. Not shocking, since it turned out Lori made a much better sub than a Domme.

Carlton would never be that lenient. She was certain. She was looking forward to it.

The door opened, jarring her from her thoughts and making her flinch. She lifted her gaze to the man she intended to submit to. He shut the door behind him with a snick that reverberated in the room and signified the beginning of a new chapter for Margaret.

Carlton rounded his desk and sat opposite her. She was surprised by his actions and thought for a moment he might have had a change of heart in his absence. His face gave nothing away.

However, when he steepled his hands and met her gaze over the top of the desk, he smirked. "You're going to be a tough nut to crack, aren't you?"

Perhaps he could read her better than she thought. "I hope not, Sir. It's not my intention." She jerked her gaze to her lap when she realized her infraction. That brought her attention to her thighs, glued together at the knee. *Okay, so maybe I'm a little out of practice. Nothing I can't handle.*

"You still in this?"

"Yes, Sir."

"No change of heart?"

"No, Sir. I want this." She squeezed her thighs with both hands, feeling the sting of her nails where they dug into her skin. She was nervous. There was no hiding it. But titillated at the same time in a way she hadn't felt for months, or perhaps ever. She had no doubt about this decision.

"I'm a very controlling Dom, Maggie. You need to know I'm demanding. I expect a certain level of perfection you aren't used to." He paused. "Judging by the tremble wracking your body, I assume you crave what I'm offering. You're tempted." Seconds ticked by. "Tell me, Maggie. Is your pussy as wet as I'm imagining?"

She flinched. He wasn't going to give an inch right from the start. "Probably more so, Sir."

"Good. I like that. I'm not going to pretend this arrangement won't be sexual. It will. I want you. But I'm firm. I'm hard-nosed. I'm tough. I'll make you want to slap me on occasion." He leaned closer to her from across the desk and lowered his voice. "You've been a sub long enough to know you have the control. You're gifting me with your submission, but the choice is always yours. And I'll make it all worth your while."

He may have noticed her trembling before, but at that pronouncement Margaret's entire body shivered as though a sudden draft of extremely cold air had blown through the room.

"Two weeks with me and you'll know what it's like to live under the thumb of a real Dom—not just a male, but one who expects everything from you. That's what you need, isn't it? To experience total submission."

"Yes, Sir." Her voice was weak.

"You understand that's what I'm offering you, right? Two weeks of experimentation where you can safely explore your desire to be completely dominated."

"Yes, Sir." She swallowed. He was absolutely spot on. And it unnerved her he could read her so well. She had no idea what sort of sub she might be after this trial, or even if she would want to continue being anyone's sub, male or female, but she craved this experience so badly she could taste it.

"It's been a while since I've had a sub. But don't let that fool you. I'm not out of shape on the ins and outs. I've worked with a lot of women over the years. I would expect you to relinquish yourself to me completely if you decide to consent. Except for work, your family, and any necessary friend-related events you clear with me first, I want you to give me one hundred percent. Are we clear?"

"Yes, Sir." She felt light headed. This was real.

"If you were anyone else, I might take things slower, be more gentle. But you're not. I've known you too long. I've seen you in more scenes than I can count. I know your reactions to about every imaginable practice." He paused. "What I can't be sure of is how you might react to me specifically. But that's semantics at this point.

"I know deep down you're a true submissive. You just

haven't been with the right Dom. I'll give you that experience, and one day you'll make a beautiful permanent sub for the right Dom."

"Yes, Sir." Her voice sounded foreign to her own ears. The ringing she'd sensed earlier, a residual noise from the club, returned to fill her head with imaginary sound. She winced at his words. Why did it sound as though he were already handing her off? He would groom her and turn her over to another man. The idea didn't sit well with her, even though she knew this was what she was signing on for.

"Let me list a few things I'll insist upon immediately with no negotiation to give you a feel for my rules. The list is long." He paused. "I'll expect you to stay in my home. That isn't negotiable. I'm too controlling to allow you to live on your own. For the duration of our agreement, you'll stay with me.

"I don't allow cussing, ever. I don't like to hear it from your sweet lips. It's unbecoming. I know I'm unusual in that regard, but take it or leave it."

Her eyes widened. That would be tough. She had a potty mouth on occasion.

"You won't wear clothes in my home. You won't wear underwear ever. You won't wear anything I don't approve of when you're with me. Your bras will be selected by me and worn only when necessary."

Visions of the type of lingerie Carlton would cover her breasts with made her nipples stiffen. They abraded against her bustier that suddenly seemed too small.

"You won't be required to shave because I prefer to do it myself, and I insist upon that. Not negotiable. I enjoy it.

It gives me pleasure."

*Shave? As in my crotch?* Flames consumed her face at the sudden embarrassment. No one had ever shaved Margaret but herself. She squirmed, her pussy growing traitorously wetter.

"You won't masturbate or touch yourself in any way sexual except under my strict instructions. Your orgasms belong to me and me alone. I'll decide when you come and punish you for every time you can't control yourself.

"My punishments are swift and fit the crime. You will never be permanently marked or scarred. You will not be branded or tattooed under my care. You also don't have permission to tattoo or pierce anything without my consent. And don't ask for that consent, because your unmarked body is the sexiest I've ever seen in my life. I would sooner die than tarnish it with ink, bruises or scars."

Her mind raced to keep up with his words. He spoke so fast and said so much in such a succinct manner. He wouldn't hurt her. That went without saying. She knew him well enough to rest easy on that subject. Carlton wouldn't hurt a bug. But the idea of enduring his punishments made her grit her teeth against the ball of need gathering low in her belly.

"You're not my domestic slave. This doesn't mean I won't ask you to help around the house, but not more than any normal couple would negotiate domestic duties.

"I know this is a lot to take in. Don't worry. You weren't expected to memorize or remember anything tonight. I've overwhelmed you enough." Carlton rounded the desk to resume the spot he'd taken in front of her earlier. He leaned his ass once again against the desk, out of her line of sight.

"I have one more question." He waited.

"Yes, Sir. Anything."

"Are you more aroused now than before I started my speech? Is your pussy leaking on my chair?"

"Yes, Sir," she muttered, disconcerted by the way he made her admit that as though it were something to be embarrassed about, when in reality, it was the goal. She straightened her spine. What if she'd said no?

"Good. Then I'd say we're almost done here." He hadn't touched her since earlier when he'd held her hand and then her chin. That surprised her, though it shouldn't have. Carlton was nothing if not concise.

"I assume you drove here?"

"Yes, Sir."

"I'll follow you home. Do you have any questions?"

"No, Sir." She ran through her brain, searching for anything she might be forgetting.

"Good. I want you to take a week to think about this. For the next seven days, I'd like you to concentrate on what it means to be my submissive. Take the time to consider this choice completely. When you aren't at work or other appointments you've already made for this week, I'd like you to be at home, thinking about what it means to be submit to a Dom. It's been a while since you've had that level of structure. Make sure it's something you truly want to explore." He glanced at his watch. "It's late. Let's get you home."

"Yes, Sir." Every minute she waited to be with him

would be torture now that she'd tasted his brand of paradise, figuratively, of course, but she was itching to make that real. She had no doubt in her mind she would agree to his terms. They might be harsh, but harsh was what she needed. Her skin tingled as she imagined all the things he could do to her with his words. If he added his hands, his mouth, his cock…

Now that she'd decided she wanted to experience everything he'd outlined and more, she felt an urgency deep in the pit of her stomach. She wanted him to fuck her. She wanted to know what it was like to feel a man's cock inside her. And she wanted that man to be Carlton. How had she never realized this before tonight?

Instead of making a public statement by traipsing through the lingering patrons of the club, Margaret was glad to find herself following Carlton out the back entrance. "I can find my way home, Sir. You don't have to follow me."

"I know. But I prefer to ensure you arrive home safely. Don't argue with me." He led her to her car, helped her inside and then proceeded to his own.

She followed him with her eyes as he approached a black Land Rover. She smiled. It suited him.

Her fingers shook violently as she started the engine. She had to grip the steering wheel with both hands to keep the car steady as she backed out and drove home. Carlton stayed on her bumper, as expected. Someone else rode his bumper, making her feel like she was leading an entourage.

Every time she looked in the rearview mirror, she could see both cars. Weird.

When she pulled up in front of her apartment, Carlton parked behind her. The car behind him went on by. She stared at it, feeling a chill climb up her spine as it eased by her. She shook away the paranoia.

She found Carlton at her side again immediately, opening her car door and then taking her keys from her to lock her car with the fob before unlocking her apartment and ushering her inside.

Everything the man did was deliberate. He was overbearing, as she'd known he would be. He stepped inside her space without invitation and glanced around. She watched his face, realizing it wasn't her belongings he took in, but rather the lack of an intruder. He was a safety guy. After all, safety was his job at Emergence. The fact that it would spill over into his private life shouldn't surprise her.

Carlton turned to her and spoke for the first time since they left the club. "I want you to lock this door, remove your clothes and spend the weekend meditating on this decision in the nude. Do not touch yourself sexually at any time. That's a hard rule of mine. I'm a discerning individual. If you ever masturbate without my permission, I'll know by your reaction when I question you. If you doubt me, try it. If you lie to me, I will find out.

"When you're not at work next week, follow the same rules. No clothes. No masturbating. Get your mind in the space. Consider what you're agreeing to." His gaze penetrated her to the core. She didn't doubt his words. The man was astute to the point of possessing supernatural powers.

Margaret stared at his mouth as he spoke. He was so

fucking sexy, every detail chiseled to perfection. *Might as well stop thinking four-letter words, Maggie. If you don't, they will leak out of your mouth.* She shivered. Only God knew what Carlton's punishments might be like.

"Are we clear?"

"Yes, Sir."

"I'll be texting you throughout the week to make sure you're okay."

*Why wouldn't I be okay?* She nodded instead of arguing. "Yes, Sir."

He had a nostalgic expression that glazed his eyes, and he shook his head subtly as though erasing something he'd seen from his mind.

Carlton grabbed the door in one hand, and then he turned back to face her. "Go to the doctor this week and get a clean bill of health. I'll do the same. I would never put a submissive in danger. You shouldn't allow it either." He narrowed his gaze. "Always make sure you have proof that whatever Dom you're with has been cleared medically."

She nodded.

He turned away from her and left without another word. He shut the door behind him, leaving her standing in her own home, shaking, feeling as though her sanctuary was somehow no longer sacred. He was watching her, even when he wasn't there. She could feel his intense gaze on her face, even though his car engine started and he pulled away from the curb.

She shivered for the millionth time as she took a deep breath and removed her skirt and bustier with trembling fingers. She squirmed out of her G-string, feeling his nonexistent gaze on her, admiring her body while judging her stance.

She straightened her shoulders and carried her clothes to her bathroom. She closed the door, still feeling his eyes on her body. It didn't help. He was inside the small space with her. She peed and then brushed her teeth, trying to ignore the sensation that he was all knowing. It consumed her. Although physically she was alone inside, emotionally Carlton Fisher had gotten under her skin. She couldn't escape him again even if she wasn't with him.

Margaret lay on her bed and pulled the sheet to her chin. She'd slept in the nude many times. But tonight she felt more than naked. She felt exposed.

With that lingering thought, she closed her eyes and took deep breaths to calm her racing heart. If she intended to start this new phase in her life, she needed a good night's sleep first.

Tomorrow. Tomorrow she would think about what it would be like to be with a man, someone she trusted with her both emotionally and physically. Because Lord knew she had enough baggage to fill a truck.

Should she have told Carlton about her past? He seemed to realize she had issues, but there was no way he could comprehend the depth of what she'd been through in her life. She shook the idea from her head. He didn't need to know her problems. Besides, they were part of her past. This arrangement was only for two weeks. A taste of total submission...with a man. There was no reason to drag issues with her stupid parents or her sexuality into the picture.

# Chapter Five

CARLTON DROVE STRAIGHT home, grabbed a beer from the fridge and plopped down on the couch. He set his feet on the coffee table and leaned his head back, rolling the bottle across his neck to cool his skin.

When he finally took a drink, he downed nearly half the bottle. He let his neck relax against the back of the couch again and stared at the ceiling, seeing nothing. The last few hours were a whirlwind. Maggie.

He took a deep breath, held it and then released it slowly. God, she was gorgeous. He couldn't deny that. And he wanted her. No, he needed her. He'd said he was doing all this for her, but he had motivations also. For one, he could purge himself of her by doing this. Or perhaps he was really purging himself of Karen? Either way, two weeks should do it. It was enough time to help Maggie realize her true potential while at the same time affording him the opportunity to remember why he was a bachelor. It would work. Assuming he could avoid falling for her.

He knew she had skeletons. Her breakup with Lori had been months ago. Nothing about the end of that relationship had warranted months of celibacy. There was more to Maggie than met the eye.

Hell, there was more to Carlton than met the eye. But she never needed to know the details. Sure, his past had haunted him lately, but the moment Maggie had entered his office and lifted her gaze to his, her eyes filled with submission, he'd known this was the right choice. She was aching to have a Dom show her what it really meant to submit. He could and would put his own issues aside for her. The idea of letting some other asshole Dom for her made him cringe.

She'd been floundering lately. He'd watched her at the club for weeks. She would absorb various scenes with a longing in her eyes he easily recognized. He hadn't been sure if she was torturing herself over the loss of Lori or if she needed something else.

Now he knew. She needed a Dom. A man. He had no idea how long it had been since she'd been with a man, but he was about to erase those memories from her consciousness. If a man was what she wanted to experience, then he would step up to the plate.

But fuck. Was that even wise? It wasn't like he could keep her. It wouldn't be fair to any woman for him to take on a permanent sub. He would never be able to fully give anyone his heart, and that was no way to expect a submissive to live her life.

Nope. His heart was guarded. And he intended to keep it that way. The pain was too intense. He would never forget it. He wouldn't survive the loss of another woman like Karen. And he suspected Maggie was way more than

Karen. More woman. More submissive. More...everything.

Still. How could he justify this charade? It was true that she needed a Dom. Not him though. If he were a better man, he would help her find a different Dom. Although he knew she would balk. Half the reason why she'd come to him in the first place was because she trusted him. He knew that about her. They'd been friends for a long time. Maggie had been wandering around aimlessly for months. There was no other man for the job, not in her eyes, and certainly not in his.

He could do this. Disassociate. Teach her what it was like to submit to a man and still remain friends afterward. He had to. There was no other choice.

He closed his eyes and let his mind wander back twelve years. More than a decade. Long enough to get over his past. But *her* face swam into his vision. Karen. It was fading, but it was still there. He could picture her laughing, her head tipped back as she enjoyed life to the fullest. She'd been an adrenaline junky. When they'd first gotten together, Carlton had loved her free spirit, but as the months went by she'd taken risks that made him more and more nervous. She'd given Carlton a near heart attack on so many occasions he couldn't count them.

He could still see her in the back of his head, leaping from one railroad tie to the next as she crossed a bridge meant only for trains. She'd been so high off the ground, yelling at him to follow her. He'd relented that time, but had wanted to kill her afterward for causing his heart to beat out of his chest.

Karen had more energy than any one human needed.

Another time they were out hiking, she scaled the side of a rock wall, spontaneously, just to see if she could reach the top without falling.

Most days Carlton went along with her if for no other reason than to keep her from killing herself. Sometimes he could talk her down from one of her antics. Sometimes he failed. He adored her. She was happy and fun and exciting all at once. And she shaved years off the end of his life every time she was awake.

He hadn't been with her when she died. As illogical as it was, and though no one blamed him, he still felt guilty about staying home that night. He'd been sick with the flu. She'd gone out without him. He would live the rest of his life with that guilt...

He opened his eyes. Glanced around the room. For a moment he'd forgotten where he was and what decade. *Maggie.* Oh God, that woman was under his skin. She looked like Karen. The resemblance was uncanny. Did she have the same personality? She certainly had taken a risk when she'd agreed to sub for him.

Eight years he'd lived in this house. It had been years since he'd had someone stay in his home. But Maggie was different. She needed this full-time arrangement. Or maybe he was kidding himself and he was the one who needed it. Either way, it didn't matter. She didn't know it yet, but she brought him to his knees. She humbled him.

He chuckled. How ironic. After all, Carlton was the Dom. He would have Maggie on *her* knees. Not the other way around. He finished his beer.

Tired beyond the norm, he pushed himself to standing,

headed for the kitchen and dropped the bottle in the trash. When he turned around, he glanced at his space. How would Maggie see his home? He was fairly tidy, and he doubted she would be disappointed, but he realized his space was rather boring. The furniture was bland, uninteresting, beige.

Few pictures covered the walls. How had he not noticed this before? *Who cares? It's only for two weeks* He lowered his gaze and trudged toward his bedroom. Without turning on the lights, he headed for the master bath, stripped his clothes, brushed his teeth and then returned to his bedroom.

Naked, he slipped between the sheets. He often wore boxers when he was alone, but not tonight. The material of his shorts would draw attention to his rigid cock. Even the sheet annoyed him this time, as though it were made of sandpaper instead of cotton. He kicked it away from his body.

Carlton stared at the ceiling. He lifted his arms to tuck his hands behind his neck. More deep breaths. It wasn't going to happen. No arguing with his dick was going to settle the fellow for the night. Giving up the ruse, he lowered his hands to take his shaft in one palm while cupping his balls with the other.

He closed his eyes, imagining Maggie's small hand around his length, stroking him from the base to the tip. Her pale skin would contrast with his tanned body. Soft against hard. Delicate against rugged. He pictured her mouth open, shallow breaths coming from between her lips as she stared at the precome leaking from the tip of his cock.

He held his breath as her imaginary mouth lowered over his shaft. How long had it been since she'd sucked a man's cock? Would she swallow him deep into her throat or would she be more timid, licking and tasting him with her tongue?

It didn't matter, because he would teach her how he liked to be sucked off.

Carlton pumped harder, his grip tightening as he let the head rub against his palm. He released his hold on his balls when he was no longer able to remain gentle and gripped the sheets at his side. It only took moments for him to reach his peak, and he tipped his head back, letting his mouth fall open as he gave a final thrust and came, pulsing onto his stomach.

For long moments, he continued to stroke himself, not opening his eyes so he didn't break the illusion of Maggie's face between his legs. He didn't want to shatter the spell.

When he finally released his cock and reached for a tissue next to the bed to wipe himself off, he let his gaze fall on his torso. No Maggie. Of course. But he could almost scent her in the room. He'd been close enough to her tonight to know what her shampoo smelled like, her body soap, her personal scent that would drive him crazier every day. It was embedded in his memory already and he hadn't even brought her to the house yet.

He tried to relax into the mattress and let sleep take him under. It was going to be a long week.

✧    ✧    ✧

WHEN MARGARET AWOKE Saturday morning, she moaned into the pillow as she turned to see the clock. Nine. She hadn't slept that soundly in months. Nor that late.

As she pulled herself to sitting, everything from last night slammed back into her mind. The sheet fell away, leaving her exposed. She glanced down as she remembered why she was naked. Her nipples pebbled beneath her gaze, already protesting their nudity, or pleading for attention.

Lifting her gaze, she eased from the bed and padded over to her dresser. Without thinking, she opened the top drawer like she would any day of the week and pulled out a pair of panties. And then she stopped, still holding them in the air as she remembered Carlton's instructions. *Remove your clothes and spend the weekend meditating on this decision in the nude.*

Margaret released the lingerie and let it fall back into the drawer. She glanced down at her body. *Am I really going to lie around naked all weekend?* How would he know?

He'd know. She didn't know how, but he'd know. He'd read it on her expression.

She pushed the drawer closed and headed for the bathroom. *Think of all the time you'll save not having to pull your pants down...*

After using the toilet, she took a quick shower and headed for the kitchen. It felt odd, disconcerting, to roam around her apartment naked. She didn't want to spend the day in darkness, so she managed to tip the blinds so light still filtered in, but anyone walking by outside couldn't see her. At least she hoped.

Coffee was first on the agenda. As soon as she had her

first steaming cup in hand, she flopped onto the cool leather couch. The smooth surface felt refreshing against her bare skin as she settled back against the armrest, swinging her legs up and planting her feet on the cushion. *I look ridiculous.*

Margaret had been with a few other partners before Lori. She'd even had a few experiences with other Dommes since Lori. However, none of them had ever requested she remain naked, especially not alone in her home.

Trying to ignore that aspect of her obedience, she took a fortifying drink of coffee and set the mug on the coffee table.

She'd been aware she was submissive for almost as long as she'd known she was bisexual. In her teenage years she'd read everything she could get her hands on concerning sexuality, dominance and submission.

Once she graduated from high school and moved out of her parents' home to attend college, she'd been free to explore more than her sexuality. She'd joined GSA clubs and dated several women over the next four years. It wasn't that she hadn't been attracted to men. She noticed them, some more than others. But it was simply easier to date women, less complicated.

As for submission, the girlfriend she'd had her sophomore year had taken her to her first club. Margaret shouldn't have been shocked. But in those days, she hadn't had the availability of rampant Internet articles to explore.

It turned out her girlfriend was also submissive, so their relationship didn't last long. But in those first few visits to a BDSM club, Margaret's eyes had been opened wide.

Another woman she'd met at the club had flirted with Margaret mercilessly. As soon as Margaret had broken up with her girlfriend, she began her first experience with submission.

It was easy. For the first time in her life, Margaret felt like she was being true to herself. By day, she attended class and worked hard to earn her accounting degree. She was an excellent student and had a good rapport with her professors. Anyone she spoke to touted her good business sense and believed she would make an excellent employee for any company willing to hire her after graduation.

By night, Margaret preferred to let the stress of the day's events slough off her skin by turning herself over to the will of her Domme.

Why was she submissive? She wondered if she was wired differently from other people. What made a woman want to be controlled by another? There was probably some dark, hidden reason for her fetish that lay in the fucked-up events of her childhood, but she'd never bothered to seek a counselor to explore the possibility.

Undoubtedly her father had caused her to become submissive. The man was domineering toward both Margaret and her mother. He ruled a tight ship and didn't take any lip from the women. Hell, the fucked-up church her family attended was so patriarchal it had made her want to retch growing up. She'd never fit in.

Had her father's insistence on her subservience caused her to be submissive to others?

As she relaxed farther into the couch, she wondered if she was making the right choice. Carlton? She'd never considered submitting to him. No, that wasn't entirely true. She'd watched him perform many scenes from the sidelines, her body quivering with want, wishing she were the submissive under his control.

She pictured him now, completely in his dominant mode. Easing her eyes closed, she visualized him circling his submissive, a flogger in his hand, stroking the strands of leather through his fingers. Her nipples pebbled. Without thinking she reached with her free hand to fondle one. She pinched down, hard, as though she could somehow prepare her mind for what was to come.

She clamped her thighs tighter as she pinched, a growing need developing low in her belly. When she slid her right hand down her body to reach between her legs, she froze.

*Oh God.* Her eyes flew open.

*"You won't masturbate or touch yourself in any way sexual except under my strict instructions."*

Margaret swallowed. Her mouth was dry. Her thighs quivered with the need that had grown between them. Her arousal picked that moment to run between her clenched ass cheeks, making her moan with frustration.

She released her nipple suddenly, as though it had burned her fingers. Her breaths came out in long pants. Her heart pounded.

Holy hell. She was in trouble. Carlton Fisher had a firm grip on her obedience without being in her home. She couldn't bring herself to finish off what her pussy begged for. Her fingers still shook, itching to stroke between the folds of her pussy. Her legs fell open farther, exposing her lower lips to the air.

She gasped and then held her breath. If she didn't concentrate on getting herself together, she was going to come without touching herself. And surely that would count as masturbation. As though there were cameras in every corner of her private apartment, she glanced around. She willed her pussy to keep from contracting.

It was irrational. Carlton couldn't see her right then. He would never have any way of knowing what happened on a Saturday afternoon alone in her apartment.

But he would. She knew he would. Somehow. If nothing else, he would question her and she would be unable to do anything but be honest. First of all, it wasn't in her nature to lie. And second of all, Carlton could draw truth from a rock if necessary.

Margaret slowly twisted until she could lie back on the sofa. She left her legs separated, knowing the friction of bringing them together wouldn't help her cause.

*Deep breaths.*

A noise outside made her flinch. She jerked her gaze toward the living room window. She couldn't see out with the blinds tipped in the position she'd left them. But adrenaline raced through her body just the same.

Probably a bird or some other small animal. *Geez. Relax.*

She closed her eyes. It was only Saturday. She had six more days of this to endure before she saw Carlton again and officially turned herself over to his care. Six long days…

Her cell phone picked that particular moment to ring.

She tried to catch her breath, staring at the ceiling and concentrating on anything but Carlton and his rugged looks. She had plenty of work she could do on her computer this afternoon instead of lying on the couch naked, masturbating.

She moaned as she pulled herself to standing and padded on wobbly legs to the kitchen table, where she'd dropped her purse the night before. She fished her cell out of the side pocket.

Two texts. The first one had been from her mother way too early this morning for her to have heard it. She ignored it in favor of the second. Carlton's. *How are you?*

Her fingers quivered as she typed a response. *Fine. Good.* She hit Send.

*Second thoughts?*

Margaret stared at the screen for several moments. She pondered that question. It wasn't that she had second thoughts. On the contrary, she'd never been more sure of anything. And that was what bothered her. She should be more leery of Carlton's intentions. She should be concerned about his level of dominance. She should be a lot of things. She knew this because society deemed it so.

She smirked. *Fuck society.* Then she smiled. She really had to curb her four-letter thoughts. If they started leaking out of her mouth, she'd find herself unable to sit for a month.

*None,* she typed in response.

*You had me worried for a second.*

*No worries, Sir.*

Margaret set the phone down on the table and wandered back to the living room. She didn't have the energy for her mother right then. She would read that message later. It made her stomach clench to combine thoughts of her mother with thoughts of Carlton. The two were like oil and water. And she had no intention of mixing them. It was her parents' own fault. Their unwillingness to accept Margaret for who she was dampened their relationship.

Twelve years she'd lived in a vacuum, avoiding anything that reminded her of the fateful night that irrevocably changed her life forever. She'd lived a good enough life since then, finished high school, went to college, entered polite society—finally detaching herself from the parental strings.

And still, every time her mother or father called or texted, she was reminded all over again. Mostly she avoided them. Occasionally she faced them long enough to keep the peace. But everything between them was stiff and fake.

Of course, if she really analyzed the situation, she knew their relationship had been awkward even before the events of that horrific night.

Her parents had always been fundamentalist Christians, a life she had never fit into. Her father, the domineering patriarch, ruled the home and demanded that everyone under his roof submit to his whims.

When the man found out his daughter was an abomination to the world, catching her in a compromising position with her best friend, Leslie, he'd gone ballistic. She'd heard everything in the book about how she *chose* her lifestyle and how the church would cure her of her sins if she just gave it a chance.

And hell, to this day her parents only knew the half of it. They thought she had *chosen* to be a lesbian to spite them. Imagine if they knew she was actually bisexual *and* a submissive? Well, forget submissive. Her mother was a domestic submissive if she stopped to think about it. Margaret knew the woman would argue otherwise, but it was all semantics as far as Margaret was concerned.

Justine Donovan had lived under the rule of her husband as though he were her Master for her entire adult life. She just didn't realize it in so many words. Even though it wasn't a sexual submission, as far as Margaret knew, didn't make her mother any less of a sub.

Ironic, considering her parents would die if they knew the level of submission Margaret had practiced and the new level she was about to embark on. What made Margaret's sexual submission so taboo?

She'd learned to accept who she was. She worried more lately that her submissive tendencies were a result of her domineering father and doubted the legitimacy of her choice, but in spite of or because of her dad, she was still undeniably submissive and preferred to turn herself over to another person after a long day to get the relief she craved.

Legitimate or otherwise, she needed this experience with Carlton on so many levels. She needed to know what it was like to be with a man, and a firm Dom. She'd never met another human being she could have considered turning herself over to as she would Carlton.

After all, she was safe with him. It was a trial of sorts. How could she go wrong? Besides getting to know herself a little better in the process, she would also have the luxury of finally knowing what it felt like to have a man inside her, someone she trusted and respected. Someone who would do right by her.

Even if he didn't know quite what he was up against. He never needed to know all the petty details of her weird life. They weren't going to be together that long. Just long enough for her to build her confidence and ease into the possibility of working under a male Dom.

She shivered again at the idea. Nerves wracked her body as though she were a teenager contemplating having sex with her boyfriend for the first time. In a way she was.

# Chapter Six

WHEN CARLTON GOT to work on Monday, Jason was immediately on his ass, following him to the coffeepot and then staying on his heels all the way to his office.

Carlton took his seat behind his desk before he lifted his gaze to meet his boss's. He smirked. "What's on your mind, boss?" he asked as though there were any question. It was nearly comical the way Jason was on him.

Jason rolled his eyes. "Just spill." He sat forward. "Not the nitty-gritty, please. Just the overall synopsis."

"There's nothing to tell."

"How is that possible? I know we didn't have time to talk on Saturday night, but you took the second half of the evening off Friday night, and now you expect me to believe you have nothing to share?"

"That's right. I met with Margaret in my office." He nodded at the chair Jason now occupied. "We talked. I gave her some things to think about. And then I followed her home to make sure she was safe."

"That's it?" Jason narrowed his gaze. "I know you better than that. What are you leaving out?"

"I did make her an offer, but I wanted her to be certain before she agreed. It's a big decision. I don't want her to be too hasty."

"That's noble of you," Jason teased. "I suppose you gave her some time to consider submitting to you before making a commitment."

"Something like that." Carlton stacked and restacked the papers on his desk. He hated that Jason could read him so well. "She'll be here Friday night, unless she isn't."

Jason nodded. "I'm proud of you. Thanks for using restraint. Take it easy on her." With that, Jason stood, patted the corner of Carlton's desk and sauntered from the room.

Easy peasy. Now Carlton just needed to live through the rest of the week before he could set his gaze on Maggie again. It was going to be a long week.

He pulled out his cell and brought it to life, thinking he would text Maggie. His finger hovered over the keyboard. And then he groaned. He didn't have any good reason to text her again. He had checked in with her both days. Today she would be at work. She didn't need him bugging her at the office.

Ah, but did she make it safely?

He typed quickly.

*Did you make it to work okay?*

He tapped his fingers on the desk while he stared at the screen.

*Yes, Sir. Thank you, Sir.*

Every day he wasn't with her made him feel antsy. He

worried irrationally for her safety. No matter how many times he told himself she wasn't Karen out gallivanting around, tempting fate with her life, he still worried. And that infuriated him. He didn't own her, and this was the primary reason why he didn't want a woman in his life. They made him worry when they made him care. He needed to cut Maggie some slack until she proved herself to be reckless.

*Either way, it doesn't matter. This is temporary. You aren't her guardian. She is not a kept woman.*

✦   ✦   ✦

MARGARET HAD TROUBLE concentrating at work. The first few days, she did nothing but fidget and check her phone. Carlton texted her nearly every day to make sure she arrived at work and then back at home safely. It seemed endearing at first...and then a little over the top. What did he think would happen to her?

He was safety conscious to a *T*.

On Wednesday when she left work, she ducked into her car and was about to start the engine when she noticed an envelope under the windshield wiper.

Thinking it would be an advertisement, she was disgruntled to have to remove her seatbelt and climb back out of the car to grab the damn paper from the windshield. She tossed it on the seat next to her and drove home.

It wasn't until she was inside the house and preparing dinner that the envelope caught her attention sticking out of her purse. She almost dropped it right in the trash, but something about it made her open it first.

It was certainly not an ad. Four typed lines in the middle of a piece of plain white printer paper.

*We're watching you. Glad to see you've finally moved on to men. You aren't a quick learner. Now, lose the kinky shit, and you'll be on your way to an eternity right with God.*

Margaret dropped the paper on the table as though it burned her. She glanced around the room, suddenly feeling the creepiest sensation she'd ever felt crawl up her spine. And she was alone. She lurched forward to ensure the blinds were completely closed and the curtains drawn together.

When she returned to the table and slumped into a chair, her dinner was burning and her hands were shaking. How many times in her life had she felt like she was being followed? Hundreds? It had seemed to increase in frequency lately. She'd always assumed she was stuck with her absurd paranoia as a result of her teenage drama, but it was more than that. And the proof was currently lying on her kitchen table.

It almost seemed as though the incident from twelve years ago was related to this piece of paper now. Irrational. Stupid. Not possible. How could anyone from twelve years ago still be following her? And if they were, why hadn't they acted before now? After all, she'd lived with Lori for a year. No one had confronted her then. Why now that she was considering a man?

A chill took over Margaret's body, making her shake uncontrollably. Her previous hunger had converted to nausea. She jumped back up, flipped off the burner where her chicken had charred black and headed for the living room.

Thank God for the throw she kept on the back of the couch. Without hesitation, she wrapped herself inside the warmth of the blanket and curled up on the couch. It took over an hour for the shaking to stop. Her mind never stopped running.

There was no good explanation for the note. It was too specific to have been a matter of mistaken identity. Should she call the police? She couldn't imagine what they would do with a single piece of paper, damp from hours in the parking garage and covered with her own prints now.

Carlton. Maybe she should call him? No. She couldn't. As though the man's ears were ringing, her phone picked that second to beep. Margaret groaned. She was supposed to text him when she got home. Now she couldn't even do that much. For one thing, she didn't have the energy to get off the couch. And for another thing, there was no way she would tell him about the note.

If she thought he was absurdly safety conscious before tonight, she could imagine what he would be like if he thought someone was following her.

Her phone pinged again. She flinched. She had to answer him. If she didn't he'd show up at her doorstep in no time.

Margaret heaved herself off the couch, tucked the blanket tight around her shoulders and headed for the kitchen to grab her phone from her purse.

*Margaret? Where are you?*

That was his second message. She didn't need to scroll back to the first.

*I'm home, Sir. Sorry. I forgot to text and I had my phone on vibrate in my purse.*

One small white lie to keep the man from going ballistic.

Now, she just needed to figure out how to keep *herself* from going ballistic.

CARLTON WAS ON PINS AND NEEDLES Friday night at the club. He'd exchanged texts with Maggie nearly every day for the last week, and he felt confident she would accept his proposal. But that didn't keep him from worrying. Until she arrived and confirmed she was all in, he would pace.

He'd offered to pick her up and bring her to his house when he got off work, but she'd declined, saying she needed her car anyway. So now he was forced to wait for her to arrive, worrying all the while that she'd been killed in an accident.

His anxiety was absurd, but he felt it all the same, just as he had on Wednesday when she hadn't answered his text after work. He'd irrationally wigged out between one text and the next.

Every time someone new came through the door, he prayed it was her. It was totally unnecessary since he'd specifically told her he had to work until about midnight. There was no reason for her to show up before he got off work. She wouldn't be doing a scene with someone else at Emergence tonight, so she'd simply be sitting around waiting on him.

But Carlton secretly hoped she would show up earlier because the idea of being able to see her in person, even from a distance, while she waited for his shift to end, made his palms sweaty. Like a teenage boy headed for a first date, he couldn't wait to get it started.

Normally Carlton worked the entire night until they closed, but tonight he'd made arrangements for someone else to take over at midnight so he could leave with Maggie.

He could kick himself for telling her she didn't need to be there until midnight. That was too late for her to be out driving around. A single woman in a car in the middle of the night was always a bad idea.

At eleven forty-five Jason stepped up to the front. "Where's Margaret?"

"No idea." Carlton looked away, pretending to be intently watching the surrounding area.

"Are you sure she's coming here? Maybe she intends to meet you at your place."

"She's never been to my place. And I didn't give her the address. Besides, we discussed it several times. She said she'd meet me here."

"Well, maybe she doesn't feel like being under a microscope, so she didn't want to get here too early."

Carlton nodded. *Hopefully that's it.* He glanced at his phone for the hundredth time and saw no calls or texts had come in.

At midnight his replacement ambled toward the front and relieved him. Even if Maggie didn't show, Carlton's nerves were shot from stressing about it. If she'd gotten cold feet, he needed to confront her anyway. Not talking to her at all wasn't an option.

Carlton headed to his office to make sure nothing pressing needed attending and to lock the door. When his phone pinged in his back pocket, he closed his eyes and took a deep breath, grateful he was alone.

*Time to face the music.*

He pulled the cell from his pants, holding his breath.

*I'm out back in my car.*

The exhale he released lasted longer than he believed possible.

And then a second text.

*Sir.*

He chuckled. God, he wanted this woman. He was so going to enjoy training her to suit his style.

And she was so going to enjoy every moment of his training.

Carlton locked his office and stepped out the rear entrance of the building. There she was, sitting in her car, a smile on her face as he approached.

*There is a god.*

He leaned over as she rolled the window down.

"Sorry. I didn't feel like facing off with Jason tonight or dealing with any Doms who thought it was their job to rescue me from my solitude."

"I should have thought of that." He nodded as he leaned lower toward her face. "Good choice. You'll follow me?"

"Yes. Sir." The pause she left between her first word and his title made him stifle a smirk. She was out of practice. And in fact hadn't called anyone Sir for as long as he'd known her, since she'd been with a series of women in the past.

Carlton tapped the side of her car and nodded behind him. The only reason he turned from looking at her face was because he feared he would fall over if he didn't pay closer attention to where he was going. Luckily he only lived ten minutes from Emergence. It was going to be the longest ten minutes of his life.

He watched her out of his rearview mirror far more than necessary during the drive, as though she might get cold feet and make a turn in another direction. Or perhaps he simply didn't like having her out of his sight.

When he finally pulled into the driveway, she inched up alongside him. He rolled down the passenger window and motioned for her to lower hers. "I cleaned out the garage so you could park on one side."

She opened her mouth but said nothing. Her eyes widened. Finally, she nodded.

Carlton eased into the left side while Maggie took the right. It felt...right. And that made him more nervous. This wasn't meant to be a permanent arrangement. He'd told himself that over and over in the last week while his every waking moment filled with thoughts of Maggie.

Nerves made his palms sweaty. Nerves that were strictly based on her right to turn him down.

He could muster up all the tenacity in the world and it wouldn't change the fact that the woman had a mind of her own and her own free will.

As he exited the car, another vehicle passed his house, a

little too slowly. He stepped onto the driveway, but the car kept going. Whoever it was apparently had an aversion to the gas pedal, or had his head buried in his cell phone.

Carlton rounded to her trunk when she popped it and removed a large bag and a suitcase. She'd traveled light. Was that a good thing?

"Come." He nodded to the entrance to the house inside the garage and headed that direction with Maggie on his heels. Seconds later he had her inside, the garage closed and the door shut. "Welcome. Follow me." He made his way through the kitchen and led her down the hallway to the master bedroom.

"Nice." She looked around his space before meeting his gaze and quickly lowering her face. "Sir."

Carlton shook his head and smirked as he put her suitcase unopened in the closet. She wouldn't need it immediately. Hell, she wouldn't need it at all in his home. Is that why she'd brought so little with her? He set her other bag at the foot of the bed. "How was your week?" He'd communicated with her through text, but he hadn't spoken with her in seven long days.

"Good. Stressful."

"Was this a difficult decision? Or did you have a lot going on at work?"

She tipped her gaze to the floor, as she should, but he worried about her current motivation. "A little of both, Sir. To be honest, no, it wasn't tough to decide to come to you tonight. I always knew I would. But I don't want to disappoint you either. That's stressful."

Carlton stepped in front of her and lifted her chin to

meet his gaze. "You could never disappoint me." He stared at her lips, wanting desperately to taste them but knowing the time wasn't right yet. Soon.

Carlton decided it would be best to jump straight into the arrangement. It would be confusing if he allowed her any leeway and eased her into her new role. "Before we discuss what I expect of you, remove everything and meet me in the living room." He turned to leave the room and give her a last moment of privacy. He didn't shut the door, however.

Minutes later she emerged and padded across the room, head bowed, arms at her sides, flawless skin taking his breath away.

It wasn't as though he'd never seen most of her body before at one point or another, but he didn't make a habit of ogling other people's submissives. Now that she was here under his care, he couldn't keep his gaze off her. He took a deep breath, reminding himself this was temporary for the millionth time. Why was that line such a blur?

She stopped midway into the room, probably waiting for instructions.

Carlton stepped up to her silently, his feet barely registering the command to move forward. Her creamy skin was so flawless she could be a model. He wondered if she ever had. "Assume a proper standing position please." He watched while she straightened her shoulders, angled her chin toward the floor, spread her feet shoulder width and clasped her hands behind her back.

"Good. You remember." He circled her body slowly. Her ass was fantastic, and he couldn't wait to mark it with the pink print of his palm, his flogger, his paddle. He'd seen her do many spanking scenes at the club. Not every submissive participated in scenes out of an actual desire to do so. Sometimes their Doms or Dommes would insist on cooperation with no regard for the feeling of the sub.

Carlton wasn't that kind of Dom. He liked to think he had a good sense when it came to selecting scenes his submissive would not only enjoy, but derive pleasure from. If he suspected his sub wasn't headed down the mental path he'd expected or desired, he tried something else.

Breaking women wasn't his game.

But Maggie was a submissive he'd seen in action. He'd watched the rapture on her face many times. He had a good idea what she liked and disliked. That knowledge was what had driven him to decide to give her this opportunity. Her needs met his style.

Did her desire to push the envelope in a variety of scenes make her a risk taker? He took a deep breath. If Karen had been a submissive, she would have gone all in like Maggie, easily taking a flogging or a spanking without question. But maybe it wasn't that clear-cut. Maggie had a level of hesitation that made her seem more cautious perhaps.

With reluctance, he left the view of her ass and rounded to her front. He spent more time than necessary staring intently at her pert breasts.

He didn't move. He waited for what he knew would come. Sure enough, moments later her nipples pebbled beneath his gaze. The pretty pink stood out in contrast to her milky white skin.

This was Maggie. In the flesh, not some apparition or a ghost. There were no demons haunting him tonight.

When Carlton lowered his gaze, he found her unshaved pussy glistening with moisture. The soft curls at her apex matched the long, black, wavy hair hanging down her back. Somehow on her, the curls on her pussy looked appropriate. So pure. It made her seem innocent. Untouched. He knew that wasn't true, but the illusion was there all the same.

However, he wouldn't keep the curls. It wasn't his style. A bare pussy suited him better and left his submissive feeling more exposed.

"Do you like me looking at you?"

"Yes, Sir." Her voice was breathy. He'd affected her. And yes, she was nervous. Cautious. Smart. Karen had never been cautious about anything. Maggie had that distinction.

"Good, because you're a beautiful woman. I'll be looking at you a lot."

"Thank you, Sir."

"All right. Let's get to it then." He forced himself to step away.

He led her to the living room and pointed at the floor next to the couch. "You won't be permitted on the furniture this week. You'll earn that privilege over time. You'll earn most of your privileges around here. For now, you have none."

"Yes, Sir." She knelt on the floor, clasped her hands behind her back and rested her ass on her heels.

He sat on the couch, his leg almost touching hers.

"Good. Your posture is spot on. You know your positions. I expect minimal discussion from you this week. One of the freedoms you'll earn is the right to speak freely. For now, you will limit your speech to necessary questions for clarity or responses to my direct questions."

"Yes, Sir."

"This arrangement is going to be slightly unconventional because we aren't strangers to each other. However, although I've known you from a distance for a long time, there are many things about you of which I'm uninformed. I'd like to take a few minutes to ask you about yourself and tell you about myself. A little background. An icebreaker, you could say."

"Okay, Sir."

"Tell me about your family."

"My parents live about a half hour away. I don't talk to them often. I don't have brothers and sisters."

"Well, that was quick and easy. Why don't you talk to your parents very often?"

"We have some differences of opinion, Sir."

"I see." He didn't. But he could imagine the possibilities considering their only child just got out of a relationship with a woman. It made him sad for her if her sexuality in any way caused a rift with her family.

"Okay, so a bit about myself. I was born in Wisconsin. I have two younger brothers. My parents still live there. I moved to the South when I was twenty and I've been here ever since." Carlton never took his eyes off of Maggie. It seemed appropriate to spend some time getting to know each other, but what he really wanted to do was find out what made her body hum. "Do you have any questions?"

"What brought you to the South, Sir?"

"We had some differences of opinion." He grinned.

Maggie smiled. "Touché."

He wasn't being exactly honest with her, but he couldn't imagine a time when he might be willing to share that particular aspect of his past. So they each had a secret. He could live with that.

Carlton leaned forward and put his elbows on his knees. He could smell her personal scent, and he wanted to bury his nose in her soft curls and inhale her floral shampoo. "I want to get to know you better."

Maggie flinched. It was subtle, but he noticed all the same.

Carlton lifted one hand and stroked the soft skin of her arm above her elbow. "I'm not talking about your mind right now. Keep your secrets. I'm talking about your body." His voice was low, softer than normal. Goose bumps rose on her skin as his finger grazed the silky smoothness of her bicep.

A soft exhale escaped her lips, and she shivered. What she nervous? Or aroused?

He would know soon enough. "Come." He stood, taking her with him with a gentle lift to her arm. Without another word, he led her back to the master bedroom. He released her next to the bed and left her standing there while he slowly removed the comforter and pulled back the top sheet. "Lie down in the center, Maggie."

She did as he instructed, climbing onto the bed and situating herself on the sheet.

He chuckled at her position. "What position is that?"

Maggie sucked in a breath. "Sorry, Sir." She lifted her arms above her head and spread her legs.

Carlton stared at her for several seconds. *God, she's beautiful.* He'd known she was submissive, but so far she'd exceeded all of his expectations. Gone was the snarky Maggie he'd come to know who had reminded him so much of Karen. This woman was submissive to a *T*, softer, calmer. As a submissive, she wasn't as flippant, sarcastic and impertinent as he'd imagined her.

Stepping back a pace, he pulled his black T-shirt over his head and bent to remove his shoes and socks. He wasn't ready to release his cock from his jeans. Soon.

He climbed onto the bed and knelt between her legs. With the back of his knuckles, he lightly grazed her thighs. More tiny bumps rose on her skin.

She kept her gaze focused on the ceiling, as he'd known she would. After all, that's what the position required.

Carlton nudged her thighs farther apart with his hands. He gazed for the first time in such close proximity at her pussy. Pink. Swollen with arousal. Wet. He inched his fingers farther up her thighs, forcing them wider. With one hand, he used the tips of his fingers to examine her soft curls. Although he liked the look on her, he would shave her soon. Shaving her every day would humble her, remind her of her place. Besides, it would afford him the opportunity to fondle her every morning, even on days when he had no intention of permitting her to orgasm.

His fingers itched to shave her for the first time right now, but that would ruin his plan. The goal right now was to find out what made her body hum. If he stopped to denude her, it would change her mindset.

"You're so wet, baby. Do you enjoy the exposure?"

"Yes, Sir." She licked her lips, her words soft, barely audible.

"And what about this?" He gently danced his fingers at the apex of her thighs.

Her legs trembled. She didn't respond. It didn't matter; he had his answer.

Releasing her thighs, he smoothed his fingers toward her belly. Her stomach dipped as she gave a sharp inhale. "You're so sensitive," he whispered. He trailed his fingers toward the underslopes of her breasts. He admired their perfection, ideal for her frame, the pink areolas small, her nipples tight, although he had yet to touch them.

Her arms were rigid, her fingers threaded together, squeezing tightly.

"Relax, baby. I'm just exploring. Nothing more. Getting to know you." As he finished speaking, he flicked his thumbs over her nipples. The buds stiffened further. "You like that," he murmured. "Your nipples are sensitive. I'll remember that." He forced himself to leave her tight buds to cup her breasts gently and then with a slight pressure.

Maggie moaned as he squeezed, bucking her chest into his palms.

"Stay still, baby. I'll train you not to move. You'll learn to control every flinch. Do you know why?" He punctuated those last words by pinching her nipples between his thumbs and index fingers.

Maggie bucked her chest again. It wasn't in her control.

He couldn't fault her for that tonight. She was new to him. Perhaps no one in her past had ever insisted on that particular compliance.

"Because it's what I demand. And because obeying me increases your arousal." He leaned his face over hers and met her gaze. "Your breaths are shallow. Your skin is flushed. Is it my voice? Or my touch?" Still squeezing her nipples just enough to make her writhe, he dipped his head and licked first one tip and then the other with his tongue.

"Both, Sir."

Releasing her breasts, he watched the shiny tips for a moment before he lowered his gaze back to her pussy.

Carlton tucked his hands under her knees and pushed them higher until they were bent at a ninety-degree angle. When he released them, she opened like a butterfly. He pulled her folds apart with both hands. "So fucking sexy." He drew one finger through her slit, almost moaning at the amount of moisture already gathered there. "Are you always this wet?"

"I-I don't know, Sir."

Carlton used one hand to hold her folds apart. Her sex glistened. He ached to run his tongue through her arousal. But he would wait. As soon as he buried his face between her legs, he would be lost. Unable to gauge her reactions.

Her thighs stiffened, her muscles contracting as she fought to keep from squirming. Good. He liked that.

He circled her clit with her moisture, not quite touching the little bud. And then without warning, he dipped his finger into her pussy. He stiffened and gritted his teeth as his finger froze inside her depths. So tight. He narrowed his gaze, slipped in a second finger. Too tight. He lifted his face to find her watching him, her lips tucked under her teeth, her eyes wide. He stroked those two fingers inside her.

Maggie lifted her ass into his touch.

Carlton considered his next words carefully. "How many cocks have been in this pussy, Maggie?"

✧   ✧   ✧

SHE SWALLOWED, RELEASED her lips. "I have several types of vibrators in my apartment, Sir."

He stroked her some more.

Her brain scrambled. She willed him not to stop.

"That's not what I asked." He eased those two fingers out and then back into her pussy and dragged them across her G-spot. When he lifted his gaze to hers again, he must have read something in her expression. It wasn't hard to imagine. She had her bottom lip between her teeth, biting to the point of pain, knowing this was the moment she had to face the truth. Would he be angry with her for keeping this from him?

Carlton froze, his eyes widening, his mouth dropping open. He yanked his fingers from her sheath.

She waited.

His initial expression made her heart pound faster. Disbelief? And then the corner of his mouth turned up slightly before he spoke. "Fuck." He leaned back, ran the hand he hadn't just jerked out of her through his hair. Frustration took over his expression, but it was too late. She'd already seen his approval before he'd been able to school his response. "You haven't been with a man." He wasn't asking. He spoke the words out loud, seemingly to let them sink into his own psyche. "How did I not know this?"

Margaret blinked. She remained silent while he processed.

He glanced around the room, searching for answers. He wouldn't find them. "There's a story behind this."

*He's astute.*

"I'll want to know." He met her gaze, set his hands on her thighs once more. "I won't make you tell me now, but soon. You need to think about your answer. I want to know about your past and why you've never explored this side of yourself."

She nodded. "Yes, Sir." She understood. She didn't blame him.

"Was Lori your first experience with submission?"

"No, Sir."

"Have there been others?"

"Other what, Sir?"

"Other women."

"Yes." The word came out on a breath.

His gaze penetrated her deeply. She owed him an explanation. She knew that. But not now. Not yet. She wasn't ready.

Carlton's face dipped.

"I'm not a lesbian, Sir. If that's what you're thinking. I'm bisexual. I've just never been with a man. Never met one I trusted."

"And me? Do you trust me?"

"I do, Sir. I really do."

A smile spread across his face as he shook his head. "Do you realize how horny that makes me?"

"Show me, Sir." God, she was bold. She'd never been this brazen. Hell, she'd never been perused like this by a man. And she liked it. No, she loved it. Many men had ogled her over the years. She'd seen their eyes. She'd seen the way they leered at her. They admired her body. But more often than not, they were only thinking sex. No, not sex. Fucking. They wanted to fuck her. That was all.

Carlton's gaze was different. It always had been. She knew he wanted to dominate her. That went without saying. It was in his nature. Just as surely as she wanted to submit to him. But his look...his look was of adoration. Oh, he wanted her. There was no doubt about that. But his needs went far deeper than just a fuck. He might not be ready to admit it, but his eyes gave him away.

And that fact alone brought her to her knees.

She now admitted to herself she'd lusted after him for months. And now, she wanted to see what lay under those jeans. He might not have ever entertained the same thoughts about her, but his eyes were open now. Wide. She had proposed this herself, and the man had taken her up on the offer. She would never regret a thing. No matter how this turned out, she vowed to enjoy every moment while it lasted.

One side of Carlton's mouth rose higher. He chuckled. "Who's running the show?" He gripped her thighs again. It was a good sign. She wasn't made of porcelain.

"You, Sir."

He lifted one eyebrow. "And yet you're asking me to remove my jeans?"

"I am, Sir."

"Kind of bold, aren't you? You just got here." Laughter filled his eyes.

He ignored her request. In fact, he settled himself between her legs once more. Without further comment, he lifted the hood of her clit. He blew a breath against it.

She tried to control her reaction, but it was impossible. She'd never been this horny. This needy. His gaze alone drove her to the edge. His fingers made her vision cloud. And now... "Oh... God..." When his tongue swiped through her sex and across her clit, she nearly came. She didn't have permission. It didn't matter.

"Red," she mumbled. "Red," she said louder. Her thighs trembled. She would lose this battle if he didn't stop.

His mouth lifted off her. "Red because you want me to stop?"

"Red because I'm going to come, and you haven't given me permission."

"Maggie..." That one word, so reverent. "You're so responsive. What am I going to do with you?" He blew on her sex again.

Her entire body shook with want. No, with need. She released her hands from the grip they held on each other to squeeze the sheet beneath her. She needed something more substantial to hold on to. But there was nothing. Nothing but the sensation as if she were falling. It wasn't logical. After all, she was lying on his king-size bed.

"I'm so proud of you. We should have discussed a safe

word. But you're one step ahead of me." He stroked her thighs again.

Every gentle touch, every caress, heightened her arousal. The first time he touched her there she'd been climbing the hill. Now that she'd reached the peak, every skim of his fingers across her skin might as well have been pressing on her G-spot. She was that sensitive. "I'll come if you keep touching me. I'm so close. I don't think I can stop it, Sir."

No warning. Not even a look. One second she was speaking, and the next second Carlton thrust two fingers deep into her pussy. She bucked her hips. She moaned, a loud, deep, vibrating sound that didn't seem to come from herself.

When Carlton removed his fingers only to thrust them back in again, he spoke one word: "Come."

Margaret screamed. Her channel gripped his fingers as she came around them. Again and again the pulsing continued.

Still he thrust, dragging across her G-spot with each swipe of his fingers. He moved with her rhythm, slowing as the orgasm subsided.

When her vision cleared, she looked at him. His smile was barely noticeable, but there all the same.

It wasn't as though that had been her first orgasm. Of course not. She had a sexual appetite that rivaled most women. And probably some men. She wasn't kidding about the vibrators. She had several. And she used them. Besides, she'd had sex with numerous women. The fact that she hadn't been with a man had nothing to do with it.

The reality was no orgasm she'd ever had could compare to the one Carlton had just delivered. Perhaps it was the intensity in his gaze, or the release of pent-up stress from a week of denial. In any case, she was now putty in his hands. He couldn't know that, of course. After all, he hadn't been present for any of her other sexual encounters.

True, he'd seen her at the club. She'd never been chaste, not even in public. But still, at no point would he have been close enough to witness the difference between those instances and this one.

"So sexy. Maggie, there aren't words." He removed his fingers and held her gaze as he brought them to his mouth and sucked them clean. "I meant for this little session to educate me on what gets you off. Now I have a new question. What doesn't get you off?" He leaned over her, planting his hands on both sides her face. His stare, deep, consuming, bored into her. "You're going to make me a very tired man, aren't you?"

"I hope so, Sir."

He chuckled, his head shaking slightly. "I'm going to enjoy every minute of it. But for now, I'm going to kiss you." In slow motion, as though they had all the time in the world, he lowered his lips to hers. The first touch was gentle, more like a chaste peck. And then between one second and the next, the kiss took on new life. He angled his head to one side and consumed her. His tongue slipped between her lips as though he were starving.

Also ravenous, she met him halfway, her tongue dueling with his in a battle to see who could take in more of the other's scent and flavor.

Carlton moaned.

She swallowed his sound. She lifted her hands from above her head and threaded her fingers into his hair. She knew she shouldn't, and would probably suffer the repercussions of her actions later, but it was worth it. She needed to deepen the kiss, as if that were possible.

Carlton didn't seem to mind, at least not in this instance. When he eventually pulled back—millimeters, not enough to separate their lips—he met her gaze.

Finally, he nibbled a path down her neck, across her chest, and over the swell of her breast. As he sucked her nipple between his lips and flicked his tongue over the tip, she gasped. How was it possible his every touch lured her body deeper into his web?

They were just lips. A tongue. Hands that roamed over her body. What made them different?

She knew the answer to the question almost before she finished the thought. It wasn't because that tongue, those lips and hands, belonged to a man instead of a woman. No, that was too simple. It had nothing to do with his gender.

It wasn't even because she hadn't been with a Dom for a while, male or female.

It was Carlton.

She shuddered.

He would have mistaken her shudder as a response to him sucking her nipple.

She'd let him think that. It was safer. But the reality was something she wasn't willing to face yet. Her heart would get broken if she fell for Carlton. Besides, just because one man made her come apart didn't mean she was in love with him or anything. It was simply sex. He'd made that clear from the beginning of this arrangement.

What she wanted, though, was to make sure he gazed at her with the same reverence in his eyes every single day while she was under his care.

# Chapter Seven

CARLTON LIFTED BOTH HANDS to extract hers from his hair. Surrounding her small hands with his, he tugged them over her head. With one hand, he clasped both her wrists and held her steady. Stretching out, he eased to one side of her, leaving his thigh between her legs, knowing the friction of his jeans against her pussy would unravel her. "Was that your first orgasm with a man?"

She nodded.

He fought to keep the idea from going to his head. Holy shit.

He glanced at the clock on the bedside table. It was after two. "You must be tired, baby." With his free hand, he brushed a lock of her hair from her forehead. He continued stroking her skin, lightly dancing his fingers down her cheek, her neck, her shoulder. When he circled her nipple, goose bumps rose all over her skin.

"Not really, Sir."

"It's late, Maggie. I have a lot planned for you for tomorrow. You need to sleep." He stared into her eyes, the deep brown drawing him closer, like a magnet.

Maggie's eyes widened. "You're not... I mean... You're not going to...?"

"Fuck your virgin hole at two o'clock in the morning? No, baby." He spread his fingers wide across her belly. "I'm not an ass, Maggie. You'll learn that I'm demanding, a perfectionist. But I'm still a gentleman."

Maggie licked her lips as she nodded. As though chilled, her body shivered beneath his palm.

Carlton lowered his voice to nearly a whisper. "Is that what you expected? Were you hoping for me to make love to you tonight?"

She bit that lip again, the bottom one, or really just one side of the bottom one. But she didn't respond.

He smoothed his hands to her hip. "Were you hoping I wouldn't notice?"

"I... I thought it might be easier."

He stroked her thigh now, his own pressing firmly against her warmth. "Easier for whom?"

"I... Both of us, I guess."

Carlton released her thigh to grasp her chin and force her to meet his gaze. "I'm not an asshole. I'm firm. Many have said I was cold. Some have even liked that aspect of my personality. I do expect obedience. You will learn my likes and dislikes. However, I'm no bastard."

She nodded again.

He released her chin and let his fingers smooth over the contours of her body until he reached her pussy. He drew his thigh to one side, dragging her leg closer to his body. And then, still holding her gaze, he pressed two of his fingers deep into her tight warmth.

"Do you know how hard my cock is, knowing I'll be the first man inside you? Do you have any idea how humbled that makes me? I don't take that task lightly. I'm not a small man. I'll want to prepare you some before I enter you."

Maggie seemed to hold her breath.

He furrowed his brow. "You were hoping to get it over with."

She nodded subtly.

"Never." He shook his head. "You mean more to me than that. Do you understand?"

She blinked. Whatever that meant.

Carlton curled his fingers across her G-spot. Languidly, he dragged them back and forth. He watched her face as her arousal rose once more.

Her eyes glazed over. She released her lip from between her teeth, and her mouth hung open.

"Not tonight, Maggie." He set thumb against her clit and pressed firmly, never breaking the gentle strokes of his fingers inside her. Against his better judgment, he would draw a second orgasm from her. He needed to watch her face as she came. Her arousal was like a drug.

Her head tipped back, her eyes closing halfway.

"Uh-uh." He shook his head. "Eyes on me."

She jerked her gaze back to his, her mouth open in surprise.

"You'll come again, baby. But on my terms. I want to watch your face." He pumped faster, adding a third finger and fighting to keep from gritting his teeth at how fucking tight she was. What the hell size vibrators did she own?

His cock wasn't small. Thank God he still had his pants on. If he'd dropped his jeans, her eyes would have bugged out of her head. He'd seen enough naked men at the club to know he was well-endowed. There was no doubt he would need to prepare her before he entered her the first time, and even then she would experience some pain.

That kind of pain wasn't something he liked his submissives to endure. But this wouldn't be avoidable.

A small whimper escaped her lips and she lifted her greedy hips into his hand.

He stilled. "Lie back down. I run this show. Not you." He waited until her ass was firmly on the mattress before he continued.

Maggie panted. Her whimpers turned to soft moans.

He reached deeper, pressing his palm flat against her pussy. "So wet, baby. You like my touch?"

She didn't respond. A deeper sound came from her mouth. She was close.

"Not yet. Concentrate. Think about how good it feels. Control the urge to come. Your orgasms are mine. I say when. That's part of submitting to me."

Her face flushed as he spoke. The pink raced down her cheeks and across her chest. Her nipples pebbled harder. He didn't have a free hand to fondle them with. If he'd thought she could control her urge to move her arms, he would have released his grip on her wrists. But she squirmed too much, her hands pressing upward frequently. She didn't have the willpower yet to control her limbs while he tormented her with his touch.

He dipped his thumb lower to gather her moisture and

then circle her clit again. Suddenly, he changed the pace, fucking her pussy fast and hard with his fingers. "Now, baby. Come."

Maggie in the throes of orgasm was a gorgeous sight. Her mouth opened farther as she let go, her eyes unseeing, though she trained them on his.

"Carlton." She uttered his name on a breath.

Carlton was the luckiest man on earth. No one would be able to convince him otherwise.

✧ ✧ ✧

THE SUN WAS rising over the horizon as Carlton stared down at his little sub.

After her second orgasm, she'd been exhausted. It had been easy to tuck her back against his front and wrap his arm across her small frame in a protective mode.

She remained in that position now, dark locks of hair spread against his pillow like a fan. He wanted to run his fingers through the silky curls. Later. He would have time for everything later. There were so many experiences he wanted to have with her. There was no need to burn all his firsts in twelve hours.

He explored every inch of her with his eyes. He stiffened as he found himself comparing her to Karen again. But he quickly found there were fewer comparisons than he'd always thought. Her hair lay in waves. Karen's had been straighter. Maggie's cheekbones were higher, her skin a paler shade. Her nose was more blunt, a tiny button on her face. Her lips were fuller, a deep pink. How had he ever thought the two were nearly identical?

The first time he'd seen Maggie, he'd done a triple take, sucking in a breath he held for so long his face must have been red. It had seemed like a ghost had walked into the room to haunt him. He'd had to look away just to breathe. When he saw her smile the first time, he melted. Flashes of Karen tortured him. He wondered if God was playing a trick on him to make him suffer more than he already had.

Now, he found Karen's memory fading, replaced with Maggie's sweet body, her softer angles, her sighs as she slept so peacefully next to him. Instead of purging himself of her, or Karen for that matter, he found himself falling under her spell.

Maggie squirmed, her soft ass rubbing against his cock as she wiggled in her sleep. In her innocence she had no idea what she was doing. All thoughts of the past vanished.

Carlton smoothed a hand down her side, grazing the edge of her breast and continuing until he rested it on her hip.

She sighed, but didn't rouse.

Slowly, he inched his fingers toward her core. When he reached her soft curls, she leaned into him, her top leg shifting to give him better access.

He smiled. Her mouth fell open on a soft moan as she lifted her top arm over her head and she eased farther onto her back.

God, she was going to kill him. Her lithe, sexy body all stretched out on his mattress made his cock pulse against her hip with need. When he'd decided to sleep naked next to her, he hadn't considered the hard-on he would wake up with. He slipped his fingers lower until they met her wetness. When he parted her folds with his thumb and pinky and then stroked his middle finger through her pussy, she moaned louder.

He glanced at her face. Her head was tipped back now, her mouth open wider, her eyes still closed but fluttering beneath the lids. She lifted her free hand to skim across her belly, up the slope of her soft breast, until she reached her nipple.

Carlton sucked in a breath as he watched the tip harden while her finger flicked over it rapidly.

Not releasing her gaze, he dipped his finger into her tightness, reaching as far as he could until his palm pressed tight against her clit.

"Ohh," she murmured, her hips rising to press into his touch. She still wasn't completely lucid. He doubted she would be so wanton if she were.

With his leg still wrapped around hers, he pulled her thigh more firmly against his cock. Precome leaked from the head, giving him some friction against her leg, but he tried not to move more than necessary for fear he would come on the spot.

As he added a second finger to her sheath, she pinched her nipple. It was so fucking sexy he couldn't muster up the energy to reprimand her for touching herself without his directive. Could anyone castigate a nearly sleeping woman for fondling her nipples?

She rocked her hips forward, and he pressed in deeper, getting a better angle.

And then he couldn't take the suspense any longer. He needed to see her come. And he wanted her lucid when she did so.

It was so easy. As soon as he began to pump his fingers, her eyes opened. She froze for a split second, and then her hand above her head shot forward, and she wove her fingers into his hair, gripping his head.

"Good morning." He smiled down at her, not pausing the motion of his fingers.

She licked her lips, her deep brown eyes still wider than normal.

"I started to wonder if you could actually come in your sleep."

She lowered her gaze, a flush stealing across her cheeks. "God." She must have spotted her fingers on her nipple because she jerked her hand from her breast and grabbed the sheet at her side, fisting it.

"So sexy…" He scissored his fingers inside her, stretching her tightness, reminding himself how fucking slender she was.

She bent her free leg, lifting her knee into the air and planting her heel against the bed. "Please…"

Carlton wished he could capture this moment in his mind forever. So pure. Wanton. Needy. He slowed his movements, not letting her reach her climax yet. "My schedule, baby. Not yours. You'll come when I'm ready."

His slow, languid torture was obvious by her squirming and the soft sounds she emitted from her lips. She was close.

Suddenly he didn't want to tip her over the edge yet. He wanted to see if she could control herself. He removed his fingers from her sheath and threaded them into the curls above her sex, waiting while she lowered her gaze to meet his.

"Please…" The word was almost too soft to hear.

"Not yet. Don't move." He lifted off her, watching as her entire body shivered at the removal of his touch. He climbed off the bed, mindful of the rigid length between his legs. He ached to stroke himself, but that would only make matters worse. Instead he let his cock bob in front of him while he concentrated on his mission.

He padded to the bathroom and grabbed his supplies.

As he returned, he watched her face and gauged her reaction. It didn't shock him when she pulled her knees together and scrambled away from him several inches. "Now?" she asked.

"Yes, baby. And every day. I told you I would shave your pussy myself." He spread the towel he carried onto the mattress and crooked a finger at her. "Center yourself on the towel, baby."

"Oh God. Sir, I'm so aroused it hurts. Please, let me come first. You can shave anything you want, but I need to come so badly."

"I know," he murmured to soothe her. "And I love the way your skin flushes when you're aroused. Your nipples bead on their own, although you helped them along, I might add, without permission. You're the sexiest woman I've ever laid eyes on, and I'm humbled you're in my bed, submitting to me.

"I told you I'm strict. You will follow my directions, because if you don't you'll find yourself worse off than you feel now. I can make you *want* like you can't begin to imagine, and hold you in that state for hours if need be. The choice is yours.

"So, if you have any intention of getting relief from that tight ball that must be forming in your stomach, you'll situate yourself on this towel, spread your legs wide and hold them open for me." He watched her face.

Shock lasted only a moment, and then she complied, scooting to his side of the bed and planting her perfect ass on his towel.

"Good girl." He pressed her legs wider. "Set your hands on your knees and hold yourself open."

Her fingers trembled as she did as he said, her breathing ragged.

He wanted to cup her breasts as they jiggled when she moved. But he needed to concentrate on denuding her before he lost the ability to control himself and slammed into her hot pussy.

He grabbed the shaving cream, making her flinch as he squirted a glob of it on his palm and then spread it over her mound. He wiped his hand on the corner of the towel and then held her skin tight and firm with one hand while dragging the razor over her with the other.

"Breathe, baby. Don't move, but you need to breathe."

Shallow little spurts of air whistled from her lips. It would get easier. This first time was trying for her. He knew that. But he also knew he needed to set a precedent immediately so there would be no doubt what his expectations were.

He would shave her like this every morning. Sometimes he would get her aroused first. Other times he wouldn't.

Rarely would he let her come before he used the razor on her folds. Though in the future he would often take his pleasure first to avoid the stiff cock now bobbing between his legs as he concentrated on shaving his sub.

Maggie's knuckles turned white as she held herself for him. He was proud of her. She didn't protest or make a sound. He knew this was difficult. She'd been submissive to other people, and even long-term, but not for Carlton. Not for a man. It would be challenging for her every day for a while, exposing herself to a man, and not just any man, but a strict Dom.

Carlton went over her folds several times to ensure she was completely bare. It would be easier tomorrow, but today, for this first shave, he needed to be more careful and thorough.

When he finished, he wiped her clean with a warm washcloth. He stroked his fingers over her newly bared skin, enjoying the look and feel longer than necessary.

Maggie held still for his inspection. He was proud of her. He rewarded her by slipping his fingers inside her tightness again. "Still so wet for me…"

She gasped at the renewed invasion, her fingers flexing on her legs and pulling her knees farther apart.

"I love this look. Your curls were precious too, but a naked pussy is so fucking sexy, baby." He stroked her outer lips with his free hand while grazing her G-spot with the fingers tucked inside her. He needed to stretch her pussy. It was so tight. He didn't want to hurt her with his cock. Some pain would be unavoidable, but if he got her to relax and open up to him, it would help. "See how much more sensitive you are?"

"Please… Sir… I need you inside me. I'm so fucking horny." Her eyes shot wide as that last sentence slipped out. "Sorry, Sir. I wasn't thinking."

"You won't cuss out loud, Maggie. Don't even let yourself think in four-letter words so they won't be tempted to slip from your lips. I don't like it."

"I know, Sir. Sorry, Sir."

His fingers had stilled at her infraction, and now he removed them.

Maggie's head rolled back as she released her thighs and moaned. She knew she'd taken a step in the wrong direction.

Of course this wasn't the direction he'd had in mind either. His cock hurt now. He gripped it with one hand and squeezed, gritting his teeth. As he watched her frustration, he stroked his palm up and down his cock. Finally, she lowered her gaze to meet his. Her eyes widened as she watched him, tipping her face farther to take in his work.

"Watch me, baby. Learn how I like to be handled. In the future, I'll expect you to do the work."

Startling him, she lifted onto her elbows to get a better view.

"Do you have any experience with cocks, Maggie?"

She shook her head. "No, but I'm ready." Her bold words shook him to the core.

"Good. Watch." He thrust back and forth through his palm as he grew harder. Letting his dick slip almost all the way through his hand, he grazed his thumb over the precome leaking from the head and spread it around. He pressed his thumb into the slit, gritting his teeth against the moan forming in his chest.

He pumped faster now, his hand moving rapidly over his length. With his free hand, he cupped his balls and rolled them around beneath his cock, enjoying the feel as they drew up tighter to his body.

He stepped closer to lean on the edge of the bed with his thighs. He wanted to be near her, but more importantly he wasn't sure he could keep his legs from buckling if he didn't provide some support.

Maggie scooted her ass away from the edge and sat up straighter. She watched, her hands gripping the bedding on both sides of her body.

Carlton didn't touch her, nor did she touch him, but the way she looked at him gave him the sensation of having her small hands on his body. Her long hair fell over her shoulders. When she licked her lips, her gaze riveted on his cock, he groaned. His balls drew up tighter, and he pumped faster. It took only seconds for his orgasm to reach the point of no return.

He squeezed gently as he came, his release landing on the towel between Maggie's legs. The vision was picturesque—Maggie's spread thighs, her rapt attention, his throbbing cock, and the stream that landed so close to her virgin sex.

When he was spent, his arms shook. He no longer enjoyed the distance between them. He needed to consume her. In essence he wanted to swallow her innocence, both figuratively and literally.

It was going to be a long day filled with sex, but he couldn't concentrate on training her to follow his directives until he got her out of his system. Although that might have been wishful thinking. He doubted she'd ever be out of his system. And her pussy called to him.

MARGARET'S MOUTH WAS dry. She tried to lick her lips, but her tongue had no moisture. She'd seen cocks before. Plenty of men had been naked on occasion at the club. She'd watched scenes where they let everything hang out.

But nothing compared to this one. Carlton was huge. She should have known. His entire body was huge. Part of her was frightened out of her mind to imagine him putting that inside her, but the other half of her wanted him to do it so badly she could almost taste the semen he'd deposited between her legs.

"Are you on any form of birth control, Maggie?"

She yanked her gaze from where he still stroked his cock to his face. "Yes." She'd been getting the shots for years. With her small frame and little body fat, she'd needed the regulation of hormones. She rarely had a period, but at least her cycle was controlled.

"Good. Did you get your doctor's records this week?"

"Yes, Sir. They're in my purse."

He stared at her and raised an eyebrow.

She licked her lips. "Did you, Sir?"

He smiled. "Good girl. Yes." He grabbed the pages he'd set on his bedside table three days ago and handed them to her. "Never take a man's word for it, baby. Always read the fine print. Safety first."

She looked down at his medical report. All clean. She handed the pages back to him. "Thank you, Sir."

The ache low in her belly had subsided while she'd watched Carlton in action and then listened to this frank discussion about logistics. She still wanted him, but not with the same intensity of before. At least her vision had cleared and her mind was less foggy. For a while, until she'd blown the moment with her cussing, she'd been ready to beg him to enter her.

Now that she was more level-headed, she realized why he'd masturbated instead. Indeed whatever he had in mind to stretch her pussy and prepare her to take his length, she was game for. She wasn't stupid. It was going to hurt the first time, but there were surely ways he could make it better.

As she watched, Carlton rolled up the towel between them and tossed it on the floor. He grabbed her thighs and pulled her to the edge of the bed. "You must need the restroom. I haven't let you out of bed yet."

She'd been so consumed with her arousal she'd hardly noticed, but he was right. She nodded.

"Go. Come right back." He dipped his head toward the attached bathroom, and she slipped from the bed to head that direction.

A moment alone would help her regain her senses. The first thing she did was pee, acutely aware of her naked pussy. It felt strange having her hair gone, but arousing too. She washed her hands and face and brushed her teeth before returning to Carlton.

"Get back on the bed, baby. Same position."

She did as he instructed, placing herself sideways on the mattress, her legs spread, her hands at her sides.

He stared intently at her pussy, sending her mind into a needy orbit in two seconds. He was right. She felt far more exposed and vulnerable shaved. It heightened her arousal for him to stare at her so blatantly. Normally, it would unnerve her, if it were anyone besides Carlton. But the intensity in his expression relaxed her. He looked upon her with true desire to possess her, lovingly.

And it should have scared her. After all, he'd said this was a temporary exchange of needs. He had no intention of keeping her. And she had no intention of staying.

Reverently he stroked her thighs again, bringing her back to the edge of need. He pressed them wider, held her open to his gaze, not touching her.

Slowly his thumbs moved over her inner legs. He drew them to her center and pulled her lower lips apart. She felt the exposure immediately, the cooler air in the room meeting the wetness at the opening to her channel.

Still he stared. His gaze made her heart beat faster. She gripped the sheets in her fists at her sides for the umpteenth time, as though doing so would ground her in this world.

All she knew was the need to come as it ratcheted up with each passing second.

Carlton leaned his face closer to her pussy. His breath hit her sex where it lay open. She flinched. *God, please fucking touch me...* She sucked in a breath at the foul word as it entered her mind. He'd instructed her not to even think in that language. How would he know?

Somehow he would. Honesty was important to him. If he asked, she would be forced to admit her infraction as though she were in a confessional dragging up the sins she'd committed.

The difference was, in this case, Carlton was God. She'd be confessing directly to the one in charge. He would dole out her punishments as he saw fit. There would be no denying her culpability.

Carlton lowered farther. *Please...* She wanted his mouth on her. If she couldn't have his cock yet, she at least wanted this deep need to dissipate in any way possible. He could easily put her over the edge with his lips.

She wasn't a stranger to having someone go down on her. In fact, she loved it, had always preferred it over penetration any day. The bulk of her orgasms came from her clit anyway. Having a dildo or vibrator in her pussy at the same time had always been icing on the cake—fun, but not necessary.

Until now. Today she wanted more. She could sense she was going to have to be patient, but if he would just lick her with those full lips...

Finally, the wait ended. Carlton reached out with his tongue and pulled it through her opening and across her clit.

She whimpered, her legs shaking beneath his grasp. Holy mother of God, the man could tease. His touch wasn't quite like a woman's. His tongue was larger, wider, stronger. "Do you like that, Maggie?" He lifted his face.

"God yes, Sir." Her vision swam, making it difficult to focus after only the one touch of his tongue. To be fair, she'd been close to coming without the attention.

He lowered his face again and flicked his tongue over her clit, pushing the hood back to gain access with each stroke. "You're delicious, baby. I'm going to want to do this a lot." He released her thigh with one hand and pulled the hood away from her clit, gazing at her from such a short distance she gasped. "Ah, such a perfect pink pearl. Wet. Pulsing with your need. I can see it moving with each beat of your heart. You enjoy being licked."

She nodded, though she doubted he noticed. It wasn't really a question. There was no denying the effect he had on her.

He dipped his tongue lower and reached inside her.

Margaret moaned. She gritted her teeth to keep from pleading with him. She thought she'd needed to come earlier, but now the need was consuming her.

He pulled away. "How close are you, baby?"

"Very." Was it a good idea to tell him that?

"Don't come yet, Maggie. I haven't given you permission." He squeezed her thighs to emphasize his words. "Do you know what my favorite form of punishment is?"

"No, Sir." She bit her lip and released it, the pain from her teeth drawing her away from the need in her pussy. She gasped as she realized what the answer would be. "Edging, Sir?"

"Exactly." He smiled proudly. "I want you to experience that this morning."

She shivered, unsure if he could accomplish what he set out to do. She didn't think she had enough control to keep from coming even if he demanded it.

"I want inside here." He tapped her pussy as he spoke. "I know you want it too. And we'll be on pins and needles until we accomplish that feat. Are you with me?"

"Yes, Sir." Was she ever.

He leaned down to get something at his feet. She heard the rustling, and her heart beat faster. How had she not noticed the addition of new items when she'd come back from the bathroom?

When he returned to his full height, he frowned at her. "Keep your legs spread, Maggie. It's one of my primary rules. Keep your pussy open to my view whenever possible. Concentrate on that task above all others for the first few days until it becomes a habit."

She jerked her knees apart, not realizing she'd closed them. The unknown at his feet must have given her the subconscious nudge to protect. "Sorry, Sir."

Carlton prodded her entrance with something she couldn't see. He hadn't bothered to lift it to her gaze first. "Don't panic. It's just a dildo. You said you have several. I know you haven't had a man's cock in here before, but you've at least experienced the fullness."

It was true, but nothing she owned compared to his size, and furthermore, no plastic, glass, or rubber was the same as his warm flesh. She was certain.

She thought the item at her entrance was rubber. The wide end swirled around her pussy, dragging her wetness in its wake.

Margaret concentrated on the pressure as he held the dildo firmly at her opening.

He kept moving it around, gathering more of her moisture and driving her to crave whatever he held inside her.

"That's it. Just relax. Feel." His words were gentle as he set his free hand on her belly and held her down. "Legs apart. Keep them wide, baby. Feel the cock as it works its way inside you." He pushed at her entrance, letting the first inch slide into her pussy.

Margaret squeezed her fists. It was a fucking dildo. Why the angst?

Somehow the man managed to make everything he did so much more intense than it had to be. It was intentional. She knew that. But her body screamed all the same.

Another inch. He pressed forward and pulled back out as she accommodated the girth. So tight. So fucking filling.

She tipped her head back, elongating her neck, praying he wouldn't ask her to watch. Her eyes weren't likely to follow any commands.

"Breathe, baby. Is it too much?"

"No, Sir," she managed to whisper.

He pushed farther. God, it was tight. When his thumb landed on her clit, she nearly shot off.

"Easy." He removed his thumb. "Don't come. Just let the cock enter you. Feel it slide between your tight walls. Breathe."

Little by little he continued until the dildo was pressed deep inside her. As it hit the farthest place against her cervix, she moaned. Without his instructions she spread her knees wider to accommodate the girth. She didn't know they made dildos that wide.

After catching her breath, she opened her eyes to find Carlton staring intently at her face. His brow was furrowed, but a smile of pride lifted the corners of his mouth. She loved that look. She wanted to see more of it. If she followed his instructions, she would.

"See, you're okay." He stroked her belly, pressing gently, making her aware of the fullness in her pussy.

She wanted him to pull the dildo back out and thrust it in. Why wasn't he moving?

"Get the feel of it. It's big. Not as big as me, but large enough to help you accommodate me."

*Move.*

She was more than ready for the feel of it. Time to move.

Instead, Carlton grabbed something next to her. When had he placed something else on the bed? *Geez, girl, you're so aroused you can't see straight.*

It was leather. A strap of some sort. Looked like a harness…or a collar…

She watched as he brought it between her legs with one hand, the other holding the enormous dildo deep inside her. For the first time she realized it was almost flush against her. No part of the huge cock was sticking out. If he let go, it would slide out, giving her the relief she needed.

He pressed on the center, pushing it deeper, and she heard a snap. She jerked her head off the bed to see what he was doing.

"Relax, baby." He was fond of that word. Especially using it when she wasn't capable of anything close to relaxing. "It's just a belt. It will hold the phallus inside you. You don't have the muscles in your pussy to grip it yet."

*Yet?*

How would she ever have the muscles to hold something like that in place? She panted as realization dawned. He intended for her to wear the dildo. He secured it inside her as he spoke.

"Lift your hips, baby."

She did as he instructed, her torso shaking with the effort.

Carlton slid a section of the leather strap under her body and then buckled it at her waist.

It wasn't so bad. She could do this.

And then he cinched up the strap that ran across her pussy and up her rear crack. She almost came. The leather rubbed her clit and slid between her ass cheeks so tight she couldn't control her reactions.

"Sorry." Carlton nudged the strap over her clit to one side. No, both sides.

She blinked as she took in the apparatus. The strap running up the front was actually two sections of leather, designed to straddle her clit so that it was trapped but not directly in contact with the leather.

She eased her head back onto the mattress. She'd seen enough. How long would he leave her lying like this?

"Come. Let's get breakfast." He tapped her thigh as he spoke.

It took Margaret a moment to realize what he'd suggested. "Get up? Sir, you want me to walk in this?"

"Of course. And I want you to think before you speak. You don't have permission to question my decisions. If you can't control your excess talking and your bad language, you'll find yourself gagged. I know you won't enjoy spending the day with your mouth full of my rubber ball or a bit." He lifted one eyebrow.

Margaret nodded. She lifted herself to sitting, cringing as the dildo shifted inside her, seeming to go deeper than she knew was possible.

She moved quicker to get off the bed, hoping if she weren't sitting, the pressure would abate. She was right. As soon as her feet hit the ground, she found marginal relief. The pressure on all sides of her channel was intense, but at least it wasn't pressing so forcefully against her cervix.

And then the next struggle began. She had to walk awkwardly, her legs spread wider than usual.

Carlton turned and left the room. He didn't look back as she followed, small steps in his direction, every movement pinching her clit between the straps and rubbing against her rear hole. She kept her thighs spread and waddled behind him in an awkward gait.

Carlton grabbed a pillow from the couch on his way by and pointed to a chair at the table. "That's mine. Please kneel next to it. You know the position." He set the pillow on the floor.

She lowered herself to this spot. She spread her knees, perhaps wider than required. It made it easier to direct her attention anywhere but toward the huge phallus inside her. If she stayed very still, she could even ignore the leather pressing around her clit.

The smell of bacon filled the room. Her stomach rumbled. She'd been so preoccupied with her pussy she hadn't stopped to consider how long it had been since she'd eaten. The sun streaming in the window of the breakfast room was high. It was late morning. She'd slept long and hard.

It didn't take long for Carlton to finish cooking and sit next to her with a huge plate of food. Just one, but she knew his intentions. He would feed her at his whim, and she would accept each morsel he offered, eating the amount he found appropriate.

She tried to relax her body, leaning on her heels, her hands clasped behind her back, her chin dipping enough to suit her master. It was difficult. Her body hummed with unrequited need.

Carlton lifted a giant glass of orange juice and held it to her lips. "You must be thirsty."

She was. And she drank about half the glass as he offered it. He waited patiently until he was sure she was finished before he set it down. Next he picked up his fork and took a bite of eggs. He offered her a forkful after he'd taken his own, and she moaned around the flavor. They were just scrambled eggs, but food always tasted better when either someone else prepared it or she was very hungry. In this case, she met both criteria.

Bacon followed, and then a bite of toast spread with strawberry jam. She was in heaven.

Carlton was generous. He didn't stop feeding her until she shook her head. "Thank you, Sir. That was delicious. I'm stuffed."

He finished the rest himself and then stood to clear the table.

"May I clean the kitchen, Sir? You did the cooking."

"Another time, baby. Not today. Today you need to concentrate on you. I want to ensure we're on the same page in this arrangement and have a mutual agreement."

*And then you'll fuck me?* That was foremost on her mind.

"You may use the bathroom. Shower. Brush your teeth. I'll be there to help when I'm done here."

Help? She was more than capable of taking care of personal hygiene alone, though she doubted there would be many things she did alone for a while. As she stood, she closed her eyes against the renewed pressure inside her. Did he want her to wear the dildo even in the shower?

He hadn't said otherwise, so she made her way to the bathroom and turned on the shower. She stood awkwardly in the bathroom once again, waiting for the water to warm. The belt around her waist was tight. It had to be to keep the rubber phallus from slipping out. *How long does he want me to wear this?*

Margaret stepped into the shower, keeping her legs spread, and let the water sluice over her skin. It felt soothing after the stressful morning. Her body pleaded with her for release. Even the running water teased her clit as it landed on her nude skin between the leather straps.

She reached for the shampoo, smiling at the girly brand Carlton had obviously selected for her this past week. As she massaged it into her scalp, she closed her eyes. Before she could finish, the shower door opened. She turned her face toward the entrance, not completely surprised. Her eyes remained shut to avoid the burning shampoo.

Carlton stepped in behind her. He settled his hands over hers on her scalp and massaged with her. It was so sensual the way he didn't touch her skin at any other point yet, just her head.

And then his lips landed on her shoulder. He nibbled as he pulled the suds through her long hair to wash the ends. "Your skin is so smooth. It's beautiful. I'm a lucky bastard if you agree to wander around here naked for my gaze all day."

Agree? Was there any doubt really?

His hands were still covered with shampoo when he smoothed them over her shoulders and then around to cover her breasts, grasping her chest firmly and squeezing until she moaned.

"I love that sound you make, and the way you lift onto your tiptoes when I pinch your nipples." To emphasize his point, he did just that. Had she reacted in a similar way last night?

Sure enough, she found herself rising onto the balls of her feet, straining for more of his touch.

He spread his fingers and caressed her skin down her belly until he reached her thighs. His hands were so large, he seemed to cover her entire torso. "Step out farther, baby."

She obeyed, spreading her legs wider as he reached between them and fondled her open pussy lips. When his thumb brushed against her clit, she lifted off the floor again. "Sir..." Her voice had no power. But she needed him to know she was close. He would be disappointed otherwise.

He met her gaze, lifting one eyebrow.

"Red, Sir." She couldn't keep from coming. Her safe word would be used any time he pushed her too far or she got too close to the edge. It was her responsibility to make sure he stopped before she came.

"Good girl." He smoothed his hands away from her clit and down her legs and then up her arms. "Step under the spray, baby."

She leaned into the water and let it flow over her head until he was satisfied. When he pulled her back toward him again, he reached for the conditioner and worked it into her hair next. "My turn. Let the conditioner sit. Wash me, Maggie."

She shook as she turned around. She stared at his body for a moment, absorbing the size of him from chest to cock. His shoulders were so wide he could have been a linebacker. Maybe he was.

She reached for the masculine shampoo in the black bottle, noting it was a 2-in-1 with conditioner. He ducked his head for her to reach his scalp better, and she shampooed his hair, loving the way the thick brown locks, shades lighter than her own, slid between her fingers.

After she angled his head under the spray to rinse, she grabbed the bar soap and explored his body thoroughly for the first time. She smoothed her palms over his chest, amazed at the rock-solid feel of his pecs. Only a smattering of hair coated his skin. His nipples stood erect as she brushed them with her fingers.

She wanted to kiss him everywhere, feel his skin against her lips, flick her tongue over his nipples as he had hers. But he hadn't given her permission to do that right now. Instead she worked her way around him, circling his body as she soaped his back and then his tight ass cheeks.

She bent her knees to soap his legs, the dildo inside her making itself known as it pressed against her cervix.

She left the best for last, coming back to his front and lathering his cock with both hands. It stiffened in her grasp, though she hadn't seen it deflated at any point yet. She licked her lips, wondering what he would feel like in her mouth.

"That's enough exploration, Maggie." He gripped her wrists and removed her from her temptation. "Later. After I've had you. I can't tolerate that much fondling before my cock has had a chance to breach your tight pussy."

She met his gaze.

Carlton stepped under the spray and rinsed the soap from his body. "Rinse your hair, baby. And then get out." He exited the shower without another word, leaving her bereft of his presence. The man could fill a room without saying a word. In the shower he'd squeezed the oxygen out.

Margaret eased under the spray and let it wash down her frame until she was convinced she could safely exit without her knees buckling.

Carlton handed her a towel. He was already dry, and he leaned his naked frame against the counter as he watched her.

Self-conscious, she wrapped the towel around her middle and patted her skin through the terry cloth.

"Did you get modest on me?" He chuckled, yanking the towel from her body and drying her himself. He even wrung her hair out until it stopped dripping. "Open your eyes, baby. Look at us in the mirror." He inched into her space, his front to her back. The towel fell to the floor. His cock nudged the top of her ass as he wrapped his arms around her and cupped her breasts.

Margaret lifted her gaze and found herself staring at a framed picture of the two of them from the waist up. Her pale skin contrasted with his tanned shoulders. Her nipples, the same shade as her lips, puckered between his fingers as he stroked them. She watched as his lips descended to her shoulder and he nibbled a path to her ear.

"So sexy," he mumbled against her skin. "Come back to bed." He turned her toward the door and gave her butt a small swat to get her to move.

She hoped he was going to take her now. If he didn't, she would self-combust. "Is this where you're going to keep me, Sir?" She tipped her head at an angle after she climbed onto the bed and turned to face him.

"For today." He smirked. "And maybe tomorrow. We'll see."

He climbed up after her, tugged her around until she lay sprawled in the center, and then spread her legs. "How do you like the rubber cock?"

"Not very much, Sir. I'd rather it were the real deal."

"I think I can accommodate that." He unbuckled the leather belt around her waist, stroking her skin where it had left its mark. Before continuing, he lowered his face and kissed the indentation on her belly.

Margaret squirmed as the leather strap fell away from her clit, leaving behind the heightened awareness of its existence.

When he finally pulled back and unsnapped the belt from the base of the phallus, she held her breath. Instead of letting the cock slip from her body, he circled the base with one finger, drawing her wetness out and then spreading it around her clit. "Did you enjoy the way it filled you? I'm going to do the same thing."

"I did, Sir." Her voice was gravelly.

"Lift your arms over your head, baby. Grab the rungs of the bed. Don't let go. If you touch me, I won't last."

She followed his directive, loving that she affected him that much.

"Keep your knees wide. Don't squirm while I remove the dildo. I don't want you to come."

He gripped the rubber base with his fingers and pulled it out so slowly she had to hold her breath. Every nerve ending inside her came to life. If this was what it would feel like having his cock in her, she wanted that now.

She burned for him.

Finally it popped free of her, leaving her wanting and needy as her pussy gripped at nothing. He set the phallus aside and then used both hands to tease her entrance. "So wet."

She didn't dare move.

"So pink. So hot." He pressed a finger into her. "And still so tight." He removed his finger and sucked it clean.

She shivered. It was so erotic.

"I'm going to push you to the edge before I take you, Maggie. Don't come until I say so. Understood?"

"Yes, Sir." Though she had no idea how she would obey that command. The "edge" had long since been reached.

He pressed his finger back into her and drew out her

arousal to spread it around the entrance and across her clit. "I love how your clit jumps to attention when I touch it." He flicked it several times.

Maggie stiffened. So close. Too close. "Sir…"

"Patience. Control."

She gritted her teeth and prayed she could do as he wanted.

"I'm going to taste you again now. Don't come yet." He lowered his face and flattened his tongue over her sex, stroking it against her clit as he licked her.

Margaret moaned. She bucked her hips toward his mouth. Or rather her hips bucked themselves. It wasn't as though she had control over her torso.

Carlton said nothing, but he threw his arm across her waist and held her down as he tormented her again.

"How close, Maggie?"

"Too close, Sir." The pulsing that proceeded an orgasm began deep in her channel. She wouldn't be able to hold back. "I'm going to come…" She tipped her head back and bit her lip.

"Now, Maggie. Come for me." He pressed his palm to her clit and held it against her.

The pulsing increased in speed as her orgasm swept through her body.

In seconds, Carlton was on top of her, his cock nestled at her entrance before the orgasm was over. "Look at me, Maggie. Take me in." He eased forward, stress evident in the furrow of his brow as he made slow progress into her channel.

The pressure was intense, more than she could have

imagined. And on the heels of her orgasm, she wanted him to thrust into her fast and hard.

But he didn't. He kept a steady, slow pace, inching into her a little more with each pass.

She squeezed the rungs above her head to keep herself steady. The sensation was both too tight and beyond awesome at the same time.

Finally, he was all the way in. Sweat beaded on his forehead as he held himself over her. He breathed deeply. "God, Maggie. That's..." He didn't finish. Instead, he pulled out and thrust back in. "So..." He did it again. "Fuck..." His eyes closed as he thrust again.

Margaret lifted her hips to deepen the penetration. If there had been any pain, it was so fleeting she'd already forgotten it. After the initial stretch passed, she wanted more. She wanted everything he would give her. As often as he would offer. A new orgasm built on the heels of the first, taking her by surprise. It was deeper, not coming from her clit, but from inside her.

Her pussy clenched to savor the feeling. Heaven on earth. How had she managed to miss out on this activity for twenty-seven years? All she could think was *more*.

Carlton opened his eyes finally. He cupped her face with his hands and let his body consume hers more thoroughly, enveloping her in his warmth until his chest pressed against hers and his torso pinned her completely to the bed. "You're so beautiful, Maggie. And not just your looks. Your soul is precious. I'm a lucky man."

She thought she had the better end of the deal here, but she didn't argue.

He moved languidly, not fast enough to push her over the edge, but enough for her to know what was to come.

Finally, he exhaled long and hard. "I can't hold back, baby. Come with me." He increased the pace, thrusting deeper.

She wrapped her legs around his ass and held him tight.

"That's it, baby. Come. Now."

She shattered, the deep orgasm shaking her body, unlike anything she'd ever experienced before. It lasted longer too. And one orgasm became two as she felt Carlton stiffen deep inside her and pulse against her cervix. A low groan escaped his lips.

Moments later, as they both gasped for breath, he kissed her reverently on the lips. "Thank you, baby. That was the best gift I've ever received. I'm humbled by you."

It seemed she should be the one doing the thanking, but she nodded instead.

He lowered his lips to hers again and claimed her mouth, angling his head to one side so he could get deeper. His tongue slipped between her lips and tangled with her own. His cock remained inside her, still rigid. Like a starving man who hadn't just eaten breakfast, he feasted on her. And she gave as much as she took.

When he finally pulled away from her lips, they were swollen and slightly bruised. It was worth it.

"I don't want to leave your pussy." He stroked a finger down her cheek until it tickled, and she tipped her head into his touch.

"Don't." She couldn't think of anything better than keeping him inside her. If she died now, her life would have been worth it.

"You must be sore."

She shook her head. "Not a bit. The stretch was tight, but only for a moment. And then pure heaven. Sir."

# Chapter Eight

CARLTON SHIFTED HIS BODY to one side so she could breathe. He was too big to keep from smashing her. He kept one leg between her thighs, not willing to completely eliminate his presence. He brushed a lock of damp hair from her brow. Lord, he was in so much trouble.

He squared his face with hers and narrowed his gaze. "Tell me why you haven't slept with a man before."

She shrugged, though he knew what she was about to share was worth far more than a simple shrug. "It's not all that interesting really." She licked her lips.

"I don't care how boring it is. Spill."

She nodded. "I'm getting there. Give me a second." She closed her eyes, fortifying herself or looking into her mind for the words. "When I was fifteen, I had a girlfriend, Leslie…"

"Girlfriend girlfriend?"

She smiled again. "Sort of. We had experimented a bit, kissing and groping. We were young. We weren't sure what we were."

"Go on."

"One day my dad walked in on us. He was livid."

Carlton leaned closer, keeping his eyes on hers, watching every move she made. He caressed her arm as she spoke.

"You'd think he caught me killing someone or gunning down a community the way he ranted. He told Leslie to leave his house and she wasn't welcome to return."

Carlton sucked in a sharp breath. He ached for the girl who'd not been accepted for who she was. Now he understood better why she was slightly estranged from her family.

"Leslie scrambled out of my room as if the house were on fire. She glanced back at me and mouthed *call me*." Maggie paused. "I listened to my father scream at me for over an hour about what a sinner I was and how I needed to get myself straight with God if I wanted to avoid my designated spot in hell. He didn't let me say a word, which was good because I didn't have anything to add.

"I was livid with his reaction. It wasn't as though I expected anything different, but I had hoped. I'd known I was attracted to girls for a long time. I was attracted to both girls and boys. Either really.

"My dad never let me explain myself. Of course nothing I could have said would have mattered to him. When he finally left, he shut me in my room and told me I was grounded until he could decide what to do next. I wasn't to leave the room or call anyone.

"Before he could get down the hall, I had Leslie on the phone. I apologized for my dad, afraid she wouldn't speak to me again. But she was more understanding than I gave her credit for. We'd been friends for ten years before that

126

day. We'd started fooling around only recently.

"I wanted more. I wasn't done. And nothing my father said would stop me. I thought I was in love with Leslie at that moment. We agreed to sneak out late that night and go to a rave.

"My mother brought me dinner, not meeting my gaze or saying a word. Dad must have told her to avoid me. He controls her like a puppet. She kept her lips pursed. Her eyes were red. I think she'd been crying. I never knew if it was in disappointment over what she'd heard about me or sadness about the way my father reacted. I've never known her true thoughts. She only mimics what my father insists upon.

"When the house was silent, I dressed in the sexiest outfit I had, a short black dress and high heels my parents didn't even know I owned. I slipped out my bedroom window and ran down the block as fast as I could, carrying my shoes until I reached the meeting place.

"Leslie stood there already, waiting. She smiled at me, kissed me on the lips as though nothing had happened. And then we took off for the rave. It was the best night of my life. We danced until two in the morning, laughing and groping on the dance floor.

"Nobody at the party cared about our sexual orientation. The place was filled with every sort of couple imaginable. And some threesomes. We were among the youngest, but no one said a word.

"When we finally left, it was the middle of the night. Our feet were killing us. We carried our shoes and started on the long walk back to our neighborhood." She stopped.

Carlton kissed her temple, sensing she needed a moment. There was more. He ached for whatever she was about to say.

Maggie took a deep breath. "Three guys followed us. I don't know where they came from. Maybe they had been at the rave. Maybe they had simply seen us walking and decided to trail us. In any case, we walked faster, holding hands and whispering our fear to each other.

"They approached closer. They were larger. There were three of them and two of us. And when I finally turned, I found them wearing masks. I screamed and started running, tugging Leslie alongside me. But they were faster, stronger, bigger. There was no way we could outrun them."

Carlton stiffened as she spoke. He wanted to punch those assholes for whatever they did next even before he heard the words.

"We got trapped in an alley, confused about which direction to turn, unfamiliar with the area. And the guys taunted us as we backed into a corner, still gripping each other. They shouted anti-gay slurs, calling us lesbos, homos, sinners...

"I thought at first they intended to rape us or rob us, but that wasn't the case. It was purely a hate crime. They shoved us against the brick wall at our backs. They swung at us, slapping against our faces as they shouted that we were sluts and whores, an abomination against the Lord.

"Finally we heard sirens. Someone had heard our screams and called the cops. Before they ran off, the guys punched and hit and kicked us. They spit on us and then took off as the sirens grew louder."

"Oh, baby. I'm so sorry." Carlton's throat felt tight. He held her closer, drawing her body into his as though he could make the pain dissipate.

"My injuries weren't severe. Two black eyes, a bloody nose, some bruised ribs. When the cops arrived, two ambulances were on their tail. Before I knew it, Leslie and I were separated and taken to the hospital. I could hardly see through the slits in my eyelids for twelve hours. I don't even know if she was transported to the same hospital or not."

"She didn't tell you later?"

"I never saw her again." A tear trailed down Maggie's face and she pursed her lips tight.

"Why? How?"

She sniffed back a choked attempt to keep from crying. "My parents picked me up the next morning, beaten and bruised. We never returned to the house. They drove straight to an apartment in a city an hour away and we started a new life without anyone so much as mentioning the incident."

"You never spoke of it?"

She shook her head. "Not even once. My mother looked forlorn, sad for me, but she did as my father said. School had just gotten out for the summer. They kept me in the apartment for three months, not letting me out for any reason. Not that I ever asked. I had no phone, no life. I didn't even know where I was.

"I was dead inside. I didn't care about anything. I slept the summer away, wondering what happened to Leslie and praying she was still alive. I didn't know. I didn't ask. I knew it would be useless.

"In the fall, they enrolled me in a local Christian school, bought me a uniform and dropped me off at the door. Every afternoon my mother picked me up. I learned quickly that if I was ever going to have any freedoms again, I needed to play by their rules, act the perfect daughter.

"I never went so far as to repent, but I did behave perfectly. I got straight As, studied hard, maintained no friendships. I went to church every Sunday with my parents and listened to the pastor drone on and on about his kind and loving God. I attended counseling a few times at the church with a sweet lady who meant well, but entertained the same beliefs as my parents. I said nothing to her.

"She encouraged me to talk to them, but I never did. It seemed totally useless. I counted the days until my eighteenth birthday. When I got a scholarship to a local four-year college, I was ecstatic. I was even more impressed when my father consented to let me go there.

"I believe in his mind, I was cured. After all, I'd caused them no more problems, walked the straight and narrow and provided him with no reason to complain. I didn't date. I didn't do drugs. I didn't smoke. I studied and went to his godforsaken church and waited for my opportunity.

"I knew if I ever wanted to get out from under his thumb, I needed to go to college. And I needed their support. It would have been nearly impossible, even with my scholarships, to attend without the financial backing of my father.

"I'd never had a job. I had no money. No prospects. I didn't even own regular clothes. There was no need. I came and went from school in my green skirt and white blouse. On Sundays I dressed in whatever my mom deemed appropriate for church."

"What happened in college?"

She smiled, her tears dry. "I flourished. The world was my oyster. I moved onto the campus, kept a low profile, studied hard and opened up. I made friends for the first time in years."

"When did you start dating again?"

"My sophomore year I met a woman in my philosophy class. She was twenty-one. I was nineteen. She approached me, but only because she said I was constantly staring at her. We went out for coffee and discussed the class. At the time I didn't want anyone to know what I'd been through. In fact, I never told her. We dated a few months. It opened me up to the possibilities out there for me."

"When did you realize you were attracted to men?"

"I was always attracted to men. I knew that. Even before Leslie, I knew it. I think messing around with her was easy. We were already friends. When she began to show an interest in me sexually, I followed her lead. I suspect she was a lesbian. She probably thought I was too. I was confused.

"I knew about women liking women and men liking men. Everybody joked about homosexuals. But no one ever mentioned knowing anyone who liked both, or, as I prefer to think of it, 'either'. It's not that I'm into threesomes, just that I can be attracted to either sex."

Carlton wanted her closer. She was already so close there was no space left to fill. He tucked her head against his chest and inhaled her scent. "I'm so in awe of you."

Maggie pressed against his chest and lifted her face. "For what?"

"For everything. For living through what you've been through and coming out a victor on the other side. For not denying your true self in the face of adversity. For giving me this opportunity to help you see another side to BDSM."

"You won't get rid of me very easily. Plus, I just gave you my virginity, so to speak." She punched his arm playfully.

"Crazy that. I still can't believe it." He lifted her chin and kissed her lips. "What happened to Leslie? You never saw her again?"

Maggie shook her head. "No idea. At first it hurt so bad I couldn't breathe. I would wake up at night gasping for air, picturing those assholes chasing us into a corner. I never told my parents about the nightmares. I could sense immediately for them that chapter in my life was closed. It was like walking a tightrope. I either had to suck it up and live by their rules or leave home broke and alone and live on the streets.

"If I had asked for phone or computer privileges, I was afraid it might backfire on me."

"It took a lot of courage to do what you did. It's been twelve years. Have you tried to Google her or find her on social media?"

"Yes. I haven't been able to find her. I've tried so many times over the years. She isn't even on Facebook. And I have no idea what I would say to her if I found her after all these years. It scares me to death. She must be so angry."

"Baby, I can't imagine her being mad at you. You did nothing wrong." He stroked a hand through her hair, his throat clogged with her pain.

Suddenly Maggie wiggled free of his clutches and sat up. She stared down at him, her expression grave. "Listen, Carlton. I need you to know that I'm a work in progress. I don't trust easily. I don't trust men at all. Allowing you to do this for me is huge. I can't tell you how big a step this is for me."

He reached for her to reassure her he was on her side. "And I swear I'll make this experience worth your while, baby. Especially now that I understand better what makes you tick. I'm not surprised you've never been with a man. After living with your domineering father and experiencing that horrific attack, I can't blame you. But we aren't all assholes. I'm not." He lifted her fingers to his lips and kissed them.

"I'm beginning to believe you."

He tipped her head up to meet her gaze. "And you still see your parents now?"

She nodded. "Not often, mind you. It's awful. Just enough to keep the peace."

"And you've never confronted them about your sexuality?"

Her eyes widened. "Hell no. It's bad enough confronting them about the weather."

"But that's toxic, baby. It's no way to live. Doesn't it weigh you down?"

"Yes. All the time."

He pinched her chin and smiled. "You owe me for the cuss word too."

She smiled back and rolled her eyes.

He would remember to address that slight later. "I want to help you. That's why I agreed to be your trial Dom. You have so much to offer someone, female or male. And you're a strong submissive. You just need confidence and direction. Some Dom is going to be unbelievably lucky to have you.

"But part of helping you is going to include facing whatever challenges you're up against that are holding you back. It sounds like your parents are an anvil you've carried your entire life."

She tucked her lips between her teeth. Her body shivered and her gaze lowered. "That's more than I can handle, Carlton."

He shook his head. "I think you're stronger than you give yourself credit for. You're just scared."

"Terrified."

"Of what? Think about it. If you confront them, what's the worst thing that can happen?"

"They could cut me out of their lives."

He nodded. "So, let's presume you go see them, tell them who you are. Tell them you're bisexual and that you need them to support you and your sexuality. Let them decide if they can live with it. If not, what have you lost? They're toxic, especially your dad."

"And his brother is exactly the same if not worse. Uncle Rocky is a few years older. He's the one who convinced my parents to attend the freaky church they go to. Every time

I'm around my uncle and my righteous cousins, I want to vomit. But they're the only family I have, so confronting them has been difficult, especially since I can almost guarantee the outcome. It isn't going to be pretty."

"I can't imagine that kind of stress. I live far away from my parents and extended family, but they're always a phone call away. I can count on them if I need them."

"That's why I've gone twelve years as a fake. The idea of completely going it alone is frightening."

"Is there any chance at all they might accept your choices?"

She shook her head. "Not likely. But I know I have to face that or lose myself entirely. I've just been putting it off."

"I understand. And I'm here for you now. I'll support you in whatever way you need."

Another tear fell to her cheek. She wiped it away with the back of her hand before he could do so himself.

"You're the strongest, bravest woman I've ever met. No wonder you're such a fantastic submissive."

"Are you sure I'm not simply submissive because of the way I was raised?"

He reared back, squinting his eyes at her. "What? Your dad and his domineering ways? No. Not a chance. One thing has nothing to do with the other. Being a sexual submissive takes incredible strength and courage. Your dad's a bully. Your mom is browbeaten. That's not the same thing at all."

She shook her head. "I don't trust that to be true."

He pulled her closer and tucked her head against his

neck. His chest ached for her misconception, but all he could do was show her. She needed to learn that it was really the submissive who held the power in a D/s relationship, not the Dom.

He stroked his hand up her back until he wove his fingers into her hair. "You're safe here with me. I promise you a soft place to fall and a safe environment to be who you are... Submissive, I mean..." He pulled her face to his and met her lips. He kissed her gently. "Give me a chance to show you how it can be."

She nodded.

He kissed her again, deepening the intensity, dipping his head to one side and swiping his tongue in to tangle with hers. She tasted of the mint toothpaste she'd used and Maggie. How was he ever going to let her go when she didn't need him anymore?

He held her tight as he thought about his own misconceptions about her. She wasn't Karen at all. She was strong and smart. She'd been through hell and come out on the other side. She was a survivor.

Her hands wandered down his back as he kissed her.

He knew he was giving her too much freedom, but she also needed a chance to explore. He was her first man. If she wanted to touch every inch of his skin, he would let her.

When her fingers wrapped around his cock, he moaned into her mouth.

She separated their lips. "Are you always this hard?" She grinned before adding, "Sir."

"When I'm with you, it seems." He wrapped his fingers

around hers and stroked up and down his cock, showing her how he liked it. "Now, stop talking and get back into the role."

"Gladly, Sir." She scooted down the bed as she spoke, taking his dick in her sweet hand. She lowered her face the last few inches and licked the tip of his cock, making him moan.

He released her hand, knowing he needed to let her explore at her own pace. To pressure her in any way would make him feel like an ass.

"Is this right? Sir? Tell me what to do."

Now *that* he could accommodate. "Baby, everything you do that involves your mouth, your lips, or your tongue near my cock is *right*. As long as you keep your teeth away from my skin, you can do no wrong."

She licked a path from the base to the tip, gripping the bottom of his cock gently. She hummed around his shaft as though he were a tasty treat. "Like this?"

"Uh-huh." Words fled his mind. He only knew the feeling of her tongue.

When she sucked the head between her lips and drew him into her mouth, he nearly shot off the bed. A powerful aphrodisiac in the form of Maggie Donovan rocked his world.

She wrapped her hand around the base of his cock and let him slip deeper into her mouth. Her tongue was everywhere at once, curling around his dick as she sucked and then through the slit in the head as she pulled back.

Carlton gripped the sheets at his side, anything to keep from grabbing her. He forced himself to let her set the pace.

He wouldn't always be so accommodating, but this was her first blowjob, he reminded himself.

As she grew accustomed to his girth, she increased her pace, her mouth molding around his cock as though it belonged there.

Carlton held his breath. It was all he could do to keep from coming prematurely. He didn't want her to stop. But he was too close. "Maggie…"

She shifted her body around to straddle his legs, never breaking the suction.

"Maggie, you have to stop." He lifted a hand to her shoulder and pushed gently.

She didn't budge. If anything, she doubled her efforts.

"I'm going to come, Maggie."

She hummed around his shaft.

He gave up the fight and let his body relax into the mattress. If she wanted to swallow him, who was he to argue? The pressure built as he focused on his cock. He tensed his torso, knowing the inevitable was just a suck away.

His balls drew up tight as he reached the peak. And then he crashed over the top, his come shooting down her throat.

Maggie kept sucking. She swallowed as he came. And when he was spent, she continued, though with less pressure.

When his vision cleared, the room looked a little brighter, his world a little sharper. He wrapped his hands around Maggie's shoulders and hauled her up his body until their faces were aligned.

Now that she straddled his torso, his cock nestled in the notch of her pussy. Her warmth and the wetness leaking from her body drove his cock to stiffen once again. Still holding her shoulders, he pulled her in for a kiss. He delved into every recess of her mouth, tasting his saltiness within her and thinking he'd never known a headier instance in his life.

Maggie smiled down at him as she released his lips, a coy expression spreading across her face as she cocked her head. "Was it good?"

"It was better than good, baby." He held her face in both hands, stroking his thumbs across her cheeks. "I've never known anyone so…pure, I guess is the word. Uninhibited, maybe that's it. It's so fucking sexy. I hope you enjoyed it, because I'm going to want you to do that frequently."

"Anytime, Sir." She twisted her face to one side and sucked his thumb into her mouth, teasing the end of it with her tongue.

Between one heartbeat and the next, he flipped her onto her back, reversing their positions. His cock still nestled at her entrance, but now *he* was the one in control. Not that he'd ever relinquished control to her in the first place, but he didn't want her to believe she'd somehow topped him.

He gripped her hands and pulled them high above her head, just as he'd done earlier. He pressed them gently into the mattress and then tapped them as he let go, intimating that she should leave them there. He glanced down at her chest. "I love the way your tits rise when your arms are lifted."

Her body shivered. Good, he affected her with his crude words.

He stroked his hands down her arms, across her armpits, the outsides of her breasts, until he reached her belly. Goose bumps rose across her skin. He loved that about her. Her nipples stood at attention. God, how he loved that too. He was falling for her. And he needed to get control of himself. He couldn't keep her for so many reasons. He just needed to get her out of his system.

Lord, how he wanted to fuck her again. But he wouldn't, not yet. She would need some time to recuperate from before. But that wouldn't stop him from playing around. He cupped her breasts, pinching her nipples between his thumbs and pointers. He twisted them and held them tighter until she bucked her chest toward him. "Do you like that, Maggie? The slight, sweet touch of pain?"

"Yes, Sir." Her voice was breathless.

"Are you wet?" He knew she was. The question was rhetorical. But he also knew voicing it would arouse her further.

She licked her lips and met his gaze. "I've been wet since last Friday night, Sir."

He froze. Again, he knew he shouldn't be shocked. But voicing it…

The emotions racing through Carlton, slamming into him from all sides, were too much. She had a spell on him. He was slipping, allowing her too much free rein. *Get it together. Be firm. You're getting too lax.*

Carlton climbed off her. He released her entirely and slid off the bed to stand beside her. "Enough lying around. Let's go shopping."

Her eyes widened in shock. He couldn't blame her. One moment he'd been two seconds from sliding into her warmth and the next he dropped her like a hot potato. "Shopping? Sir?"

"I have to work tonight. You're going with me. I want you to have new things, outfits that I buy, that I pick out, that I instruct you to wear."

"What will I do while you're working, Sir?"

"Whatever I tell you to do." He flashed a grin. "Now, come on." He turned his back on her and padded toward the closet. Once inside, he thumbed through a few dresses he'd purchased for her during the week. He grabbed a black one and held it up. Perfect.

When he stepped back into the room, he found her standing next to the bed, her gaze downcast in proper submission. His cock hardened again at the sight. When would he ever get enough of her? *Two weeks, dude. Two weeks. Get her out of your system in that time and not one day more.*

If he didn't, if he let himself fall under her spell, she would hurt him. Inevitably she would leave to find another Dom. As she should. No one should stay with the first Dom they submitted to. Even though she'd had several experiences with female Dommes, it was obvious she was ready to switch. She needed to use this experience as a stepping stone to grow from. If he stayed with her longer than a few weeks, the pain of her loss would grow incrementally. No matter that she batted those fucking sexy eyes at him like he hung the moon.

"Lift your arms, Maggie," he said as he approached.

She obeyed promptly, her breasts rising with the action, her tits standing at attention.

*Fuck me.* She unmanned him every time he saw her. He needed to get a grip. He repeated his mantra to himself again. *This is temporary. You can't keep her. She deserves more than you can offer. And besides, she would break your heart.*

Carlton slipped the dress over her head, easing her hands through the armholes and settling the material over her shoulders. The hem landed inches beneath her ass. Perfect. He stepped back to get a better look. "You can lower your arms, baby. Spin around slowly."

When she faced him again, she lifted her shoulders and clasped her hands behind her back.

Maybe this hadn't been a good selection after all. The dress fit too well. Perfectly. Her young breasts still sat high on her chest, small enough they didn't sag. He could see the pucker of her nipples. The dress wouldn't be appropriate for the grocery store or the library. But she'd be practically overdressed for the place they were going.

Satisfied, Carlton turned back to the closet. He selected a pair of worn blue jeans for himself, shrugged them on without bothering with underwear, and then grabbed a red T-shirt. He toed his shoes into the center of the closet and slipped his feet into them.

Returning to the bedroom, he found his sexy submissive still standing demurely in the same spot. "Come," he said as he passed her.

She followed him into the bathroom.

He nudged her to sit on the small bench at the vanity. And then he picked up a brush and worked through the tangles in her barely damp hair.

"Thank you, Sir." She lifted her gaze to stare at him in the mirror as he finished and set the brush on the counter.

He wrapped his hands around her bare shoulders. "You're beautiful just like this. Do you mind going without makeup?"

"If it pleases you, Sir."

He smiled and bent to kiss her forehead. "It does."

He eased his hands down her arms until he reached her hands. Threading their fingers together, he tugged until she stood to follow him before he released her in the bedroom. "Stay." He went back to the closet and stared at the boxes of shoes he'd bought for her, trying to remember what was in each one. A pink box caught his eye and he flipped off the lid. Perfect. He returned with the dainty scandals and handed them to her, making her smile. Good. Hopefully that meant she liked his selection. He wanted her to do his bidding, of course. But he also wanted to make her happy.

As she finished slipping them on and stood upright once again, he stroked his thumbs over her nipples. "I'm a nipple guy, Maggie. I like to see them. And when I can't, I like to see their indentation. When it's appropriate, I'll stroke them to keep them stiff or ask you to."

"Yes, Sir."

He led her from the room and grabbed his keys from the kitchen counter as he headed for the door to the garage.

Maggie cleared her throat behind him. "What sort of

shopping did you have in mind, Sir?"

He turned to see her chewing on her lower lip. He stepped toward her and took her chin in his hand to lift her face. "I know we've slipped out of the role several times this morning. It will happen occasionally, especially in the beginning when we're still getting to know each other. There are discussions we need to have. Things about you I want to know.

"But when we're in the role, I'll expect you to obey without question. Trust my judgment. Do you understand?"

"Yes, Sir. I'm sorry, Sir."

He nodded. "I'm very astute. I *will* make good choices. I'll dress you appropriately for wherever we're going. I'll never have you in panties. I abhor them. I will however, permit you to wear a bra when the situation deems it necessary. I've told you that. That isn't the case this morning."

"Yes, Sir."

Carlton led her to the car. He allowed her to pass by him between the vehicles, and then he opened her door for her, shutting it after she settled in her seat.

As he rounded the hood, he fought once again to control his emotions.

*The sexiest woman I've ever seen is also the perfect submissive.* She had knocked his pants off him, literally. He couldn't imagine a scenario in which this arrangement wouldn't work out. And that thought alone scared him to death.

# Chapter Nine

MARGARET SAT ON her hands to keep from fidgeting while Carlton drove to the outskirts of town. She realized soon where they were heading. A fetish shop. Not surprising. And it was one she'd been to before, but not for a while. The entire time she concentrated on her surroundings to occupy her mind and keep from thinking about how wet her pussy was, naked beneath her skirt.

She stared at the buildings they passed, counting them. She watched a black sedan behind them follow them for miles, not saying a word to Carlton. Surely she was overreacting. Who the hell would be following her everywhere she went?

Eerily it continued to follow them, all the way to the shop outside of town. She shivered as they parked and the car went on by. She needed to stop obsessing over vehicles in her rearview mirror. She couldn't shake the niggling in the back of her mind that someone had left her a very nasty note, and perhaps that somebody was following her. Ridiculous. Because who would do that, and who the hell cared so much about her private life?

"What's the matter, baby?"

She glanced over her shoulder as Carlton helped her from the SUV. She shook off the strange feeling and turned to him with a smile. "Nothing." No way was she going to tell him she felt like they'd been followed both last night and today. For one thing, it was absurd. For another thing, he would freak.

A complete safety nut, Carlton had an obsession with locking doors. He also buckled her into the car himself when they left the house this morning. He drove the speed limit and came to a complete stop at every sign.

When they stepped inside the store, Carlton greeted the owner as though they were old friends.

Margaret stood behind Carlton, her gaze downcast enough she couldn't see the woman's face.

"Carlton, it's been a long time."

"Yes, it has."

"And even longer since I've seen you with a sub."

Carlton chuckled. "Kelly, this is Maggie. She's not new to the lifestyle, but she is new to me."

Margaret said nothing. She wasn't expected to. The introduction was purely for Kelly's benefit, not Margaret's.

"What can I help you with today?"

"We need a few outfits, and I'd like to try a variety of nipple clamps."

Margaret stiffened. *Try?* She didn't need nipple clamps if he was going to talk so bluntly. Her nipples perked up on their own at the mere mention of torturing them.

The urge to cover her breasts by crossing her arms was strong. She had to fight to keep her arms behind her back with one hand grabbing the opposite wrist. But Carlton had accomplished one thing—if he liked stiff nipples, she currently sported them.

"Follow me," Kelly said as she meandered through the rows of bondage equipment and clothing. "I'll get you a fitting room and then bring you a selection of outfits."

When they reached the back of the store, Kelly used a key to open a door and ushered Carlton and Margaret through. "I'll be right back."

The room was large, with plenty of room for Carlton to stay and watch. She wasn't sure if she found that disconcerting or comforting. Probably a little of both.

Margaret stood in the center of the cubicle and waited.

"Relax. You've purchased fetishwear before. You wear it every weekend." He chuckled. "I haven't brought you to the guillotine."

He was right, of course. But she'd never purchased anything with anyone hovering over her. Nor had she let anyone else select her garments. Her previous Domme hadn't been that strict. She'd let Margaret choose whatever she was comfortable with.

Within minutes, Kelly returned. She knocked softly on the door.

Carlton responded. "Come on in."

Kelly entered, discreetly slipping through the entrance so other patrons in the shop wouldn't be overly privy to what happened inside.

Margaret had been a sub for a long time. She'd been in public wearing all manner of clothing, some more risqué than others. She could only assume her nervousness this morning stemmed from the commanding presence of Carlton. When he was totally in the role, he was stern and serious. There was no telling what he might select for her to wear.

Kelly held up a variety of items. Carlton took them and shuffled them around. "This one, I think."

He handed it back to Kelly and stepped up to Margaret. Without a word, he lifted the hem of her dress. "Lift your arms, baby."

In an instant, Margaret was naked, with the exception of her sandals. Cool air from a vent blew across her skin, pebbling it with bumps. She shivered, though not entirely from the cold. Thank God she was required to keep her gaze lowered. She didn't relish the idea of facing Kelly head-on.

Kelly sucked in a breath. "She's exquisite."

"She is," Carlton responded. "I'm a lucky man."

They spoke of her as though she were a porcelain doll, though she knew Carlton didn't see her that way. He knew her better than to only see skin-deep.

Kelly didn't, though. "If you tire of this brute, girl, give me a call," Kelly teased.

Carlton chuckled. "Don't even suggest such a thing. I'm liable to lose her to you before I've had my fill."

Margaret flinched. His suggestion left nothing to the imagination. And it stung a bit that he could so flippantly pawn her off on Kelly.

Oblivious to the sting of his suggestion, Carlton took the black leather garment from Kelly's hand and held it over Margaret's head. "Arms again, baby."

Margaret obeyed, lifting her hands in the air, completely aware of the rise of her breasts and the fact that her nipples stood erect again. They'd begun to do it on their own as though they knew Carlton liked it and wanted to please him.

Black leather slid over her body, not nearly enough of it.

Kelly stepped forward and smoothed it into place while Carlton circled Margaret. "Let your arms settle at your sides so I can see how it fits."

"Yes, Sir." She lowered her hands, her fists clenching as she stared down at the front of the "dress". Thin straps held the leather over her shoulders. The bodice was almost nothing with the black material reaching around from under her arms to cover the outsides of her breasts. The two sides were connected with a crisscross of thin leather that snapped together at her cleavage to hold the material in place and keep her nipples barely covered.

Her entire belly was exposed beneath her breasts where a giant oval of leather was missing. The short skirt hung just low enough to cover her pussy and her ass, but only if she remained standing and didn't lift her arms.

She could feel the breeze on her back, so she knew it matched the front with the missing oval of leather. If her butt crack was covered, she'd be surprised.

"God, baby. That's so fucking gorgeous on you. Turn around. Look in the mirror."

Margaret spun toward him. She lifted her gaze to see herself. On her tall, slender frame, the dress indeed looked like it was worn by a model. She wasn't modest enough not to notice.

"I could sell a ton of these if you worked for me and modeled it all day," Kelly said.

Margaret glanced at Kelly's face, using the mirror as a way of discreetly checking the woman out. She was hardly less attractive herself. The woman was blond and skinny and only about an inch shorter than Margaret. She wore the outfit she currently modeled at least as well as the dress Margaret wore. Surprisingly, Margaret didn't find herself particularly interested in Kelly, and that was saying something.

"I don't think she's looking for a job," Carlton said. He reached forward and caressed between Margaret's breasts, letting his finger dance across the inside swell of each. When he dipped his finger under the leather to flick over a nipple, Margaret gasped. "So sexy. I love it. Do you love it?" He lifted his gaze to her, surprising her that he would care about her opinion.

She couldn't lie. It was fantastic. "I do, Sir. I feel as sexy in it as you think I look."

"Will you wear it to the club with me?" Again, he asked instead of insisting. Unusual for him. "I only ask because every man in Emergence is going to hit on you wearing this. You'll have to fend them off. Can you handle that?"

"I've managed for several months, Sir."

"Yeah, but you weren't wearing this." He reached under the material to tease her nipple again. "I especially love how easily I can fondle you." He leaned closer, letting his thumb join his pointer under the leather until he pinched her nipple firmly.

Margaret sucked in a sharp breath and held it.

"Now that's sexy." He released her nipple and smoothed his palm down her torso until it flattened across her naked stomach. "Perfect." He turned to Kelly, whom Margaret had all but forgotten. "We'll take it."

Margaret didn't move a muscle, loving the way his splayed hand on her belly made her tingle in every cell.

"Can you bring us some clamps to choose from, Kelly?"

"Of course. Be right back."

Margaret watched in the mirror as Kelly slipped out the door, the queen of discretion.

"You won't wander out of my sight in this dress. Understood?"

"Yes, Sir," she whispered. She had no intention of wandering out of his sight under any circumstances. The dress had nothing to do with it.

Almost soundlessly, Kelly stepped back into the cubicle. "I have several selections here. The best thing is to try them on and see how they feel. Give them a few moments each to make sure they don't pinch too hard or too lightly. Everyone is different. Nipples are all different in size and sensitivity."

Carlton lifted the hem of the dress and drew it over Margaret's head, leaving her naked once again.

She was calmer this time, but still self-conscious stripped like this in front of Kelly, her pussy so recently shaved.

Kelly handed the first pair to Carlton. He gripped one in his left hand and played with the opening of the other.

"Those are tweezer-style, the most common. They

pinch the nipple from underneath and dangle onto the breast below. They can be simple or ornate, depending on how much weight you want on them and how obvious you want them to be. You can adjust the intensity."

Margaret doubted Kelly had anything to say that Carlton didn't already know. But Margaret appreciated the explanation anyway, and perhaps that had been Kelly's motivation for the providing such explicit details in the first place.

Either way, it helped prepare Margaret for what she was up against. Even after all these years as a sub, she'd never worn nipple clamps. She'd seen them on other people, but Lori hadn't asked her to wear them, nor had any previous Domme.

Carlton cupped Margaret's breast in one hand, weighing it as he stepped closer to her until less than an inch separated them. He leaned down to graze her ear with his lips and whispered, "Relax. We're going to try several pairs and choose the best ones. I want you to wear them for me. I know they'll look fantastic on you, no matter which ones we choose. Can you do that?"

She nodded, biting her lower lip as she fought the shiver his lips threatened to send down her body with each breath against her earlobe.

He stepped back a few inches and grasped her nipple with his thumb and pointer. She was growing accustomed to the sensation. He pulled outward, drawing the tight bud away from her body, causing her to sway forward.

"Stay still, baby." His voice was gentle. Low. "Your nipple needs to be stiff when I clamp it."

He rolled the offended tip in his fingers both directions, languidly, almost too far.

Meanwhile Margaret's pussy grew wet with need. She inched her legs closer instinctively, praying a line of her moisture didn't drip from her lower lips.

Carlton didn't say a word, but he did step between her legs with one foot and nudge them apart again. While she was concentrating on her sex, he attached the clamp to her nipple. He let it go, leaving it to hang down from her breast.

Margaret gasped at the sudden sharp pinch.

"Breathe. It isn't that bad. Concentrate. I want to find the right ones that hurt just enough to keep your attention, but also make you more aroused. If they're too tight, you won't be able to get beyond the pain to the pleasure."

Margaret nodded subtly, not willing to move more than necessary and not trusting her mouth enough to separate her lips for fear she would moan.

He switched to her other nipple and worked it in a similar fashion until she had to press her lips together. When the pinch came, she was more prepared.

"How do those feel?" Kelly asked.

"Um..." Margaret wasn't sure. "Okay, I guess." She held as still as possible.

"I like these. Do they come in different styles?" Carlton turned toward Kelly.

"Yes. Different weights and a variety of dangles. I can show you a selection."

"Okay. Let's try another set." Without warning he unpinched first one nipple and then the other.

Margaret gasped. She fought the urge to come. It seemed ludicrous she was that close without him touching her pussy.

"Better give her a second to recover, Carlton," Kelly warned.

Thank God, because Margaret didn't think she could have made her lips move to advise Carlton similarly.

Kelly opened another package. "Try these next. They tend to be a little more intense. I wouldn't recommend starting with them, but you might want to purchase them for later. They're called clover clamps. Their pinch is firmer, and they aren't adjustable."

Carlton didn't give Margaret much time to think. He pinched one already offended nipple between two fingers and quickly clamped it with the new device of torture.

"Oh God. That's tight." Margaret squeezed her eyes shut. She hadn't had permission to speak out like that, but she also couldn't help it. "Too tight."

Carlton removed it within seconds and he leaned forward to take the swollen bud into his mouth, licking it and sucking it until the sting eased. "We'll leave that one for now. I don't want you in so much pain you can't derive pleasure. I'm not that kind of Dom." He took her cheek in his palm and kissed her lips. "You know that, right?"

"Yes, Sir," she said breathlessly. She was learning his ways. It hadn't been twelve hours yet, and already she knew she could trust him. Actually, she'd known before last night, but the reinforcement was reassuring.

Carlton turned around. "I'll look at a few tweezer varieties up front, and we'll take the dress."

"Perfect." Kelly slipped out of the room again, leaving Margaret with Carlton's intense gaze on her naked body.

"I can't wait for you to wear those for me." He stepped closer. "Did they make you wet?"

"Very, Sir."

He shocked her by stroking a finger through her pussy and bringing it to his mouth. He sucked it clean, moaning as though her cream was the tastiest of treats.

He stepped even closer until she breathed the same air as him, a chill shaking her as he wrapped an arm around her back and forced her to step backward as he continued to approach. In seconds, he had her back against the wall. He leaned into her with his body, wedging one knee between her legs. "Step out, baby." His voice was gravelly, low, almost hoarse.

She obeyed, widening her stance.

"Clasp your hands behind your neck."

She lifted them and threaded her fingers together to anchor her arms behind her head.

And then he was inside her, his fingers thrusting so deep so fast he took her breath away. His thumb landed on her clit and pressed hard enough to bring her up onto her toes. "Not a sound. If you can stay perfectly still and quiet, I'll let you come. If you make a single peep, I'll stop."

She nodded. Her eyes fell shut as he thrust again, deeper if that was possible. He fucked her hard and fast as her arousal built to a sharp peak.

A tiny, high-pitched squeak pierced the silence.

And then his fingers were gone.

Her eyes shot wide open, as did her mouth. "No," she

blurted. She was so close. Her body shook with need.

Carlton calmly sucked his fingers clean of her wetness and kissed her forehead. "You'll learn to stay quiet if you want to come."

Sweat gathered on her temples as she tried to catch her breath. Her pussy pulsed, the need still there. She pleaded with her eyes, but he ignored her. When he released her body, she nearly collapsed, her wobbly legs not willing or able to support her. All her blood pooled in her sex, demanding release she wouldn't get.

Carlton turned to grab the dress she'd come in wearing. He slipped it over her head as though she were unable to do so herself. And he probably had good reason. She doubted her arms would have been able to keep from fumbling if she tried to lift the material over her head.

Her pussy still pulsed. Wetness ran down her legs. She stepped forward awkwardly, not closing her legs for fear they would rub together and create even more friction she would be reprimanded for.

Carlton took her hand and led her from the room so fast her face still felt flushed with need. Her feet barely followed directions. The dress felt too tight. Her nipples abraded against the cotton as though it were sandpaper. The front of the skirt grazed across her naked clit, torturing her further.

Carlton smiled at her as he checked out, completely ignoring what had just happened. If he said anything, she couldn't hear him over the roar in her ears.

She watched him select a pair of clamps that had something dangling from them. She couldn't say what it was.

She was in a fog as though drugged. A sexual haze that wouldn't abate until she came. And he'd denied her that opportunity. And it was her own fault for not controlling her mouth.

He wasn't angry. It was a matter of fact. He wouldn't punish her for her transgression. She could tell it was over for him. Her punishment for not obeying his order had already been doled out in the form of denial.

*Orgasm denial.* He was fond of it. He would use it against her to train her. She understood that clearly. And any part she didn't quite grasp would be very sharp in her mind within days. He was a fair master. She'd known he would be. He hadn't done anything other than what he'd expressly promised.

Carlton led her to the Land Rover and helped her inside. She winced as she sat on the seat, her pussy sticking against the leather. She spread her legs to avoid any friction and to please him.

When he entered his side, he turned to her. "Do you understand what happened?"

"I do, Sir," she mumbled.

"Tell me."

She felt her cheeks heat under his intense scrutiny. "You asked me not to make a noise. I failed. You stopped the orgasm."

"How do you feel?"

"Denied."

"Does it feel good?"

"No, Sir. It actually hurts." She wasn't kidding. A tight knot had formed in the pit of her stomach that wouldn't lessen as long as she remained on the edge. And that could be a long time.

"You think you can control yourself next time?"

"I'll try, Sir." She couldn't promise anything. When he touched her, she lost all sense of anything but his fingers. Her mouth hadn't seemed to be connected to her brain anymore.

He smiled. "I know you will." He touched her cheek with his fingers. "You're so gorgeous when you come. I don't like to deny you."

She swallowed and nodded.

Carlton started the engine and pulled out of the parking lot.

Margaret tucked her hands under her thighs again and tried to breathe normally.

It was going to be a long day.

# Chapter Ten

CARLTON PULLED THE CAR up to the back entrance of Emergence without saying a word. He'd kept one eye on the rearview mirror and one out the windshield the entire drive. Either he was growing paranoid, or the same car always seemed to be on their tail every time they drove. *The world is covered with dark sedans, dude. Loosen up.*

He shook the irrational fear from his mind and parked. He had things he needed to take care of at work. Saturday was a busy day, and he needed to make sure everything was attended to before they opened in the evening.

Maggie fidgeted in her seat.

He knew what she was thinking. "The only person here is Jason. I don't think Jason cares if you're out for the day without a bra. Do you?"

"No, Sir."

"Then let's go inside. I'll order lunch. It's late. You must be starving."

Carlton took her hand as he led her inside. He loved the feel of her small palm against his. He totally swallowed her hand with his. As they passed Jason's office, Carlton greeted him. "Hey, boss."

Jason glanced at his watch and smirked. "Getting a late start today?"

"We had some things to take care of." He leaned on the doorframe, keeping Maggie at his back as he rolled his eyes. "I'll be in my office if you need me."

Carlton knew Jason well. The man was teasing. And Carlton deserved the ribbing after the number of years he'd gone without a sub, even a temporary one.

Carlton led Maggie to his office and pointed toward the love seat against the wall. "Sit, baby. I'll order us some sandwiches."

He watched as she carefully lowered herself onto his soft, beige leather couch.

"We aren't at home, Maggie. Sit however you like. I don't expect you to hold any particular form here unless I specifically shut the door and tell you so."

She nodded and tucked her legs under her.

The first item of business was lunch. Carlton called his favorite deli down the street and ordered sandwiches to be delivered. Then he powered up his computer and proceeded to check his email.

"What exactly do you do for Jason?" she asked.

The door to the office was open, and at that moment Jason happened to walk in. "Everything," he said with a smile. "Without him, I'd still be in the small, run-down location where I started. He arranges the cleaning crew, stocks the beverages and snacks, keeps up the membership, sends out the bills, handles payroll, checks the backgrounds of any perspective members. He's God around here." He lowered his voice to barely above a whisper. "Secretly, he runs the show. I'm just a pretty face."

"I'd hardly go that far, but thank you, Jason." Carlton shook his head. He'd been with Jason so long he knew the man inside and out. He could guess what the man needed before he asked. And now was no exception. "Did you get my list of guests for tonight?"

Jason laughed again. "See what I mean? He's one step ahead of me," he said, facing Maggie. Then he turned toward Carlton. "I did. Anything I need to know specifically?"

"I don't think so. Nobody stands out for tonight."

"Good. And you'll be here?"

"I will," Carlton said. "Maggie will be here also."

Jason turned back to Maggie. "Let me know if you need anything. And you know you're free to come and go from the back rooms any time, right?"

Maggie nodded. "Thank you."

Jason backed up toward the door as he directed his attention to Carlton once again. "Make sure you have enough staff available to handle things up front. Delegate, man. You've been here for ten years. You deserve to enjoy yourself. Spend time with your sub. Don't work your ass off at the front door. I've been telling you that for years. Now's the time to get other people to do the grunt work for you. They can come to me if they have a problem. The place won't fall apart if your huge frame isn't blocking the entrance." Jason chuckled as he left the office.

Carlton smirked and turned back to his computer.

"You're like family to him," Maggie said.

"Yeah."

A buzzing noise at Maggie's feet indicated her cell was ringing in her purse.

Carlton watched her face as she cringed, a slight flinch indicating she wasn't pleased.

"Are you going to get that?"

She shook her head. "No."

"Who is it?" Obviously she had the ringtone set up for someone or she wouldn't have reacted in that fashion.

"My mom."

He watched her face as she lowered her gaze. "Does she call often?"

"Yes."

"And you don't answer?"

Margaret rolled her eyes. "She wants me to come over for dinner usually. She has hounded me more often lately."

"And your dad?"

"Nah. He doesn't call. He probably thinks I'm a lost cause."

"Do you ever go? To dinner, I mean?"

"Never."

"Maybe you should?"

She smiled. "Are you going to bug me about this?"

"Maybe. If it's that painful for you, you need to put it to rest. At least with your mom. Who knows? Maybe she isn't as rigid as your dad. Maybe she secretly wishes she had a relationship with you. Maybe if you give her a chance, she'll show you a side of her you never knew existed."

"Or maybe she'll tell me not to let the door hit me on the ass on the way out."

"And would that really be worse at this point? You have to ask yourself if you're better off with or without people sometimes. This is one of those times."

"I know all this, Carlton." She wasn't angry, but exasperated.

He decided not to push the subject further right then.

The sandwiches came and they ate together. They were both starving and polished the meal off fast.

"Those are good. I've never been to that deli before," Maggie said as she wiped her mouth with a napkin. She leaned back on the couch. "Now I'm exhausted. You've worn me out."

"Take a nap. That love seat is small, but you're hardly bigger than it. Lie down and rest. I've got a few more things to do before I can wrap up for the day." Jason was very understanding, and Carlton knew the man meant every word he'd said about Carlton taking time for himself, but his work ethic wouldn't permit him to fool around all day. He needed to spend the afternoon making sure the place was ready to open.

"Mm. I might do that." She leaned to one side and curled her legs under her. Her cheek rested on the arm of the sofa, and she tucked her hands under her chin and closed her eyes.

God, she was precious. He was so fucking screwed.

Carlton glanced up every few minutes to watch her sleep. So peaceful. When she was asleep, all her worries disappeared and her expression relaxed. The only other time she let go of her problems was when she was aroused.

He liked both looks on her.

About an hour later, he finished checking on everything for that evening and shut down the computer. He rounded the desk and padded to his sleeping sub. For a few minutes he simply stared down at her, not wanting to disturb her. But the need to touch her was larger than his will to hold back.

He soundlessly backed to the office door, shut it with a slight snick and turned the lock on the knob.

When he returned to Maggie, he kneeled at her side and set his hand on her smooth, creamy thigh. The dress was so short, it barely covered her ass, and he didn't intend for it to do even that now.

He caressed her skin as he eased his hand higher.

She moaned into the arm of the couch, and her top leg rose just enough to separate her thighs and give him better access to her pussy.

Panties were the dumbest invention of man, and Carlton was glad he'd banned them. When he wanted pussy, he didn't want the hindrance to get in the way.

She didn't come fully awake until he grazed his fingers through her folds, finding her wet heat beneath.

And then she moaned as her eyes flittered open. She smiled at him. "Is this how you're always going to wake me?"

"Mm. Maybe. Do you mind?" He lifted an eyebrow in question.

She shook her head. "Not a bit." Her face grew serious and her mouth fell open wide when he pressed two fingers into her channel. She drew her knee up farther, giving him better access.

"I love the look on your face when I reach inside you." He stroked her G-spot as she stretched her body longer. She gripped the arm of the sofa with both hands.

"So, this is my office," he said as he continued to torment her with two fingers. "Jason is just down the hall."

"Mmm hmmm." Her eyes grew glassy as she sucked her lower lip in between her teeth.

"You don't want Jason to hear you, right?"

"Mmm."

Carlton removed his fingers and grabbed her lower thigh until he had her attention. As her eyes landed on his, he continued. "No noises. Not a sound. If you can control your voice, I'll pleasure you. If you can't, I'll stop."

She nodded.

Carlton nudged her waist with his free hand, easing her onto her back. "Keep your hands above your head."

She grasped the leather with the flat of her palms, trying to anchor herself with little success.

He bent her back knee and leaned it against the back of the sofa. He pulled her other leg to let it dangle over the edge of the seat. And then he pushed her dress up to expose her pussy. "So sexy." He held her open with one hand on each thigh. "So wet for me. I know you need to come. You never got to earlier. I hope you can this time. I don't like to leave you hanging."

She gave only the slightest whimper.

He shifted his gaze from her wetness to her face. "Tell me, Maggie. Can you stay quiet?"

"Yes, Sir," she murmured.

"Let's see." With both hands splayed on her thighs, he

smoothed them up to her waist and then pushed the material of her dress above her breasts. Her nipples stood stiff and eager for his touch. Carlton circled them both at the same time, careful not to touch the tips. He didn't stop until he got the desired result. She bucked her chest into his hands.

"Stay still." He knew he set her up for failure by teasing her, but this was her first full day as his submissive, and he wanted to set the stage with no doubts about who was in charge. He wanted her to writhe with need, but be able to control her movements and noises. He would use restraints and gags to accomplish the task until she complied, but for today, he would demonstrate he meant what he said.

She wouldn't get to come right now, or even later when he tested her again. There was no way she would be able to control her throat or keep her body still. She was too new to his ways. And she would test him. And she would fail every time.

And in the end, she would beg him to strap her down and block her mouth so she could come.

But not this afternoon. She wouldn't be ready yet. It wouldn't occur to her. After a few more instances like this, she would realize what she needed to ask for to get relief.

Carlton left her needy nipples, stiff from circling them with no direct contact. He wanted her closer to the edge before he pulled back. If her legs weren't too shaky to stand, he wouldn't have done his job well enough.

He caressed his way back down her body to her hips, pressing them into the couch while blowing on her open pussy.

She flinched, the smallest squeak leaking out of her mouth.

He pulled her lower lips apart with his thumbs and then dragged them through the copious gathering of moisture. "Always ready for me." It was true, and her wet heat made his cock swell to the point of almost unbearable pressure beneath his jeans.

He circled her clit with his pointer, holding the little hood up with his other index finger. Again, with no direct contact, he made her squirm. "Still, baby. No movement."

Her rigid body fought for control. She was losing the battle. As he knew she would. But his intentions were to establish complete control over her and let her know he was the Dom. Her orgasms were his, to be doled out on his terms under his directives.

In a few days, she'd easily be able to orgasm under his command with more frequency.

Carlton thrust two fingers into her sheath. He pressed the spot at the base of her clit enough to send a wave of shock to her system.

Success was immediate. Maggie's mouth fell open, releasing her lip. She was so close to screaming, her face appeared to mimic the action without making a sound.

"Good girl." He was impressed. And proud of her.

He thrust again, twisting his fingers inside her. He released the pressure on her clit, knowing it would be too much. He didn't want her to topple into an orgasm without his permission. He had no intention of letting her go over the edge just now.

He thrust harder, pressing deeper.

Maggie dug her heel into the couch and lifted her ass to meet his thrusts. A loud moan filled the room.

Carlton let her go, pulling both hands away from her body at once, leaving her hot, swollen, exposed to his view.

Her heart beat so hard he could see the rise and fall of her breasts as her gaze met his, her mouth open in shock. "No. Oh God. No. Please."

Carlton licked his fingers of her arousal. "Those are the rules, baby." He pulled her dress down over her breasts, though he'd rather continue to watch her nipples, swollen with need. If he didn't remove the temptation, he'd likely take her against his own rules.

He backed up and stood, his cock protesting at least as much as her pussy. He needed relief and soon. "Let's go home for a while before we have to be back here. Maybe I'll give you another chance."

Maggie's arms shook visibly as she pulled herself to sitting. Her eyes remained wide with shock.

Carlton reached for her hand and helped her stand. He kissed her forehead. "You'll learn, baby. The first few days will be hard while you get accustomed to my rules. I make them. You don't have any leeway to break them."

"Yes, Sir." Her steps were unsteady as she followed him from the office and out to the car.

In no time, they were on the road. Carlton put his hand on her thigh as he drove, knowing his touch would keep her on edge.

Maggie kept her hands at her sides, saying nothing. Her legs eased open enough for him to reach between them. Her body pleaded with him, willing him to touch her. He knew the signs. And he ignored them.

He glanced at her peripherally several times. God, she was fucking gorgeous. Sometimes he thought he saw a flash of Karen, but only for a second and then it was gone. Her memory was easing away, replaced by this woman beside him who was not Karen. Her own personality was showing through. She wasn't reckless at all. He still felt nervous every time she wasn't with him, but at least he knew she wouldn't be out drag racing or mountain climbing without a rope. Maggie was more mature. Hell, she was older. Would Karen have been similar at this age?

He shook the thought from his head and turned to watch Maggie's profile while he waited at a red light. *She's not Karen. Not even close. And she's so much better.* Karen wasn't submissive. She didn't have a submissive bone in her body. Hell, back then Carlton wasn't even a Dom. The idea hadn't entered his head yet.

Maggie flashed him a smile while he stared at her. It lit up her face, and he gripped the steering wheel tighter.

When they got home, he led her to the bedroom, pulled her dress over her head and told her to lie across the bed sideways. "Spread your legs wider, baby. Arms over your head."

She followed his instructions, still shaking from earlier. Her pussy as wet as it had been in the office.

"You want to try again?"

She nodded. "Please, Sir."

He stared down at her, loving the way her body flushed under his gaze. Her nipples stood high and tight without touching them. Her pussy was still swollen and needy. Her clit peeked out from under the hood without assistance.

"There will be times when I want you to scream and writhe, and I'll let you know when you may do so, but other times I want to catch you unaware and watch the rapture spread across your face without anyone else knowing."

He leaned over the bed to get closer. "I'll bring you to orgasm in public when you least expect it. And to do so, you have to stay still and quiet. It's the single most sexy view in the world to me. I'll train you to do it."

"Yes, Sir."

"And you'll thank me."

"Yes, Sir."

"I'll give you another chance to practice now. Your job is simple. Don't move unless I say so, and don't make a sound."

She nodded, but she didn't look convinced.

Carlton pulled her ass to the edge of the bed so her pussy glistened right in front of him. There was no place for her legs, so he held them open and bent with his hands on both thighs. "Do you want me to touch you, baby?"

"Please, Sir."

Her pussy called to him. He needed to taste her again. He leaned in and dragged his tongue over her slit and across her clit.

Maggie jerked, her entire body lifting off the bed, the only purchase coming from her shoulders. And she screamed.

Carlton released her, letting her legs dangle over the edge of the mattress and stepping back.

"Oh God. Carlton. I'm sorry. I'm so fucking horny. I need you inside me. Please."

He waited while she realized what she'd said.

Her eyes went wide. "Sorry, Sir," she stammered.

"You aren't allowed to cuss. That's twice today."

"I know, Sir."

"It's not pretty. You're a gorgeous woman. I don't want to hear foul language coming from you. You'll learn to curb that instinct."

"I will. I'm sorry, Sir." She scooted back, pleading with her eyes.

"If you're going to cuss, you'll be punished. I've made that clear."

"Yes, Sir." She let her gaze fall, her head tip toward her lap.

"How will I punish you for cussing?"

"I don't know, Sir."

"What do you think I might use to keep you from speaking?"

"A gag, Sir." Her voice was barely above a whisper.

"Would you like to get that punishment out of the way now? Or wait until later tonight?"

"Now, Sir."

Carlton crossed the room and grabbed his toy bag. He brought it closer and pulled out a bit. He wasn't sure how much experience she had with gags, and he didn't want her to choke, so he would start small. Anything holding her mouth open would keep her from talking. It didn't matter what size it was.

"Lean forward." As she did, he put the bit between her

teeth and fastened the strap behind her head. "It's not comfortable. It isn't meant to be. It's meant to remind you of your lapse of judgment. My punishments will fit the crime. You cuss, you lose your ability to speak. Simple."

She nodded.

"Lie back. Keep your legs open. Don't move while I shower." He walked away, leaving her sexy body on the bed. It was difficult, but he had pushed the limits on his own needs. He needed to come so bad he was about to spew into his jeans.

His hands shook as he removed his clothes and flipped on the shower. In seconds he was inside, letting the cool water race down his body. He didn't wait for it to warm. He needed the lower temperature anyway.

Without hesitating, he took his cock in his hand and pumped. He needed fast and furious. There would be no slow rise to heaven. Not this time. He thrust into his palm hard until his cock grew stiffer and he came in long jets that burst from his body as though he'd been waiting weeks for the release.

When he was finally spent, he stood for a while to catch his breath before he could reach for the soap and wash his body. His dick stayed hard, mocking him as though thinking it was humorous that he thought he might be able to ease his need with a short orgasm in the shower.

Carlton rolled his eyes at the stiff length between his legs. "I know. I know. You'll have her again soon."

He stepped from the shower, dried quickly and padded back into the bedroom with his towel around his waist.

# Chapter Eleven

MAGGIE DIDN'T MOVE a muscle while Carlton was in the shower. She adjusted to the rubber between her teeth and played with it with her tongue, trying to keep her mind off the pressure in her belly. She'd been horny for hours, it seemed. And getting no relief.

She was familiar with his demands. He'd made himself clear. But knowing what he expected and following through on his directions were two different things. It was nearly impossible for her to stay still and quiet while having sex. She'd always been rather loud and squirmy in the bedroom.

Carlton seemed to think her orgasms would be more intense if she tried his way.

She pulsed with renewed need as he padded back into the room. He glanced at the clock before he leaned over her, lifted her head and unstrapped the bit.

She swallowed and stretched her jaw when it fell free as she hauled herself to a sitting position.

"Have you learned your lesson?"

"Yes, Sir."

"Will you be cussing anymore?"

"No, Sir."

"Okay then. You have two choices. We can go get dinner before going back to Emergence. Or I can replace the gag and you can use it to help you get relief without speaking. The bit won't keep you from moaning, but it will keep you from using words."

*Oh God.*

"It's early. We have time for whatever you choose."

She glanced at his cock. There was no chance in hell he hadn't just masturbated in the shower. And she remained as needy as ever. She wanted to cuss at him again, but she didn't dare.

"I'm not used to coming without moving, and I'm noisy, Sir." She lowered her gaze.

"And I love that about you. And I want you to be able to do both." He leaned forward until his forehead almost touched hers over the bed. "Your next orgasm will be quiet and still. Once you've accomplished that task, I'll let you have loud and squirmy as a reward."

*Fuck.* How was she going to do this? Earlier in the day she'd hoped he would budge on this subject, but not any longer. He was serious. She didn't stand a chance. Under her own free will, she knew she couldn't remain still.

"Tell me what you need, baby." He stroked her chin. "How can I help?"

*He knows. The bastard wants me to say it.*

She swallowed hard, mustering up the courage to ask for exactly what he was waiting for. She had no choice. She wanted to come, and he held the cards. She exhaled slowly.

"Restrain me, Sir. And put the bit back in. I-I need to come."

"Good girl." He released her to reach back into the bag. What he held up next made her hold her breath.

She'd seen and experienced more forms of bondage than the average human. Her previous Domme had enjoyed bondage. But whatever he held in front of her now was foreign. The pile of straps and cuffs made no sense to her.

And then he started attaching them. He encircled her wrists with Velcro cuffs and then put a belt around her waist and cinched it tight. Two more straps attached to the belt under her breasts, and he lifted those, drew them over her shoulders and crisscrossed them in the back, sort of like suspenders. He attached them at the back of the belt. The front sections nestled over her nipples, making her more than aware of the pressure.

When he lifted two more cuffs, she expected them to be placed on her ankles, but that wasn't what happened. He attached them high on her thighs.

For a moment she didn't see how any of this was causing her to be restrained, though just the thought of all those straps made her hornier. But she hadn't noticed all the connections until Carlton took her wrist and attached it to both her waist and her thigh. He did the same on the other side.

*Oh God.* She was indeed trapped now, and her thighs had no chance of closing with her wrists attached to them like that. She also couldn't anchor herself in any way. Her hands were of no use to her.

His face was intense as he worked. He yanked the towel he wore away and dropped it on the floor as he completed the attachments. "So sexy, baby. Do you know how horny it makes me to restrain you?" He stroked his cock to emphasize his words. Instead of waiting for a response, he put one hand behind her shoulders and eased her onto her back.

Her legs fell open wider. Her feet were free, but only for a moment. Two more cuffs came from the bag and Carlton wrapped them around her ankles, spun her to the center of the bed and secured the final cuffs to the bedposts. "There. That will keep you from kicking me." He smiled.

Carlton grabbed the bit from the bed and reattached it to her mouth. "And that will keep you from talking." He handed her a soft, squishy ball, setting it in her palm and wrapping her hand around it. "When you're gagged and we're engaged in sex play, you'll need something to use if you need to stop. If you're in pain or can't tolerate anything I do, you drop the ball and I'll stop. Got it?"

She nodded. She couldn't imagine anything he could do she would need to halt, but it gave her peace of mind to know the option existed. She was so much more aroused than she had been earlier. The only thing she could think about was getting the relief she needed.

Carlton set a finger on her clit and tapped it. "So vulnerable. Do you like being open to me like this?"

She nodded.

"When I reach inside you, will I find you soaking wet?"

She nodded again.

He climbed between her legs, his cock bobbing in front of him.

Margaret swallowed the saliva building up in her throat. The urge to suck him was strong. If only she could exchange favors… But that wasn't Carlton's game. He didn't make trades. He followed his rules and his rules alone. Sometimes that involved getting her off and sometimes it didn't.

Carlton leaned over her and tugged the straps that lay tight against her nipples to the sides. The effect of that shift was that her breasts pressed to the center. They felt heavy and tight, and her nipples ached to be touched after the abrasion of the straps disappeared.

He set his hands on her open thighs and then caressed her skin everywhere, gently. Her arms and legs and torso. Everywhere but where she most needed his touch.

"So smooth. The most flawless skin I've ever seen." His fingers fluttered over the curves of her breasts.

She willed him to stroke her nipples. Anything to bring relief from the need growing inside her.

Relief was on his time schedule though.

*That's not entirely true. If you would stay still and quiet, he'd grant you that orgasm.*

She communicated with every part of her body, begging her muscles to relax and let him do as he pleased. She promised her synapses the reward would be worth it if only her limbs would obey.

Deep breaths.

Carlton suddenly tapped her nipples.

She inhaled sharply, but she didn't move.

"Good girl. You're learning." He danced his fingertips down her body. "What about here?" He tapped her clit next.

She remained still. It took all her will, but she closed her eyes and concentrated on each stroke of his fingers, absorbing the feeling, gathering the need, letting it settle in her pussy, waiting…waiting…waiting…

Back to her nipples. He pinched them this time. "Love these pink buds. You'll wear the clamps tonight. I want to see them on you. You'll wear them to remind you of your role."

She swallowed again. Her nipples hardened further. The suggestion of clamping them should have made her nervous. But instead, she grew more aroused. She found herself wishing he would clamp them now. It would be easier to accept while she was restrained.

Later, he would take them while she had free will. Later, he would expect her to offer her tits up to him.

Back to her pussy. He toyed with her lips, pulling them open, stretching them until she felt the air rush across her wetness. "I'm going to push my fingers inside you now. Don't move. Don't moan. I'd hate to stop this. It's so sexy." He said that as if it pained him more than it did her.

She braced herself, willed her throat to remain silent. Staying still wasn't a problem. She couldn't even buck her body in this position. With her feet in the air, she had no chance of gaining any sort of purchase against the mattress.

And then he was inside her again. So good. Too good. She bit hard on the gag, her teeth clamping down to keep from moaning.

"So proud, baby. Feel the strokes. Relax... Let my fingers make you feel so good." His voice was low, soothing.

She concentrated on his words...his fingers.

His movements were slow, deliberate, agonizing. His fingers fucked in and out of her at a pace that drove her mad. Wetness leaked to run between her ass cheeks. With his other hand, he held her hood off her clit, exposing it to the air also. "Your clit is swollen, baby. Needy."

He didn't touch it. His fingers kept their easy rhythm.

She needed to come worse than ever in her life. She'd go insane if she didn't get the relief she needed soon. She'd do anything, including remain still and quiet. It was getting easier, partially because deep in the recesses of her brain, she was learning. There would be no relief if she didn't obey this command.

"You're doing so well. I know you're close. Don't come until I say so." He thrust deeper, but not faster. "Your pretty ass is sexy as hell, but it will be even sexier when I spank you. If you come before I say, I'll flip you over and spank you until the sting keeps you squirming all evening. Do you understand?"

She widened her eyes and nodded. Did he think those words would keep her from moaning? If anything they antagonized her, goading her into ruining the building orgasm. Hell, she would come in an instant if he spanked her.

"You like to be spanked. I know this. I can see it in your eyes. I've also watched other people spank you at the club. It gets you off." He emphasized his words with a deep penetration of his fingers, adding a third.

He lowered his voice. "I've seen you come from spanking at Emergence. I know how much you like it. You won't come when I spank you though, baby. Not unless I say so. If you were someone else, it would be different. But I know how much you enjoy having your ass smacked. I won't deny you the experience from time to time, but spanking is a punishment in my house. I'll use it to correct unwanted behavior. I know it will arouse you, but I won't let you go over the edge."

Her pulled his fingers from her pussy and stroked them across her perineum until he met her lower hole.

Maggie winced. It had been a long time since someone had breached the puckered entrance. She knew it would raise her arousal. She'd experimented with it before. His finger pressed against the entrance without slipping inside, perhaps gauging her reaction. When he removed the pressure, she had to strain not to sigh.

"You like that. You like having something in your tight ass. I'll keep that in mind." He tapped the entrance with his fingers. "Spanking and plugs get you off. Hmm."

Two fingers plunged back into her pussy.

The smallest squeak caught in her throat.

"Good girl. Control. That's the way." He thrust again. "You need to come. I know that." Again. "So close. Hold on to the edge." Again.

She thought she would burst. Her thighs shook and a quiver built in her pussy like a dam about to explode.

Finally, he relented. "Come, Maggie." He fucked her fast and hard with his fingers, adding a third once more and pinching her clit with his other hand.

The intense orgasm washed through her like a tsunami, breaching the dam and flooding the universe with its force.

Maggie rode the waves, biting the bit so hard she would leave indentations in the rubber. But she didn't scream. She fought and she won. Her pussy clenched around his fingers hard, milking them.

It wasn't enough, though. Before Carlton, she would have found such an orgasm to be the last stop on the train to heaven, but not since she'd had his cock inside her. Now she wanted to feel that fullness again.

Maybe it was just him. Maybe she craved him like a drug, but as the waves of pleasure subsided, she pleaded with him inside her head.

And then he surprised her by lifting her head and removing the bit. He pulled it away from her mouth, stroking her jaw and massaging it with both hands. "You did so well, baby. I'm so proud of you."

She nodded. *Please, please fuck me.*

"I'm going to fuck you now. Okay?" He watched her face. "Hard and fast. You have me so stiff I can't think."

"Please, Sir. God, please."

And then he was inside her, thrust to the hilt, his cock pressing so deep she thought she'd split in half. So full. So perfect. So tight.

He moved, thrusting hard, reaching deeper with each pass, if that were possible. He held her shoulders, reaching under her armpits with his hands and curling them around her body so she couldn't scoot away from him with each thrust.

She was helpless to participate, so she stared into his eyes and watched his face as he grew closer to release.

Her clit slammed into the base of his cock with each thrust. Without the protection of her curls, her naked skin was supersensitized by his coarse hair.

A second orgasm built fast, rushing to the surface less than a minute from the first. She knew by the strain on Carlton's face and the way his gaze seemed to see nothing that he was close also. His jaw was set and tight.

Finally, he thrust in deep, held himself rigid, and met her gaze. "Come, Maggie. *Now.*" He shouted that last word.

Her body followed his command, toppling into oblivion once again.

On a groan, Carlton followed her, as if he'd been waiting for her release before enjoying his own.

Maggie's throat constricted. No sound came out.

Instead she was swamped with a new thought that kept her from uttering a sound.

*I'm totally ruined for any other human.*

Moments passed while she heaved for oxygen, Carlton doing the same above her. His lips found hers and he consumed her with a kiss that told her without words how much he felt about what they'd just done. She felt the intensity of his emotions in every stroke of his tongue.

When he finally released her lips and pulled out of her to remove all the Velcro restraints, she was exhausted.

He chuckled as she let each limb collapse onto the sheets. "I'll run a bath for you. The warm water will help your muscles."

"God, that sounds amazing."

Carlton left her lying limp on the bed and padded from the room. When he returned, he swatted her ass gently. "Come on. We have to get to the club. We don't have all night, lazy."

She pulled herself to sitting. "Somebody wore me out with sexual antics."

"Somebody has to take all the blame herself for getting into such a predicament."

"Ha." Margaret stood on wobbly legs and dragged herself to the bathroom. The moment she slipped under the steaming water, she sighed. It felt fantastic. No bath in history had ever felt so welcoming.

She lay there for several minutes before reaching for the soap. During that time, she watched Carlton take a second shower and emerge looking larger than life. "You just going to lie there?" He smirked.

Margaret held up the soap. "I've managed to get this one palm clean, but I haven't found the strength to do the rest yet. These things take time."

He leaned over and kissed her forehead. "You were wonderful. You deserve a break. I'll go make something for dinner. You take your time."

She watched him disappear around the corner, thinking she was the luckiest person alive.

And this man would destroy her when he let her go.

# Chapter Twelve

A T MIDNIGHT, MARGARET propped herself onto a bar stool and asked the bartender for a soda. She rarely drank the sickeningly sweet beverage, but she needed both the caffeine and the sugar tonight.

She sat very straight, keeping her back as rigid as possible to avoid causing the front of her dress to gape open and give everyone around her a peek of her tits.

Her newfound sensitivity was absurd. She'd been coming to Emergence for over a year. She'd revealed every inch of her person to the crowd many times, including her nipples. Why on earth was she suddenly self-conscious about her body?

She turned to glance over her shoulder at the man managing the front door. His appraising gaze was on her, and he sent a chill down her spine from across the room.

That was why. Carlton was the reason for her change in attitude. She was no longer responsible for deciding who saw what and when. She was under the direction of a Dom now. He would decide what she wore and when she would display her assets at Emergence. Tonight she wore the new dress that concealed her most private parts, and nothing more.

After one full day, already she was an emotional mess when it came to Carlton. She hadn't meant to fall for him. This was meant to be an experiment in her sexuality and submission. And she needed to get her head back in the right place because Carlton had never once insinuated that for him this was anything more than temporary.

Warm hands slipped around her middle, making her flinch an instant before she relaxed into Carlton's embrace. He kissed her ear and whispered, "It's just me, baby." His fingers splayed across the expanse of bare skin at her belly and grazed the inside of her breasts.

"Mmm." She closed her eyes, relaxing into his touch.

"Come back to my office." He lifted her off the stool with both hands as though she were nothing more than a feather. In the high heels she wore, it took her a second to get her feet under her.

He winked as she steadied herself against him, and then he clasped her hand and led her through the throng of patrons to the entrance to the back rooms.

The moment the door shut behind her, silence relaxed her. Normally she loved the bustle of the main room, but tonight, she'd counted the minutes until she could be alone with Carlton again. It seemed her wait was over.

He led her down the hall and into his office, where he kicked the door shut and immediately turned to press her into the wall. He cupped her face with both hands. "Baby, you've been driving me crazy all night. Every move you make gets me harder." He took her mouth in a powerful kiss that left her weak.

His hands spanned her waist again, both supporting her against the wall and teasing the undersides of her breasts.

When he finally released her lips, he righted himself and reached into his pocket.

She knew what was in there. He'd warned her earlier.

Sure enough, he held up the small clamps he'd selected earlier in the day. She'd tried on a similar pair.

Carlton wrapped one large hand around her neck and set his forehead against hers. "I want to put these on you. Just knowing they're there will take my breath. Will you wear them for me?"

"Yes, Sir." Her voice was breathless. A moment ago, she'd been leery about the clamps, and now that he'd asked her with such affection, she felt only the desire to please him.

"Ask me."

She licked her lips. "Please, Sir. I'd like to wear the nipple clamps for you."

"Excellent." He stepped back, brushed her hair over her shoulder, unsnapped the tiny crisscross straps holding her dress together in the center and easily slid the leather material to one side to expose her nipple.

Margaret gasped as he toyed with the already erect bud, pinching and twisting it until it hardened further. Holding the tip with one hand, he drew it out from her breast and slid the little clamp into place.

The pinch was instantaneous, and she fought against the urge to squirm.

"God, that's sexy, baby." He spread the other side of

her dress open farther and repeated the attention on her left nipple, clamping it to match its twin.

A tiny tinkling sound caught her attention, and she glanced down to see each clamp had a small bell dangling below her nipples.

Carlton stepped back. He surveyed her from head to toe. "Lift your arms and cross them behind your head, baby."

She did as he instructed, knowing what the action did to her tits.

"That's so goddamn sexy." He reached to flick first one bell and then the other, making them sway and pull on her nipples.

They weren't unbearable. The pain had been sharp but short lasting. Now she was left with a pinching sensation that was simultaneously sending a message of arousal to her pussy.

He stepped forward and cupped her chin, tipping her head up to meet his gaze. "May I take a picture?"

She sucked in a breath, her eyes widening at his suggestion.

"I want to remember this moment and the expression on your face while wearing my adornments. I would never breach your trust in me. Any photos I take are purely for your pleasure and mine. No one will ever see them."

She found herself nodding consent.

"I need a verbal, baby."

She swallowed. *Him and his verbals.* "If it pleases you, Sir, I'd like you to photograph my new nipple clamps."

He smiled as he stepped back and used a small digital

camera to capture the image. "Keep your arms behind your head, your elbows spread. There. Perfect." He took a few shots. She wasn't sure how many. It was so titillating having someone take nude pictures of her breasts she almost moaned.

As he put his phone back in his pocket, he spoke again. "You liked that. The pictures, I mean."

"I did, Sir."

"Good. I like pictures. I want to be able to catch moments of our time to look at later. Especially when you do something new that makes your face light up with a blush." He gave her a quick peck on the lips. "You can lower your arms now." He reclipped the straps between her breasts, drawing the sections of material over her nipples and trapping the clamps against her skin.

"Will you come to the front with me? I hate you being halfway across the room. When I can't see you, I worry some asshole is going to harass you. I know it's boring, but I like having you close."

"Of course, Sir." She hadn't wanted to get in his way or distract him from his job. The first step she took made her gasp. The clamps forced her nipples to rub against the leather and tug on her breasts with each movement.

Carlton set his lips on her neck and nibbled. "I love knowing the clamps are under there, just inside, where I can easily swipe a finger and remind myself."

Margaret wished they could stay here in his office and do any scene in the world he desired. The last thing she wanted was to walk back out in public and wait patiently for him to get off work to give her his attention again.

She followed him to the front, however, wondering the entire time what on earth she'd been thinking concerning his attentiveness. The man could work a crowd, manage the club, speak to every member as they entered the front door, and still leave Margaret feeling as though every ounce of his attention was focused solely on her.

Carlton set her on a stool behind the front desk. He leaned in to whisper in her ear again. "Spread your legs, baby. Nobody can see you from the other side."

Again she thought how silly it was for her to care who saw her. Patrons had seen her pussy before. They'd seen her nipples. Heck, half the people in the club tonight could probably describe her ass cheeks and their color in great detail. Most of the members were aware of the intricate aspects of her nipples—their color, the size of her areolas, the way they stiffened when provoked.

But those parts of her weren't for public viewing right now. Carlton hadn't said as much in words, but he had treated her with discretion from the moment they'd begun this arrangement.

The man didn't share. It almost made her giggle.

And it forced her to feel as though the intimate, private parts of her body were for him and him alone. She didn't feel the need or desire to share with anyone else all of the sudden.

She spread her legs as he requested, allowing her ass to rest naked against the stool. The dress was too short to keep tucked under her butt cheeks anyway, and she had to sit straight again to avoid letting the front of the dress gape open and display more than Carlton had in mind.

Between customers, he would reach for her, stroke her thigh, her arm, her cheek. Without warning, he would run a finger through her pussy, gather the wetness and bring it to his lips.

Every move he made heightened her arousal. When he slipped two fingers into her dress to jingle the bell hanging from her nipple, she fought the urge to come at that simple gesture.

"Am I distracting you?"

She nodded. "Yes, Sir."

"Good. Because you're distracting the hell out of me." He turned and greeted the next customer.

Lord, she was in so much trouble. She was falling hard. Why did Carlton have to be so fucking temporary? She couldn't imagine calling an end to this arrangement and then returning week after week to Emergence and not having him as her Dom. It made her sick to her stomach just picturing him with someone else. And there was no way she could switch to another Dom at this point. He owned her. He just didn't know it.

She'd been a member of this club for over a year. She'd never seen Carlton with a sub of his own. Sure, he dominated many women. She'd seen him dozens of times. But to her knowledge he'd never taken on a permanent submissive. Perhaps he didn't like the idea. Maybe that was why he insisted this arrangement was temporary.

She chewed on her lower lip, wondering if there was any way she could make him see reason and keep her. She had two weeks to convince him. And she intended to make good use of that time. She knew he felt more for her than he was willing to admit, but he was stubborn. She didn't know why. But she intended to find out.

After a while another employee came to the front. "Carlton, Jason sent me over here to tell you you're a crappy delegator and if you don't turn the front desk over to me, you're fired. His words." The man held up both hands in innocence.

Carlton laughed. "Fine. You take over. I have some business to take care of in my office anyway."

*Business, my ass.*

Carlton lifted her off the stool, manhandling her to the ground for the second time in the evening, and making her acutely aware that instead of feeling like a child, she felt cherished, loved, respected.

She followed him to the back office again, waiting patiently while he shut and locked the door.

She still didn't say a word as he tugged on the black tie he wore and jerked it over his head. He removed his shirt, one button at a time, not taking his gaze off her.

Margaret squirmed beneath his gaze as he removed first his shirt, then his shoes and socks and finally his pants. He wore nothing under the black denim.

When he stepped forward to lift her arms over her head, she realized she'd been holding her breath. He pulled the dress up her body, slowly, teasing her with his touch on every inch of her skin. "How do your nipples feel, baby?" He tossed her dress aside and lifted her breasts to examine the jewelry.

"Exotic, Sir."

"Really?" He lifted one eyebrow. "Exotic, huh? Interesting."

He toyed with the dangling bells and then leaned forward to flick his tongue over her nipples, one at a time. "You may touch me, Maggie." He took her hands in his and set them on his cock.

She loved the smooth feel of his skin pulled tight across his length. She loved how firm and virile he felt, as though his life force were expressed through this one appendage. She even loved how the smooth tip leaked the milky-white precome.

She longed to taste him again. "May I suck you, Sir?"

"Is that what you want?"

"I do, Sir. Please."

He nodded. "I would never deny a woman a blowjob."

She lowered herself to her knees, careful to keep them spread apart to his requirements. She wrapped her palm around the base of his cock and licked the tip.

Bolder this time, she sucked him in deep. Her pussy grew wetter when Carlton moaned.

She loved the way he threaded one hand in her hair, not pushing or pulling, just caressing her scalp.

She sucked harder, as though she were starving. In a way, she was. She needed him with a force that wouldn't stop. She needed him inside her, around her, over her... As she continued, she relished the taste of his precome leaking from the tip. His fingers stiffened in her hair.

Suddenly he groaned louder and jumped back to dislodge from her mouth. He hauled her up in front of him.

"Did I do something wrong, Sir?"

He pulled her lips up to meet his. "No, baby. You did

everything way too right. I need to be inside you."

The throbbing in her core increased tenfold as he wrapped his hands around her waist, lifted her off the ground and planted her back against the wall. In an instant he was inside her, taking her breath away.

Margaret wrapped her legs around his waist and held on to his biceps as he thrust again. He filled her so perfectly she wanted to grip him with her pussy and never let him escape. She willed him to slow down so it would last longer, but he was on a mission. He increased his pace instead, lifting her off him with each thrust until sweat beaded on his forehead and she had to bite her lower lip to keep from coming without permission.

As though on cue, he growled deep in his throat. "Come, baby. Now."

She shattered around him, hoping he could manage to hold her up, because there was no chance she could assist in any way as her channel flexed around his cock, grasping at him.

When he finally stopped moving, he remained embedded inside her, pressing her against the wall while he caught his breath.

Her nipples rubbed against his, the tiny chains and bells making their presence known, heightening her sensitivity.

He met her gaze, one hand holding her up under her ass, the other cupping her face, his thumb stroking her cheek. "You slay me."

She smiled and tightened the grip she had with her ankles around him.

He held her stare for long moments until she blushed from the intensity of his gaze. "You can put me down now."

"Not yet."

As though she weighed nothing, he continued to hold her pressed against the wall, his cock still hard and buried deep inside her.

As he watched her face, her arousal built again. He pressed his cock deeper, the base shoved tight against her clit. "That's it, baby. Let it build." He continued staring. "Lift your arms behind your head."

She didn't drop his gaze as she obeyed him, her breasts rising as her elbows rose high above her head.

Carlton leaned his chest back, only inches, but enough to expose her nipples. His torso still held her wedged against the wall. He smoothed his hand down from her cheek to her breast. With one finger, he tapped the dangling clamp, making it sway.

Margaret sucked in a breath. She lowered her gaze to her chest. While she watched, he grasped the clamp between his thumbs and index fingers. She moaned even before he moved, and then she screamed when he released her nipple and quickly repeated the action on the other side. The removal was much worse than the placement. The sharp pain was unexpected and instantaneous, but at the same time, her pussy gripped his cock harder.

He dropped the clamps to the floor and then cupped her breast again, rubbing and pinching her nipple. "Maggie, baby. That's so hot. Are you okay?"

"Yes, Sir."

Still gripping her breast, he firmly kept her planted to the wall with his other hand under her ass. She was confused, momentarily, until he removed his cock and slammed back into her.

Margaret's breath whooshed out of her lungs.

He did it again. And again.

Her pussy pleaded for more, shocking her after the recent earth-shattering orgasm.

Thumb pressing into her nipple, palm up the underside of her breasts, fingers splayed at her armpit, he held her steady as he plowed in and out of her. Relentlessly. His gaze bored into her face. She knew it without looking.

The need for another orgasm built so rapidly she couldn't wrap her mind around it. Each time his cock pulled away from her, it sucked some of her brain out of her skull. But it felt so good she never wanted it to end.

"I want... You... To come... Again." He punctuated each word with the thrust of his cock. And then suddenly he stopped.

Her mouth fell open, the protest on the tip of her tongue.

"Look at me. Yeah, baby. Look into my eyes." He waited for her to obey. "I need to taste you." Still lodged inside her, he moved from the wall, cupping her ass with his free hand.

She lost her balance and flung her arms around his neck.

Seconds later, he spun in the other direction and set her ass on the edge of his desk. He eased her back onto the cold surface. Her feet hung in the air with nothing to gain purchase against. It didn't matter because Carlton grabbed her thighs under her knees and spread them high and wide. "Arms over your head, baby."

He must've trusted her because his gaze didn't lift from her swollen, needy pussy.

And in a heartbeat, his lips were on her, his tongue plunging into her while at the same time he sucked her clit into his mouth. He moaned around her entrance, pressing harder, demanding more.

Margaret's legs shook. Her arousal skyrocketed. His own come oozed from her body. He sucked and licked her as though it meant nothing to him. The heady idea made her flush as he continued devouring her pussy. The way he consumed her made her feel cherished and more desired than any man ever had. Or woman for that matter.

If it were possible, he pressed her knees higher, wider. Splayed open and at his mercy, Margaret let herself sink into a place where the only thing she knew was his mouth loving her. She whimpered. She could hear the small sounds, but she didn't care. She only cared about the intensity of the orgasm about to wash through her.

And then it did, her entire pussy pulsing against his lips, grasping at his tongue, swelling as she teetered over the edge. She couldn't breathe. She didn't remember how. All she knew was the pulsing of her clit.

He didn't stop until every wave was sucked from her body. And even then, he continued to lick her clean. "You're amazing, Maggie. I'm humbled. You're going to make some Dom a very happy man one day." He tucked his hands under her shoulders and lifted her body until she sat on the edge of the desk, her chest pressed against his. He buried his face in the curve of her neck, every breath he took sending tingles down her spine. At the same time, she held her breath to keep from choking at his last line. He fully intended to let her go still. It was surreal. How could he be this kind and caring and proclaim he had no intention of keeping her at the same time?

When he finally pulled back enough to look at her, his face was serious. "Let's go home, baby."

# Chapter Thirteen

MARGARET PULLED INTO the driveway and then eased her car into the garage. She took a deep breath and let it out slowly. She was growing more angsty by the day. She hadn't received any more notes, but every time she was in the car going to or from work, she felt like someone was tailing her. It was crazy. Who the hell would be following her? She needed to get a grip on her nerves before she went inside.

As she lowered the garage door from inside the car, she stared through the windshield at the far wall, thinking about the past few days. Perfect. Too perfect. Carlton had pampered the hell out of her. She'd easily slipped into the role he'd demanded and loved every minute of it. After three days back at work, it was beginning to feel normal for her to come home to Carlton.

She worried she was getting too comfortable. She knew she was falling too hard for him. Was it simply because he was her first—first man, first male Dom, first firm Dom? No matter what the reason, she knew this was temporary. She reminded herself every day. Carlton was kind and caring, and she swore she could see more than just a desire to train her deep behind his brown eyes, no matter how many times he insisted otherwise.

Every morning he fixed her breakfast while she showered. She came to him, naked, her hair still damp, and kneeled at his feet. The way he fed her, smiled at her, even wiped the crumbs from her mouth, aroused her just as much as he could with his hands on her body. He cleared away the dishes while she waited and then led her back to the bedroom. Each morning he spread the towel on the edge of the bed, and she lay down and splayed herself open for him to shave. He helped her dress, her body trembling with need under his administrations.

He would kiss her gently as she left the house, his thumbs grazing over her nipples beneath her blouse. That action always left her shivering as she started her car with shaky hands. Did he know how aroused she was before she left the house each day?

And he was beyond overprotective when it came to her driving. On Monday he'd offered to take her to work and pick her up. She'd balked. "Why on earth would you do that? I'm perfectly capable of driving myself." She'd thought for a moment he was being too controlling if he didn't trust her to go to work and come home. But then he'd clarified: it wasn't trusting her that was his issue. It was her safety. "In my car?" she'd asked.

He'd held his breath and pursed his lips and then nodded. "Just be careful. There are a lot of crazy drivers out there." For that reason, she wasn't about to tell him she had the crazed idea someone was following her. He'd never let her leave the house alone if he suspected as much.

Hell, maybe he *did* suspect as much. Had he also noticed someone tailing them over the weekend? Maybe it wasn't just her. Maybe his weird fear was founded on his own creepy sensation, and neither of them were willing to admit to the other what they suspected.

He still didn't know about the note, though.

He hadn't fucked her in the mornings. To be honest, there hadn't been time. But every day she left for work trembling with need. To anyone looking on, she appeared perfectly normal. Nobody on the streets or at work could possibly know about the lacy demi-bra or her lack of panties. Those two unseen aspects alone kept her horny all day every day.

A noise jerked her attention to the present, and she glanced over to see Carlton standing in the doorway. She had no idea how long she'd been sitting in the car. Her hand still rested on the keys from turning it off, but otherwise she sat slouched in the seat.

She immediately pulled herself together, grabbed her purse and keys and climbed out of the car.

Carlton's face was hard as she approached him.

"Sorry, Sir. I guess I got distracted." She winced as she passed him. He hadn't said a word, and she feared he was angry. She hadn't seen him angry with her yet.

"Where were you? You're late. You never work this late," he said to her back.

She set her purse on the counter and turned to face him, keeping her gaze lowered, her stance appropriate for a submissive. "I had to stay longer than I thought at work,

Sir."

He paused. "You need to let me know when you do that. You worried me."

Worried? "I was fine. I'm here now." Was he that concerned with her driving?

He approached and pulled her into his arms, hugging her tight as though relieved to find her alive.

And that was strange.

"Why are you still dressed?" he asked her neck where he had his face buried, clearly inhaling her scent.

When he released her, she tried not to chuckle. *Because you haven't given me a chance.* She unbuttoned her blouse and shrugged out of it first, setting it on the counter. Next she unzipped her skirt and stepped out of it and her pumps at the same time. She added her skirt to the pile and reached behind her back to unsnap her bra, what there was of it.

When she was finished, she stood awaiting his next request. Clearly he was in a serious mood. All his words had been growled so far, and there had been few of them.

She spread her legs to his liking, linked her hands behind her back, lifted her shoulders and dipped her head.

Her nipples beaded as she stood there, feeling his gaze bore into her. Finally, he circled her body slowly, not speaking until he came back to her front.

She flinched when he reached forward and tweaked a nipple without warning. "I got new clamps today." His voice was less harsh, as though he was calming from his earlier stress and concern. He reached into his pocket and removed two silver clips, which he held up in his palm for her perusal.

"They're lovely, Sir." And they were. Still dainty enough she knew they wouldn't hurt too bad, feminine, sexy, but the heart-shaped pendants that would hang from her nipples appeared heavier than the bells.

Carlton cupped one breast with his free hand and molded it. He grasped the tip between his fingers and teased her until it stood at attention, pinching, tugging, twisting. When he was satisfied, he held it out and clasped it with one of the new clamps.

Margaret winced, but remained still. She knew what to expect and even craved the feeling, but the initial shock was new to her.

"So pretty," he murmured as he flicked a finger over the tip. "Do you have any idea how sexy you are?" He grasped the other nipple in the same fashion and gave it its due attention before clasping it also.

The same tiny gasp escaped her lips unbidden.

"You'll learn to do that without making a sound. I know it's new, but soon."

She nodded. "Yes, Sir."

Next, he shocked her by lifting her onto the counter so fast the breath whooshed from her lungs. "Spread your legs so I can see your pussy while I cook, baby."

She inched her thighs apart, grabbing the edge of the counter to keep her balance. He'd never requested this of her before. Normally he had her kneel at the table or in the kitchen, out of his way.

"Sit straight. Hands behind your back."

She followed his directives, lengthening her spine.

"Perfect." He reached inside her pussy with one finger and then dragged it back out to trail it up and over her clit.

When he sucked his pointer into his mouth, she stiffened to keep from flinching or moaning. "Excellent." He turned and pulled things from the refrigerator and set them on the counter next to her. Every few moments he touched her somewhere: her thigh, her nipple, her clit... Just a brief flick of his finger, enough to keep her on edge and drive her higher as he worked.

She remained quiet. She'd fought with him the first few nights about helping him, and he'd made it clear he was going to do the majority of the housework because she worked longer hours. He wanted her naked and horny, nothing else.

Next to her, he diced vegetables—onions, carrots, broccoli. He picked up a baby carrot and nonchalantly pressed it into her pussy. "Hold that for me, would you?" He went back to work.

The carrot was small, but its presence inside her seemed like a cucumber for how erotic it was.

When he took a break from chopping to make a drink, she watched him intently from her peripheral vision. He dropped several ice cubes into a glass, one at a time with no haste. How could he make a drink so damn sexy?

Next he added cold water from the refrigerator, the sound of it filling the glass making her shiver with desire, though she had no idea why. Perhaps because everything he did, he did with a specific intention. The man wasn't just thirsty. He had a plan. He always had a plan.

Sure enough, he offered her a drink, holding her neck

tipped back with one hand while he let the cool water run into her mouth. She found she was actually thirsty and welcomed the liquid. At the last second, the ice broke apart in the glass and sent a splash of water running down her chin, her neck, her breasts.

Carlton didn't comment, but he tipped her head back into his preferred position with one hand while the other, still holding the glass, leaned too close to her chest and pressed the cold surface against her nipple.

"Sorry, baby." He kissed the tip gently as though he'd truly committed an accidental infraction and had somehow injured her. When he stepped back, the little heart swayed in front of her. He reached into her pussy with two fingers and pulled out the carrot, which he tossed in the sink. Then he set the glass down between her legs nonchalantly, strategically placing it against her pussy, as though that were the only counter space available, and went back to work.

Every noise in the room seemed more pronounced as he turned on the stove and tossed the vegetables into the popping oil. Every smell increased as her senses went on high alert. She fought the urge to pull away from the cold glass at her pussy, knowing he would come up with something much worse if she moved even a centimeter.

He lifted the glass, took another sip and set it back down, pushing it closer to her center.

Her pulse beat in her thighs, all her blood running to her pussy, her wetness mixing with the condensation on the glass to create a pool on the counter between her legs.

Carlton ignored her plight as though nothing were

amiss. He tossed chicken into another pan, the sizzling making her jump enough to cause the glass to teeter forward before settling back against her. She cringed as he turned toward her, catching the disturbance. "Sit still, Maggie. You're too squirmy tonight."

She nearly moaned. Need grew as he worked.

The next time he picked up the glass, he let his fingers drag through her spread lips. "Baby, you're so wet. Is my cooking that sexy?" He took a drink and then reached into the glass to fish out an ice cube.

Maggie inhaled sharply and held her breath, waiting for whatever plan he had for that melting ice. She'd stared at it all this time, knowing it wouldn't end in water while resting in that glass.

Sure enough, Carlton tapped it against her nipple, making the little bud hypersensitive.

She flinched.

He set a hand on her back and stroked the other nipple with the ice. "So wiggly, baby. I need you to learn to stay still for me."

*Stay still...* His favorite words. And damn him for using them so often she was constantly a needy ball of nerves.

Back and forth he moved the ice, from one nipple to the other. And then, casually as he had tossed the carrot in the sink, he pushed the ice cube deep inside her pussy.

She braced herself. The cold was intense inside her, making her pussy clutch at the ice, which aggravated her when she'd rather push the offensive cube out.

Carlton reached back into the glass and grabbed a second, larger cube, which he added to the first. He went back to work, stirring the vegetables and chicken in the pans while she clenched at the ice cubes and fought the impending orgasm.

When he stepped back, he fished out another cube.

She didn't think she could take any more. The first two had not melted inside her.

This third one he didn't press into her though. Instead he lifted the hood off her clit with his free hand and flattened the cube against her nub.

Margaret moaned loudly, the sound coming out all on its own.

"As much as I love your noises, I haven't given you permission to make them. Curtail the sounds, baby." He spoke soothingly as though her infraction were no big deal, when she knew without a doubt she would pay later. Pay dearly. Pay with denial. His favorite.

When the ice finally melted against her clit, he lifted her face with his freezing cold hand and met her gaze with a smile. "Ah, baby. I love that look. The one where your eyes are so glazed you can't quite see me."

She blinked.

"It makes me so fucking hard when you look at me like that." He released her entirely and went back to work.

Stunned, she watched him, or tried to anyway. Her body was on fire, her thighs shaking with unfinished need. Her nipples pleaded for release they wouldn't get anytime soon.

Carlton didn't touch her pussy again while he cooked. He would know she was too close to withstand any contact. But he did jiggle the hearts dangling from her nipples several times, reverently admiring them with small kisses or displaying them by lifting her breasts up in his palms. He was without a doubt a nipple man.

With dinner finally ready, he set a huge plate on the kitchen table, as usual, and then lifted Margaret from the counter. He patted her ass. "You know what to do."

She did. Careful to keep her legs spread, she padded toward his chair and kneeled on the floor in her spot. The moisture from the ice and her arousal dripped down her leg, making her struggle to keep from fidgeting.

Carlton took his seat and proceeded to feed her succulent bites of stir-fry. He always fed her first, his own needs secondary. He watched her closely, learning her capacity better each day, making her feel treasured. In between bites, he gave her a drink of water or wine. Even when he chewed his own bites, she felt his gaze on her throat, her mouth, her lips.

It was almost overwhelming how absorbed he was. And still her body hummed with need.

When the meal was over, she bit her lip to keep from requesting that he let her clean. He'd made that clear also. Not yet. He wanted to do everything for her.

When he was almost finished, he excused her to use the bathroom.

She lifted herself off the floor, almost reluctant to leave his presence. It was absurd, but she liked the way he looked at her, denying her any privacy. Not that she wanted him to follow her into the bathroom, but she found herself missing his gaze when she was out of his sight.

He was in the bedroom when she emerged. He held her

phone out. "It rang. I thought you should know."

Margaret took it from him and glanced at the caller ID. "My mom." *Damn.* The woman wouldn't leave her alone.

"You should call her. That's four nights in a row."

She nodded. "I should."

"You want some privacy?"

Bless him for asking. She almost cried at how sensitive he was, a complete contradiction to what she would find on the other end of the line when her mother picked up. She found herself unwilling to do it alone. She had nothing to hide. He knew the score. And his proximity might even soothe her. "No. Stay. Please, Sir."

He took her hand and led her to the bed, where he patted the mattress. "Lie down. Relax your body. You're so tense when your mom calls. I hate it."

She followed his instructions, climbing onto the bed and stretching out, the phone still clutched in one hand.

Carlton, completely dressed in a T-shirt and jeans, crawled up next to her and leaned on one elbow. He set his hand on her belly and massaged. "Call her. I'm right here."

It felt weird calling the woman with Carlton at her side. Weirder still that she was naked and he could drive her to distraction if he so chose.

She hit Redial and waited, hoping by some miracle her mother wouldn't answer and she could leave a message. But luck wasn't on her side.

"Hello? Margaret? Finally. I've been calling you for days."

"I know, Mom. Sorry. I've been busy."

"Listen. I'm glad you called. We're having a family

lunch here on Sunday. I want you to be here. You haven't come to the house in ages."

"Mom—"

"One o'clock. Your Aunt Barbara and Uncle Rocky will be here. They want to see you too. It's been months since you've seen them."

"Mom, I can't. I have plans."

"Cancel them. Just this once, Margaret. Do something your father and I request."

*Your father and I...* As if her mother had a firm bone in her body. She knew her father had put her mother up to this.

Margaret cringed. She lifted her gaze to meet Carlton's. His eyes were narrow slits of concern. His hand pressed into her, anchoring her amazingly. He said nothing. He nodded. He could hear every word. Her mother was loud. He was telling her to go. Did he think she would take him with her? She wasn't ready for something like that.

On a sigh, she responded, "Fine, Mom. But only for a few hours. I have work to do. It's a busy time at the office."

"Perfect." Her mother's voice sounded so excited Margaret almost felt guilty. "We'll see you Sunday then. One o'clock." The woman hadn't asked her grown daughter if she wanted to bring anyone with her.

It was just as well. Facing her family the way she needed wasn't something she wanted to do with Carlton at her side. Not yet. Maybe not ever.

She hung up and handed him the phone.

"I'm proud of you." He kissed her lips briefly as he set the cell on the bedside table. "That gives you four days to figure out what to say to them."

She scrunched up her nose. "I'm not sure I want to tackle them yet. And besides, my aunt and uncle will be there."

"All the more reason. Isn't that your father's brother?"

"Yes."

"You said yourself those two were tight and you thought many of your father's ideas were learned from his older brother."

"Yeah." She set her hands on top of the one he still had on her belly. "They have gone to the same church since before I was born. My aunt and uncle went there first and dragged my parents down the same path."

"I'm sorry, baby." He kissed her again. "Put it out of your mind for tonight. We'll deal with it more before you go over there." He nibbled a path to her ear.

"You aren't mad I didn't suggest bringing you with me?"

"No. Not at all." His tongue landed on her earlobe, making her flinch. "I know this is something you have to do on your own. I'll be here for moral support before and after."

# Chapter Fourteen

THE NEXT FEW DAYS went smoothly, balancing work and play. If someone was following her, she tried to ignore it. Her imagination had gotten out of hand. Surely she was simply being paranoid. Staying in someone else's house, waking up in a strange bed, assuming a new role that she found herself loving—it was enough to make anyone panicky. When would the other shoe drop? She'd never been this happy. And her fear of losing all this had gotten the best of her.

She spent her days at the office as one persona and her evenings at Carlton's as another, entirely different persona. High-powered stress, number crunching, keeping customers happy took the first ten hours. After that she flipped a switch and let Carlton take charge.

It was amazing. Beyond her expectations. And she found herself staring at Carlton, wishing he could see how good they were together and take her on permanently. The man never insinuated any such thing, however. He looked at her like she hung the moon and the stars, but his words still spoke of this temporary arrangement.

Carlton was perfect in every way she could imagine. His quirks were few and far between. He was constantly freaky about her safety, but she tried to internalize every weird incident as his way of showing how much he cared rather than finding him to be controlling.

He demonstrated not an ounce of jealousy or lack of trust. He never mentioned a word about people looking at her or her eyeing them. He just seemed to genuinely worry about something happening to her. Obsessively at times.

If she admitted he was controlling, she wouldn't be able to tolerate him. After living under the controlling hand of her father for most of her life, no man was going to control her now. It scared the fuck out of her that she even allowed herself to submit to someone. She'd struggled with that her entire adult life, worrying about her motivation. Had her father made her this way? Shouldn't she fight against it, lift up her chin and take control of her own life?

Every time she considered leaving Carlton to go it alone, she couldn't visualize a life without him. Damn him and his two weeks. Damn herself and her need to be controlled. The juxtaposition was stressful.

Add to that her paranoia and she was on pins and needles.

Every night when she left work, she watched her back. Every time she approached her car, she scanned it for evidence that someone had been there, left her a note again, tampered with her car in some way.

On Friday, she went out to lunch. As she reached her car, she came to a stop, her hands shaking as she eyed another fucking note on the windshield. After several deep breaths, she picked the corner up with two fingers and carefully set the envelope on the passenger seat. Lunch would have to wait. Enough was enough. She needed to go to the police.

Her heart pounded as she drove to the nearest station. A normal person would call her boyfriend and tell him what was happening. Was Carlton her boyfriend? Not hardly. And besides, the man would freak out and insist she no longer drive alone. Losing her independence to some stalker would send her over the edge. She couldn't do it.

She wouldn't. She inhaled deeply as she pulled in to the station, resolved to turn the problem over to the police and keep Carlton out of it.

Margaret entered the police station, spoke to a kind woman at the front desk, and then waited for only moments before an officer assisted her.

"Ma'am." He shook her hand. "Officer Brantly. I understand you've received some threatening letters?"

"Yes, on my windshield. The first one I opened before realizing what it was. But this time, I didn't touch more than the corner to set it in the car. It's lying on the front seat. I drove straight here from my office."

He smiled politely. "Good choice. Give me a sec to grab some gloves and I'll follow you out to retrieve it."

Less than a minute later, Officer Brantly was back at her side, ushering her to her car. He carefully picked up the note and slid it into a plastic bag. "Did you touch the windshield or the hood much?"

She shook her head. "I don't think so."

"'Kay. I'm gonna send some guys out to see if they can

pull any prints. Come on back to my office. I'll take down some information." On the way down a long hall to Brantly's office, he stopped by another office and handed the note to someone else.

Brantly turned toward Margaret. "It's a red Camry, right?"

"Yes."

He turned back to the other man and asked him to dust for prints.

It took over an hour for Margaret to provide the officer with all the details of the first note and then the circumstances of the second. She called her boss to let him know she would be late returning.

Halfway through the conversation with Officer Brantly, a female cop stepped into his office and handed him a note. She left without saying a word.

Brantly read the note and handed it to Margaret. "Well, someone is threatening you. Does this make any sense?"

Margaret held her breath as she read the words.

*Listen, bitch. I don't think you understand. You need to straighten yourself out unless you want a repeat performance. Then again, it seems you like pain. So maybe fucking you up won't do a bit of good.*

Margaret's eyes teared up. She hated herself for not staying stronger, but she was suddenly overcome with emotions. Who the fuck was harassing her? It almost sounded like it could be the same people who'd attacked her the first time. But that was impossible. Why now? After all these years?

Brantly spoke again, gently. "I assume this means some-thing to you?"

She nodded, but it took her several minutes to form words.

"Whatever it is, you need to tell us. Would you like me to call in a female officer?"

She shook her head. "No. I'm fine." She sucked in a breath.

Brantly waited patiently. Finally, he spoke again. "Is someone hurting you? Do you know who would have left this note?"

She shook her head again. "No. Not a clue. And the creepy idea I have is so far-fetched it will sound ludicrous."

"Go ahead. Anything you can add will help."

"When I was fifteen, I was attacked by three men in an alley. It was a hate crime. I'm—I'm bisexual." She swallowed through the admission. She'd never told anyone that outright.

Brantly didn't flinch. "Well, that's not a crime." He smiled and leaned forward. "Did the cops find the men who did that to you?"

"No. I'm not sure what ever happened." She lifted her gaze. "My parents... They...um...weren't particularly supportive. They moved me to another town and never mentioned the incident again."

He frowned. "Were they trying to help you move on?"

The sound she emitted was unrecognizable to her ears, like a deep, sardonic chuckle that made her shiver. "Hardly." She lifted her gaze to the officer. "They weren't supportive of my lifestyle. They were more likely to have hired the thugs themselves than track them down to exact justice."

The second the words left her mouth, she gasped.

Brantly lifted an eyebrow. "Do you believe that?"

She inhaled sharply. "No. God, I hope not. Surely they aren't that cruel. I'd been at a rave with my girlfriend. We'd been...making out, dancing, flirting. I assume someone at the rave followed us and took it upon themselves to make sure we knew they didn't approve of our choices."

Brantly paused for several seconds, thinking, his brow furrowed. "And you've never had another problem until now?"

"No. Never." And then she shook her head. "Although I have felt like someone was following me for the last several weeks. I assumed I was being paranoid."

"Even after receiving that first note?"

She glanced at her lap, wringing her fingers together. "I guess I was in denial. I've had...some life changes lately. I tend to get paranoid when I alter my routine. I hoped it was a case of mistaken identity or something. I didn't figure there was anything you could have done about it after I'd opened the envelope and touched the paper myself. Stupid, really. I should have called nine-one-one."

Brantly leaned on his elbows. "You could have. But you're right about one thing. It's damn difficult to track down someone who leaves you a note." He hesitated. "Do you live with another woman?"

She shook her head for the millionth time. "No. In fact, the irony is that, for the first time, I've been staying with a man. That's when this all started."

Brantly drummed his fingers on the desk. "What do you think this asshole means when he says you like pain?"

Margaret swallowed and met the officer's gaze head-on. She needed to be totally upfront with him. "I'm a member of a BDSM club. If that person is following me, they would know that."

Brantly nodded. "Okay." He didn't judge her. Nothing on his face indicated she was saying anything out of the ordinary. Thank God. "Well, I think I have all I can go on for now." He handed her a card. "I'm going to contact the station that handled your case twelve years ago and see what kind of information they gathered at the time. Do you think you could ask your parents for more details? Maybe they knew things they didn't tell you at the time. You were so young."

Margaret stared at him. "Maybe," she mumbled. "I'll try." She couldn't imagine bringing up that can of worms with her parents, but then again, she had a shit ton of baggage to clear with them. Maybe this was the nudge she needed to confront them once and for all, for better or for worse.

Brantly stood. "Call me if you come up with even the tiniest piece of information that might help. And I'll be in touch with you as soon as we process the fingerprints. But I'll warn you, the chances of finding a print on that paper is slim."

She nodded as she stood also. Her legs felt like lead. "Okay. Thank you. I realize it's a long shot, but I also knew I needed to file a report."

"You're absolutely right. Always call us. That's what we're here for." He rounded the desk and opened the door. "No detail is too small. Unfortunately there isn't a lot we can do without more information. But if I were you, I would take care to avoid being alone. Don't go anywhere at night by yourself. Maybe someone at work could walk you to and from your car?"

"Yes. Absolutely." No way in hell was she going anywhere alone now. And that pissed her off more than anything. She hated having to look over her shoulder all the time. She hated that her irrational fear was perhaps not so irrational. She hated to think someone was indeed following her and knew where she went at all times.

Fuck. Her fingers shook as she left the station and headed to the parking lot. Officer Brantly saw her to her car and shut the door for her.

She dropped the keys as she lifted them to put them in the ignition. After she picked them up from the floorboard, she locked the doors and sat for a few minutes, trying to gather the strength to drive.

She had to get back to work. She needed to think. What the hell was Carlton going to say? He was going to kill her for not calling him immediately.

*Or else, keep this to yourself for now.* There was no need to tell him, really. There wasn't a thing he could do but worry. And he already did enough of that. There was also no reason to burden him with her problem when he didn't plan to stick around in her life more than one more week.

God, how she wanted him to keep her. With each passing day she grew more attached to him. She secretly hoped she could slowly convince him that *he* was the Dom for her and not set her free to find someone else. As paranoid as Carlton was, finding out she had a stalker wouldn't help her case. He'd probably wash his hands of her and not look back.

Nope. She would keep this to herself. On the off chance Officer Brantly called with any details, she would discreetly handle it when she was alone. Resolved, she headed back to the office to finish the day.

✧  ✧  ✧

CARLTON SAT IN his usual pew and stared at the row of candles flickering to his left. He imagined each one reaching toward the heavens, paying homage to whomever each was intended, including his.

When his eyes began to play tricks on him from looking at the flickering lights for so long, he switched his gaze to the front of the church.

*Please, Karen. Help me do the right thing. It's been so long. I know you would be disappointed in me for carrying a torch for you for so many years. I know this isn't what you would want for me.*

*But it's hard. I'm scared. You hurt me so badly. I never want to feel that sort of pain again.*

*Maggie. She's so much like you, and yet so different at the same time. I wonder if you would like her if you met her. She's smart and feisty and…alive. So alive. Vibrant. She doesn't take risks like you.*

He smiled. He felt a calm wash over him for the first time in years. Forever. He'd never felt this relaxed when visiting Karen.

*Maggie isn't you. She's her own person. I'm not sure why I ever thought she was so similar to you. Even her resemblance is fading as I get to know her better.*

*She would kill me if she ever found out what attracted me to her in the first place. Who wants to know that her boyfriend carries a torch for his first girlfriend?*

*Boyfriend.* He leaned back, smiling. *Boyfriend* was a term he hadn't used for twelve years. Never intended to again in this lifetime.

Until Maggie. God, he wanted her. Could he keep her?

And, hell, he didn't know if she would agree. He'd never once told her the idea was even on the table. Until today, he hadn't entertained the thought himself. How could he have told her?

*I'm done coming here, Karen. I need to move on. I'm at peace finally. And I know that would make you smile. I'm sorry, my love. I'm sorry for not being there that night. I'm sorry for not insisting you stop taking risks. I'm sorry you left me here to fend for myself in this life. But most of all, I'm sorry for spending so many years with regret and anger toward myself and you.*

Carlton stood, feeling stronger than he had in years.

*Goodbye, Karen. Rest in peace.*

He left the chapel, his chin up, a renewed sense of life following him to his car.

# *Chapter Fifteen*

O N SATURDAY MORNING, they were finishing breakfast when she announced she needed to get her nails done. It had been over a month since she'd been into the city to get a manicure. She was past due.

"Sure, baby. I'll take you. What time do you want to go?"

She rolled her eyes. "Carlton, I don't need you to take me to the salon. I can get there on my own." Inside, she knew she needed him with her. Outside, she couldn't just readily agree or he'd be suspicious. They'd had this argument too many times.

Besides, she wanted to know what his motives were. He knew nothing about her being followed—stalked really. So why the hell did he have such a fetish about her driving?

"I don't mind." He stuffed dishes in the dishwasher while she kneeled on the floor. Her submissive mode had gone out the window with his weird, quirky need to escort her.

"I'm sure you don't. You've made that abundantly clear. But why on earth would you want to go sit and wait

221

for me to get my nails done?" She stood. In fact, she put her hands on her hips.

"I like being with you." He smiled over his shoulder. But there was more to it, and she intended to find out now.

Perhaps she'd read him wrong, and he really was a jealous boyfriend. "Why do I get the feeling you don't trust me?"

"What?" He made a mock-crazy expression that wasn't sincere. "That's absurd. Of course I trust you. Why wouldn't I trust you?"

"I don't know. You tell me. You obviously hate me driving anywhere. Have I done anything to give you the sense that I'm a bad driver, or are you afraid I'm too weak to fend off anyone who might try to pick me up at the salon, or work, or any other place I go?" She threw her hands up in the air, exasperated.

"Of course not. That's ludicrous. I promise I have no latent jealousy issues. I trust you implicitly."

"Then it's my driving." She stepped toward him.

"Nope."

"What then? Carlton, stop fucking loading the dishwasher, turn around, look me in the eye and tell me why the hell you feel the need to accompany me everywhere I go." She stopped inches from his back, knowing she had goaded him by cussing.

He froze for a moment and then slowly turned toward her, drying his hands on a towel. He didn't meet her gaze for a long time. Finally he set the towel on the counter and lifted her face.

The look he gave her was pained, and totally unexpected. "I'm sorry. You're right. I do have a reason. And it has nothing to do with anything you're thinking or could possibly have imagined. I trust you completely, baby. So wipe that thought from your head."

She waited for the rest.

He took a deep breath. "And you're a fantastic driver. I can't argue that."

"So? Don't tell me you just like to hang out at nail salons and go shopping, because I won't buy it."

"Not that either." His shoulders dropped. "Come." He took her arm and led her to the living room, where he sat on the couch and pulled her down next to him.

Now she grew worried. What the hell was going on?

"When I was eighteen, I fell in love with my high school sweetheart. We were inseparable. I thought from the first date she was the love of my life. We were together two years. We went to the same college and spent every waking hour when we weren't studying hanging out with each other. I would say we were soul mates. At least I thought so at the time. But what did I know? We were young. Maybe it wouldn't have worked out in the long run anyway."

Margaret released a breath she'd been holding for too long. She took his arm and forced him to look at her. "She broke up with you?"

"No." He shook his head. "I wish." He held her gaze, his expression pained once more. "She died in a car crash one week after her twentieth birthday."

The breath knocked out of Margaret's lungs. "Oh. God. Carlton. I'm so sorry. That must have been horrible." She set her palm on his cheek and held his face.

BECCA JAMESON

It all made so much more sense now. His strange driving quirks.

"She was a risk taker. Always had been. An adrenaline junkie, her friends called her. Made me crazy all the time. That night she was out with friends while I stayed home with the flu." He wrung his hands together and then continued, lifting his gaze to hers. "Apparently she decided to race against someone else on some back roads. She lost control on a turn and slammed into a tree."

Margaret winced. "Oh God. Honey…" She leaned into him and wrapped her arms around his neck, setting her head on his shoulder. They stayed like that for a while, him wrapping his arms around her also and holding her tight.

"I'm sorry," he mumbled into her neck. "I hate that twelve years later I'm still fighting that demon."

"It's okay. It's understandable." She rubbed his back, digging her fingers into his muscles, wishing she could crawl inside him and take the pain away with her touch to his soul. Twelve years. She didn't miss the irony. It was twelve years ago almost to the day that her life changed irrevocably also.

"I try to fight my demons and let you have the space you need. It's unfounded that I get stressed when you're driving. And you always win. I always let you go." He pulled her back and met her gaze. "I'm working on it. You're the first person I've met since then that meant so much to me, I can't stand to have you out of my sight for fear I'll never see you again."

She nodded, fighting tears for his loss and his declaration. Was he coming around then? Maybe there was hope that he wouldn't let her walk away next week and go on with his life. "That's why you wig out when I'm late. You're scared."

"I am."

"I'll do my part. I promise. You can't take me everywhere, but when it's reasonable, go with me. We'll work on it together. And I'll do my best to be sure and call or text when I'm going to be late, so you won't worry." She clasped his face with both hands and kissed him.

"Have I mentioned how awesome you are?"

"Yes." She smiled. Then she lifted her hand in front of his face and spread her fingers so her nails dangled in front of his eyes. "Have I mentioned how badly my nails need to be done?" She grinned and gave him a shove. "Let's go downtown, big guy. I need a lift. There are some really old ladies with blue hair dying to tell you about their bridge club in the waiting room."

He chuckled. "I don't have to go with you. I'll survive."

"Oh no, you don't. Now you have to go." She stood and tugged him to standing. "Now I want lunch too, and maybe I'll wear some cute short dress that makes you drool all over, knowing what I'm not wearing beneath it."

He lifted his eyebrows. "How can I resist that temptation? Can I choose the dress?" He let her pull him to standing and followed her down the hall.

"Maybe..."

✧   ✧   ✧

LATER THAT NIGHT CARLTON had to work the front door at Emergence. The hours flew by. It was busy, but he didn't fail to glance at Maggie every few minutes where she sat perched on a bar stool, chatting with the bartender.

He moaned when he watched her squirm on the seat. He knew her thighs got stuck to the vinyl after a while since her ass was directly on the seat, her skirt hanging over the side, and hopefully her pussy at least marginally wet with need.

He always tried to keep her on the edge even when he was working. It made the rest of the night fantastic when he finally got someone to cover for him. Plus he loved to see her squirm, and she looked at him with those sultry bedroom eyes when she reached her limit.

And one of those times was now. She'd given him her I-can't-take-much-more-of-this-teasing look several times in the last five minutes. He knew because he'd barely paid attention to the door in that time. His cock was harder than a rock behind his jeans and threatening a revolt if he didn't release it soon.

The dress she wore didn't help matters at all, and he had no one to blame but himself for that. It was red, her favorite color. When she wore it, he could spot her easily anywhere in the room. Of course, so could everyone else. But he didn't care. No regular would approach her and few guests would either. Everyone knew she was with him by now. And God almighty, she was *with* him. To deny how he felt about her was ludicrous at this point. Did she feel the same? He thought so. He'd gone over and over her reactions to him in his head. The way she looked at him like he was the only person in the room. The way she trembled beneath his touch. It was more than he deserved, and he needed to come clean with her, tell her how he felt. No way in hell was he going to let her go.

He stared at her now. The red dress was tight across her breasts, held together with leather lacing that crisscrossed all the way from her belly button to the top, which was barely above her nipples. The bottom was almost not long enough and full, making it easy for him to slip his hand under it and stroke her skin—which he'd done a dozen times throughout the evening, causing the bedroom eyes he was getting from her now.

One of his employees came to the front and relieved him just as he was about to hunt someone down. He mumbled his thanks and meandered through the crowd until he reached her back. She was laughing at something the bartender said as he wrapped his arms around her middle and kissed her neck.

"Doesn't my submissive have the nicest nails tonight?" he asked the bartender, stroking a palm down Maggie's arm until he held her hand out for inspection.

"You guys are weird. Get a room." The man chuckled and walked to the other end of the bar.

"Good idea. What do you think?" He punctuated his question by spreading his hands down her chest to cup her breasts, and then farther until he crossed her belly and grasped her thighs to spread them wider.

She gasped.

He reached beneath the scarlet material and opened her sex with both hands, spearing her with a few fingers while he held her captive against the bar.

No one could see. Not that anyone cared. Much crazier

BECCA JAMESON

things happened at Emergence than a little groping at the bar under the lip of the counter. But it wasn't usual for Carlton to tease her like that in public, and he knew the spontaneity would drive her wild.

Sure enough, she moaned and leaned her head back to roll against his shoulder. "Carlton…" Her voice was sultry. Needy with arousal.

"Baby…" he responded, while adding more fingers to the assault and pinching her clit between his thumbs.

She lifted clear off the seat, her body going tense in an instant. And then she made that little noise he'd come to recognize preceded her orgasms. A sharp intake of breath that whistled as it passed her lips.

He released her, not wanting her to come in the middle of the crowded bar area.

She groaned as she grabbed his wrists, trying to get him to continue.

This amused him and he chuckled against her ear. "Who's on top?"

"Carlton. God. Please."

"Who's on top?" he repeated.

"You are. Always you, Sir."

"Are you sure?" He held her thighs in a tight grip, not giving her what she wanted.

"Yes, Sir. Positive. Sorry, Sir."

"You owe me a punishment." He nibbled her lip, trying not to grin.

"I do?"

"You do."

She hesitated. He knew her mind was racing around to

find the infraction.

"You cussed at me this morning."

"I did? Oh shit, I did." She threw her hand over her mouth as she did it again. "Sorry, Sir. I mean for both. I wondered if you noticed that this morning."

"Oh, yeah. I noticed. My gorgeous, sexy submissive stood in my kitchen with her hands on her hips and ordered me to stop *fucking* loading the dishwasher." He continued to kiss her neck, her shoulder, her ear while he tormented her. "It would have been comical, except I don't like such words coming out of my *fucking* smoking hot submissive. It makes her less attractive." He emphasized *fucking* the second time to point out it was okay for him to use the language, but not her.

"Yes, Sir." She lowered her gaze, deflated a little. But her thighs remained stiff.

"Granted, she was somewhat justified to be angry with her Dom at the time, but that doesn't change the rules. Do you think I should go easy on her?"

"Um, yes?"

"Are you asking me?"

She swallowed. He felt the movement in her throat with his lips. "No, Sir."

"No, I shouldn't go easy on her?" This was fun.

She didn't respond. She sat perfectly still and waited.

"And now she has cussed again. That's one *fuck* and one *shit*. Oh, and I believe there was a *hell* in there also." He continued nibbling her warm skin, easing his fingers back toward her center, pulling her thighs wider as he did so.

Her hands remained on top of his, her new nails digging into his flesh, although she probably had no idea.

"Let's do a scene." He stood, releasing her abruptly.

She twisted on the stool to look up at him. Just as quickly she lowered her head. "Okay, Sir."

The element of surprise was so totally his friend tonight. He'd planned the scene hours ago, but she didn't know that.

He took her hand and helped her down from the stool. And then he led her down the side hall that accommodated several rooms that people reserved throughout the night to enact various scenes. Each room was three-sided, leaving the fourth as a wall of glass anyone could watch through from the wide hall. All this was intentional, as intentional as what Carlton had planned for Maggie.

✧   ✧   ✧

MAGGIE FOLLOWED CLOSE behind him. She kept her gaze low and her head bent, but even if she'd straightened her neck, all she would have seen was the back of Carlton's body. When he stopped abruptly, she ran into him.

He turned toward her, took her face in his hands and kissed her chastely. "Trust me, baby?"

"Of course, Sir."

"Implicitly?"

"Yes." Her breath came faster. She stood on the edge of one of the rooms, unable to see around him to know what he had in mind.

And he held her face still. "Look at me." He released her cheek with one hand and reached into his pocket for something. When he held it up, she gasped. "May I blindfold you?"

She nodded.

"Words, baby."

"Yes, Sir. You may cover my eyes."

He lifted the black material up to her face and held it in place. And then he attached it behind her head. "I've seen you do dozens of scenes in this club. I've never seen you do this one. I want the experience for you, and I want your awareness heightened with the loss of sight."

"Okay, Sir." She trusted him with everything in her. There was no doubt of that. The titillation was wondering what he had in mind.

He took her hand and led her into the room he'd obviously reserved much earlier. "Wait here," he whispered close to her ear. "In a standing pose, baby," he added.

She nodded, quickly spreading her legs and clasping her hands behind her back. She even tipped her head, although the motion was a moot issue.

She listened closely to the movement around her, unable to discern what he might be preparing. Soon, he returned to her side and took her arm to lead her forward. He ducked down in front of her and wrapped his fingers around her ankle to remove her shoe. She set her bare foot on the ground as he removed the other one. "One step back, baby."

She obeyed, her feet landing on something metal and cool.

"Step out, Maggie."

She did that too. With Carlton still at her feet, he

grasped first one ankle and then the other, securing them to the metal base, or maybe a bar on the base. She wasn't sure.

He smoothed his hands up her thighs as he stood, reaching under her skirt but not lifting it out of the way. When he dropped the skirt and caressed her belly, he pressed her backward.

She lost her balance, but that was intentional. She found herself leaning against something else cold and metal, a pole of some sort angled just enough to force her to lean against it. It rested along her spine, making contact with her bare skin where the dress didn't touch.

Next, he took her hands and attached them to the pole at the small of her back.

She slouched, uncertainty boring into her. Whatever this apparatus was, she hadn't seen it before. It must have been new. She wouldn't put it past Carlton to have had it delivered this week.

Her slouch ended when Carlton lifted her chin and tucked something padded under it, forcing her to stand tall when he attached the restraint behind her head.

Moisture was building between her legs already. Spread like they were, she knew it would run down her thighs soon. And she wasn't naked.

Carlton touched her arms and then trailed his fingers over her frame. She never knew where they might land at any given moment while her arousal built. She didn't have to fight to stay still. She could hardly move her torso an inch in either direction with her feet spread and her chin so high.

He teased her nipples through the material of her dress.

His finger stroked down the lacing up the center until he reached her belly. "I love this dress."

She didn't respond.

"It covers more of you, but it leaves more to the imagination also." He circled behind her, dragging one finger around her waist until he returned to the front. "The skirt barely covers your pussy, baby." He reached beneath it and cupped her sex. "You're wet."

She couldn't argue that point.

"And hot. Do you like being restrained like this?"

"Yes, Sir." He knew that.

"Do you know what I want, baby?"

"No, Sir."

"I want you to learn to come in public without anyone noticing."

She swallowed. He'd told her that before.

"We're going to practice that right now." He released her pussy. "I'm going to leave your dress on because it's sexy and I'm not in the mood to share your pussy with the world. But I'm going to work you so close to the edge you can't keep from shivering. And your job is to learn to stay still. No sounds. No movement. Just feel whatever I do."

"Yes, Sir." Her words were breathy. He had a way of dragging her close to orgasm before he started the scene. His voice was effective. His word choice was even more so.

He reached for the laces between her breasts. "I can't stand the idea of not watching your nipples. If I have to do without a visual of your pussy, at least I want to see your tits." He pulled the leather thong holding the front of the dress together until it came untied. He didn't remove the laces, but he loosened them enough to cause the front of the dress to separate until she felt the cool air of the room on her nipples.

"You're already pointed and tight, baby." He grazed his fingers along the undersides of her breasts.

She concentrated hard on the feel of his hands, but she shouldn't have because the second he reached to pinch her nipples, she lifted on tiptoe, a squeak escaping her lips.

"Uh-uh. See, I need you to listen. No movement. No noise. An entire room full of people would have seen and heard that."

She lowered back down onto her heels and breathed deeply. "Sorry, Sir."

He still held her nipples. "I'm going to clamp these. Because I like to see them that way." He pinched harder. "Stay still while I apply the clamps and then when I remove them also. I'll do it a few times to help you overcome the need to squirm."

She didn't see how that was possible, especially with a blindfold, but she braced herself. Even though he'd used clamps on her several times now, she always tensed when he applied them...and then freaked when he removed them.

She felt the material of her dress grazing the sides of her breasts as she inhaled deeply, concentrating on the way Carlton worked her nipples into stiffer points and then quickly clipped his favorite accessories onto each one. She knew by the sound he'd used the bells.

He stepped back then, grazing his fingertips down her belly until he skimmed the bottom of her skirt. "I'm not going to remove your skirt, but I am going to torment you."

Something came up between her spread legs. She hitched in a breath as cool wetness hit her pussy and nestled against her.

"I put some lube on it, baby, just to be sure."

*On what?*

He reached under her skirt and pulled her sex open with one hand as he pressed the smooth, rounded *something* firmly against her open lower lips.

*Oh God. If that's a vibrator...*

His hands lifted a few inches to stroke above her clit, as though ensuring the *something* was making contact with the little nub. Oh God, was it ever.

And then his hands were gone. Her skirt fell back into place.

She tried to breathe, to think about anything but the way her Dom was about to torture her needy body. But all she could concentrate on was the *something*.

A clicking sounded at her back, each faint noise accompanying more pressure against the smooth item pressing at her entrance. It was like some sort of knob, like a wand. Too big to enter her, it nestled at her entrance, covering every inch of her skin, including her clit.

*He's tightening it. Fuck.* She lifted off the balls of her feet as the pressure increased.

When the clicking stopped, a humming began, low, almost inaudible, but that was the least of her problems. The humming was an indication that indeed the *something* was a vibrator and it was now armed and tormenting her pussy.

"Breathe, baby. Relax."

*Relax? Breathe?* Was he kidding?

Her clit climbed to hyperswollen in less than a minute. Pulsing. Needy. Wanting. She stayed very still, hoping if she concentrated hard enough on the slight vibrations, it would be enough to get her off.

"It's not time yet, baby." His voice, deep, gravelly, commanding, registered in her ear, so close she could feel his breath. And he splayed his fingers over her exposed belly where the crisscross of laces hung loose.

He waited. And then he continued, "Do you know what I want from you?"

She didn't speak, afraid if she moved her lips her clit would press harder against the vibrator. As it was, she was trying to ease her heels to the ground. Even though the pressure would increase, she couldn't stand there long on her tiptoes.

"I want still, quiet orgasms... Lots of them. I want you to take them, one after another, without moving or moaning or speaking. Can you do that, baby?"

*Not a chance in hell.* "I'll try, Sir."

"Good. I'm going to increase the speed and I want you to take it. You're allowed to come when I do this. You're allowed to come as often as you need, but you can't speak, move or scream. If you do, we'll be here all night until you learn."

Her face heated. Her mouth fell open. How many times would he want her to come?

"I'll decide when I feel you've learned. If that takes two or ten orgasm under control, that'll be my choice."

"Yes, Sir."

"Your safe word?"

"Red, Sir."

"Will you need it tonight?"

"No, Sir." Not if the goal was multiple orgasms and the only apparatus being used were restraints, nipple clamps and a vibrator.

The humming increased, as did the vibrations, of course.

*Think about the pleasure.* She sealed her lips together, fighting sounds. She couldn't block the hum in the back of her throat, but maybe he wouldn't notice.

"No sounds, baby. None," he whispered. He stroked her neck.

She swallowed and shifted her attention to her pussy. So much pressure... More speed...more vibrations. How many people were watching her? She couldn't concern herself with that. It didn't matter.

She'd done more scenes at Emergence than most of the patrons in attendance. She'd been a member for over a year and had no difficulty participating in whatever was asked of her, but this...this was different.

This was Carlton. She was fast falling in love with him. He'd mentioned many times how much he wanted to be able to bring her silently to orgasm in public. This was his way of working her toward that goal.

This was unexpected.

This was spectacular.

It felt fucking fantastic.

Her nipples tightened as her breasts swelled with need.

The tiny bells rang, sounding louder than they should to her ears.

"I know you're squirming because I can hear the bells, baby."

*Ah. Right. That.*

He kissed her neck, licked a line up to her ear. "Take it, baby. Do this for me. Show me that you can control yourself. It's the ultimate line of submission."

The speed increased.

So close. Too close. She was torn, wanting to tip over the edge for the relief, while concerned she couldn't meet his expectations and would find herself having more orgasms than she would prefer tonight. She had her limit. The vibrator would grow sensitive after a few moments. He knew that. But he also knew she could work past the sensitivity and reach a new peak, over and over.

The first orgasm swooped in fast, taking her almost by surprise as the vibrations jumped to a new level. She opened her mouth, but held back the sound threatening to escape. Her legs stiffened and then shook as she tipped over the peak and pulsed against the bulb at her entrance. She let her feet settle firmly on the floor and actually pressed her pussy against the device. Waves of bliss hit her hard.

And then the vibrations subsided to a dull trickle of energy as she caught her breath.

"Good. But you can do better. School your face. And try not to stiffen your body so hard and rigid. It doesn't look natural. Your face looks like you're in the throes of ecstasy. Which you are." He chuckled.

Before she could catch her breath, the speed increased

hard and fast.

She squirmed, lifting onto her tiptoes, although even that didn't alleviate the pressure enough.

And then it was gone, the vibrations ceased, leaving her with the knob at her entrance that no longer got her off on its own.

She started to speak.

"Not discussing my methods, baby. Close your mouth and try again. You were about to wake the neighbors."

He was right. And she strained to catch her breath, letting her body acclimate to the object between her legs currently posing less of a threat. Just when she thought she had herself under control, the vibrator started up again, a gradual increase until it reached a level slightly higher than before.

"So sexy, baby. Let yourself come. Just don't tell everyone. I know you can do it."

Pressure. More than she'd ever endured. She was closer to orgasm without going over than she'd previously experienced. *Think. Do not move.*

She let her mind settle on the bliss, felt the slow build as she approached another climax.

And then she was right there. And she absorbed the waves, keeping her body still, her throat clamped shut.

"Fucking gorgeous, baby."

The pulses continued longer this time, her clit begging for more. What she needed now was penetration. And she wasn't going to get it.

Another wave built on the heels of the second, rising faster, threatening destruction. But Margaret forced herself to enjoy the pleasure internally.

"That's it, baby. I knew you could do it." He caressed her breasts, her belly, her neck, teasing her everywhere while he praised her. "One more, baby. Do it for me."

She tipped her head into his palm as he cupped her chin. She gasped for breath as she waited for the inevitable whir of the vibrator to start up again.

He let her rest this time first. Almost too long. She was just coming down from her high when she was yanked back to full arousal.

"Control, baby. Fight it."

For him, she would. For Carlton, she would master this desire of his.

And she did, luxuriating in the deep grip of her channel as waves of pleasure took her into another dimension…without a movement or a sound.

As she endured his test, she had two thoughts. One, that if she passed this test he might declare her trained and break off their arrangement. That idea made her stomach clench. Because her second thought was that she was deeply in love with Carlton and never wanted this agreement to end.

# Chapter Sixteen

ON SUNDAY MORNING, Carlton decided she could sit on the furniture. When he first told her, she was shocked, but she'd misunderstood completely. His new position for her wasn't on a chair, but on the table itself.

She sat naked, one foot from the edge of the table at his chair, her legs bent, her feet planted, her knees spread wide.

Carlton liked to sit between her legs, and who was she to argue? It was sexy as hell having him watch her pussy while he ate and fed her.

"What time are you supposed to be at your parents'?"

She rolled her eyes. "I was hoping you'd forgotten and we could let that one slide."

He lifted a brow and smiled. "Nope. You need to face them. Your life is in a holding pattern while you let that fester." Carlton pushed back from the table, loaded the dishwasher and wiped his hands on a dishtowel. He leaned against the counter, his legs crossed, his stance making her lick her lips. "What time, baby?"

"One."

He padded forward, lifted her from the table and set

her on her feet. "I set clothes on the bed for you."

She cringed. What would he choose for her to wear to her parents' house?

"Don't look at me like that. They're decent." He headed for the living room. "Oh, I forgot shoes. They're in the orange box to the left inside the closet."

"Got it, Sir." She wiggled her ass at him as she left the room.

Margaret made quick work of dressing in the outfit he'd set out, grateful for the jeans and soft sweater that wouldn't leave her feeling vulnerable at her parents'. He'd even included a bra. No panties, but she could live without them under her jeans.

She headed for the closet next. *Orange box...* It was high and she reached up on tiptoes to nudge it forward so it would topple into her hands.

It came down, just as she'd planned, but unexpectedly it careened into her hard, the lid falling off, and the contents flying into the air.

Not shoes, to her surprise, but papers...and photos...and documents...

She squealed, but not loud as the mess rained all around her. *Ugh. Wrong box.*

She kneeled on the floor to gather all the pages and stack them up to put them back in the box.

And then she froze.

Her breath caught in her throat. Slowly, her eyes glued to several photos, she lowered herself to the floor and sat on her ass. Her hand shook as she reached for one of the pictures. Her eyes scanned the pieces of paper, memories from a lifetime ago. Carlton's memories.

*Karen.*

Her name was on everything. Soft, feminine handwriting covered the pages as she glanced around. Heart-shaped doodles scrawled on the corners of notebook paper. Love letters.

*Oh God.*

Her gaze went back to the picture gripped in her hand. She scrambled to grab several others and laid them out in front of her.

A chill went down her spine. "Fuck," she whispered.

"Baby, are you—" His words cut off as he stepped into the closet and found her there, pieces of his past circling her, reaching for her, taunting her.

For a brief second, she felt sorry for him. He'd loved this girl so much he'd kept her alive in an orange box in his closet.

But then her focus landed on the picture in her hand again and she dropped it like a hot potato. Her vision blurred. Rage like nothing she'd ever felt swarmed in to eat her alive. She leaped to her feet and jumped away from the remnants of a life that was no more. Or was it?

"Baby…" He reached for her.

She jerked from his grasp, backing into the bedroom, her fists squeezing tight at her sides. "Carlton." Disbelief crowded her brain, fogging it, making it difficult to think or feel properly. And then she screamed, "She's fucking *me*! You, you, you—"

She shook her head, trying to clear it, make sense of this insanity. She glanced back at the floor. Karen stared back at her, smiling, mocking her. Or was it a mirror?

"No, baby. Let me explain." He inched toward her, palms out, pain in his voice.

Not the kind of pain she was feeling, but more of a sorrow from being caught red-handed.

"Explain what?" she shouted. "Explain that you found a woman who looked just like your old girlfriend and thought you could replace her? That's fucked up, Carlton. Even for you." She heaved for oxygen. She needed to get out of there. She spun on her heel and ran for the bedroom door.

"Maggie, no." Carlton was right behind her. He reached for her forearm, but she yanked it from his grasp.

"No. Don't touch me." She twisted in circles, looking for her purse. It was by the door, of course, where it always was. She took long strides to get there, heedless of her bare feet.

All she cared about was getting the fuck out of the house, and now.

"Baby, stop. Sit down. Let me talk." He kept to her back, not touching her, but not giving her an inch of space either.

She rounded on him with her hand on the door to the garage. "Don't." She held up a hand. "Let me go, Carlton. I swear to God, if you have a decent bone in your body, you'll let me go." She didn't know where she would go or what she would do, but she did know she needed to get out of this house for now and think. She needed space.

He stopped, close enough she could see his chest rise and fall, feel his breath hitting her shoulders. She didn't meet his gaze. She lowered her voice. "Let me go, Carlton."

He nodded. "I hate you driving like this." His hands shook at his sides.

"I know." It was ironic that his worst fears had all tumbled together into one moment in time, but it couldn't be helped. He was going to have to get over it. "I need to get out of here. You have to let me. We'll talk later after I've had some time."

He nodded again.

✦  ✦  ✦

CARLTON GRIPPED THE steering wheel so tight his knuckles hurt. Maggie had been gone for an hour. Too long. Eventually he couldn't take the stress any longer. He'd paced a hole in his carpet.

He'd gathered up the mess in the closet and stuffed it back in the box. He berated himself for his stupidity. He was worried out of his mind.

And then he'd gotten in the car. She surely had gone to her apartment. He knew she wouldn't go to her parents yet. It was too early in the morning, and besides, it would be hard for her to go there even under the best of circumstances. Her car wasn't at her apartment or her office. That left one place, and he pulled into the parking lot of Emergence, breathing out the biggest sigh of relief ever.

He gave a silent prayer to whoever would listen up above and then turned off the car and dragged himself to the back entrance of the club.

He let the door shut hard behind him, announcing his arrival, and followed the sound of voices to Jason's office.

When he finally rounded the corner, his shoulders slumped in relief. No matter what, he was just glad she was alive. If he never had the opportunity to touch her again because of his damn stupidity, he could at least rest easier knowing he hadn't caused her to crash her car on the way over.

She sat on the couch, curled in a ball with her knees pulled to her chest, a throw tossed over her legs. Her face was red from crying, dry streaks from tears on her cheeks. She held a wad of tissues in one hand and several littered the ground next to her.

Jason sat in a chair nearby. He turned toward Carlton, a wan smile on his face. As Carlton stepped farther into the room, Jason stood. He nodded at Carlton and left without saying a word, closing the door to his own office behind him.

Carlton eased into the seat Jason had vacated. "I'm so sorry, baby."

She stared at him, wiping her eyes with the back of her hands. Her tears had probably dried up before he'd arrived and now fell anew. "Tell me."

He looked at her, trying to decide what she meant.

"Tell me when you decided I was not a replacement for your dead girlfriend. Or did you?"

"Of course I did, baby."

"When? Before you fucked me for the first time? Was it before you took me as your submissive? Was it before I fell so hard for you I can't stand to be without you?"

"Yes. Before all of those things." He sucked in oxygen at her last words.

She swallowed visibly. "I'm not Karen." Her voice was

weak. "I can never be her. And I'm not a replacement."

"I know that."

"Tell me more."

He knew exactly what she meant this time. He leaned forward, wanting to be closer to her, but not risking her wrath by touching her. "The first time you came to the club, you took my breath away. I thought you were a ghost. That was a year and a half ago. I almost couldn't stand to be in the same room with you for fear I would inadvertently reach out and touch you to see if you were real.

"You were with Lori. You weren't mine to touch."

She stared at him, not moving, so he continued. "Yes, you looked like her. Like Karen. The resemblance was uncanny at first. But then I got to know you, and you're nothing like her. Your personality is so distinct there's no comparison.

"Eventually I forgot most of the time that you even looked like her in the first place. You took on your own glamour with your uniqueness. Your smile lights up a room with genuine delight. Your complex mind is a wonder to behold when you're in the zone. And your submission…baby…your submission is humbling."

She stared at him for long moments, holding his gaze. Finally she licked her lips and wiped her eyes with her tissue. "Tell me you haven't been sleeping with a dead girl."

He let a tear of his own slip down his face. "I've never looked into your eyes with my cock inside you and thought of anyone but my Maggie. I swear." He lowered onto his knees in front of her, bringing his face close to hers.

"*Your* Maggie?"

"Yes. Mine." He took a deep breath. It was time to get his head out of his ass. "You're mine, Maggie. I've been an ass to pretend otherwise. I was scared. I never wanted to fall in love again with anyone. When Karen died, she took a piece of me with her. I've lived without that for all these years. And then you waltzed into my office and sucked the life out of me with your submission. I love you so much it hurts. You're my life, Maggie. My soul. I've never felt this way before, not with Karen, and not with anyone since then." He tentatively took her hand and turned it over to kiss her palm and then place it against his cheek.

"Do you have any other secrets lurking around you need to divulge? I can't take much more of this, Carlton."

He exhaled as a smile spread across his face. She was going to forgive him. Give him another chance. "None. I promise."

"You're sure?"

"Positive." He leaned closer. "Please come home with me."

"Get rid of the box."

"Done."

"Don't ever call me by her name."

"I would never."

"I'm my own person."

"I'm so very clear on that."

"And I love you."

"I—" His throat caught. He blinked. "What?"

"You heard me." She smiled again.

"I know. But just to be clear?"

"I love you, Carlton. Even though that was a shitty

thing to do and you should have told me, it doesn't change how I feel."

"I should have told you. You're right. Can you say that one more time?"

"I love you." She didn't wait for him to kiss her. She wrapped her arms around him and kissed him first, a deep, sensual kiss that curled his toes and made him melt into her body, right in Jason's office.

MARGARET'S PALMS WERE sweaty as she stared at her parents' front door. After a morning that had ripped her in two and put her back together, she was exhausted. But Carlton had convinced her to keep this lunch date and face her fears.

She'd worried about driving here by herself. Carlton hadn't said a word. Of course he had no idea about her other fears. She knew she should have come clean with him that morning about her concerns and the notes and the possibility that someone was following her. But she'd been too exhausted to fight that battle, and everything had been so perfect. She hated to ruin the moment. She would tell him later. Adding that to the stress of facing her parents and facing his dead girlfriend hadn't been in the cards this morning.

And she figured she would surely be safe in the middle of the day in a residential neighborhood. She hadn't noticed a single person following her today. Not now and not earlier when she'd fled to see Jason at his office.

She could hear voices inside. She knew she was the last

to arrive. She'd intentionally come late and hoped to leave early. The less time she spent at the house, the better. Especially since she couldn't very well confront her parents about her childhood issues on a day when the extended family was also present.

She finally lifted her hand and knocked. It seemed silly since these were her parents, but she didn't feel like this was her home. She wiped her hands on her jeans as she waited. She was glad for the outfit Carlton had chosen. It was perfect.

When the door finally opened, her mother stood there with a beaming smile on her face. "What are you knocking for?" She grabbed Margaret with both hands and pulled her in for a hug. It actually felt good. She hadn't seen her mother in months. "Come in, honey. Come in." She pointed over her shoulder. "Your aunt and uncle are already here. And your cousin Robbie."

Margaret cringed as she followed her mother into the living room. She hadn't seen Robbie in years. Something about him had always rubbed her wrong. Uncle Rocky and Aunt Barbara had three sons. All of them were older than Margaret. They were close in age and had seemed more like friends to each other than brothers. They'd given her the heebie-jeebies even as children.

Of course it might have had something to do with the fact that she considered them egotistical bigots like her parents and their parents. Even as a child, she'd hated them. They'd gang up on her and taunt her like a little sister instead of a special cousin. Her dad would always tell her to toughen up. He actually encouraged them to bully her, saying she was weak and needed better influences in her life.

"Hey, squirt." Robbie was the first to greet her when she entered the room, and of course he couldn't say something adult and polite. No, he still talked down to her like she was a child.

She chose to ignore him in favor of smiling as warmly as she could conjure at her aunt and uncle. She hadn't seen them in months either, not since the last holiday function. Even at twenty-seven years old, she felt as though they smiled back at her condescendingly, with some sort of misguided disapproval.

It unnerved her, but she stuffed it to the back of her mind.

Her uncle spoke first, even before her father. "How've you been?"

"Good. Work is good."

"Are you still with that accounting firm?"

"I am. I love it there."

Her father cleared his throat. "Nice of you to grace us with your presence."

Margaret fought to keep her face straight and her body from quivering. *Don't let him get to you.* She took a seat in the armchair next to the couch, crossing her legs and tucking her hands under her thighs to keep from fidgeting.

"Can I get you something to drink, dear?" her mother asked.

"I'm fine, Mom. Thank you."

Luckily, everyone's attention was diverted to Robbie when he began to ramble on about his latest accomplishments in advertising. The man was thirty-four years old and he still needed to steal the limelight to prove himself worthy of his parents' respect.

Margaret's mother spoke again when Robbie finished his discourse. "Margaret, why don't you and Barbara come out back with me? It's such a nice day. We can sit on the patio."

Somewhat relieved, Margaret followed her mother through the kitchen and out the back door. Barbara copied her, right on her heels.

It was pleasant outside. Plus, something about the open air eliminated some of the tension that filled the inside of the house like a gaseous substance waiting for the right moment to explode.

They chatted pleasantly for several minutes, and Barbara and her mother took turns questioning her about her job. Pointedly, neither one of them asked her about her love life. And thank God for that.

Margaret's mother glanced at her watch. "Oh. The roast should be about done. Margaret, would you please go give your father a fifteen-minute warning?"

Margaret tried not to roll her eyes. After all, this had been her mother's way ever since Margaret could remember. She'd always let her husband know at precisely what moment dinner would be served. The man hated when his food wasn't ready on time.

Margaret nodded and turned to enter the house, thinking this day wasn't going as badly as she'd expected. Of course, with her aunt, uncle and Robbie in attendance, she had no intention of confronting her parents about anything. That alone had lifted a huge weight off her shoulders. At least for today.

Margaret held her hands out to ease the screen door shut without letting it slam. It was one of her father's pet peeves. There was no need to encourage the man to snap at her as though she were a five-year-old today.

She could hear the men talking. They were no longer in the living room. They had moved to the study, so she turned down the hall toward her father's favorite room. Before she reached the entrance, however, she stopped dead in her tracks. Their voices were off. Not quite loud enough. And their tone was combative. And then she heard her name mentioned and couldn't move another inch. She held her breath.

"Do you really think Margaret has turned over a new leaf?" her uncle asked.

Robbie chuckled sardonically. "You would think after the way Petey, Ross and I roughed her up twelve years ago she would've straightened herself out. But I don't think so."

*What the fuck?* She set a hand on the wall to keep from falling. Her legs threatened to give out.

"You're still following her, right?" This question came from her father.

"Of course. Just like you requested. She hasn't been staying at her apartment. At least this time she's fornicating with a man. It's an improvement over that lesbian bitch she was with for over a year. But this guy ain't right either. He takes her to the same club she went to with that rug muncher. It's a fetish club."

"That could be good though, right?" her father asked.

"I mean, at least it's a man."

Uncle Rocky laughed. "I hate to tell you this, brother, but that girl ain't right. If my boys couldn't scare her straight back when she was a teenager, I don't think there's hope."

Robbie chuckled also. "I've even left her a few threatening notes to shake her up. But nothing has caused her to change her ways."

"Well, she better get on the straight and narrow and stay there soon. If I'm going to become a deacon next month, I need my family by my side. It won't look good if my own daughter is sowing her wild oats. She needs to come back into the fold and start going to church again."

Margaret was too stunned to breathe or move. She knew she needed to, and fast. But the shock was overwhelming. What the fuck was she listening to? She lifted her hand to tuck her hair behind her ear but found herself shaking so violently she couldn't even accomplish that simple task.

Her feet seemed to be stuck in quicksand.

She glanced around. The voices in her father's study continued, but she could no longer hear them. She'd heard enough. More than enough. She had to get out of there. *Now.*

Commanding her body to move, she turned silently, made her way to the front door, grabbed her purse and managed to slip out without making a sound. Even the front door snicked shut on a breath. At least something went in her favor.

Without looking in any direction except straight ahead,

Margaret headed for her car and didn't pause until she was in the seat, holding the keys up to the ignition. She dropped them and had to fish them off the floor, panic crawling up her spine for fear someone would come out of the house before she made her escape.

Shaking, she finally managed to start the car and peel away from the curb.

Tears filled her eyes when the shock wore off. She gripped the steering wheel so tight her hands hurt. When the tears fell, she had trouble seeing. She kept driving. No way would she risk pulling over.

She drove for several miles before she realized where she was headed. Suddenly, her apartment was right in front of her. She pulled over, shut off the car and heaved giant sobs, unable to open the door. She sat there for a long time, sucking oxygen in over and over—the true meaning of the ugly cry.

When she finally wiped her face and glanced around, she was relieved to find no one had noticed her. And no one seemed to have followed her. She gathered up the strength to grab her purse and head for her apartment. The moment she got inside and shut the door, she leaned against the wall, slunk down to the floor, buried her face in her hands and cried again.

She cried for the child raised by such a heinous family. She cried for the teenager viciously attacked and beaten by her own cousins. She cried for the mother who might or might not have known any of that happened to her daughter, but was just as guilty by association.

Most of all Margaret cried for herself, for her loss, for

the loneliness that crept into her and wouldn't abate. She wasn't sure at first why she'd come home to her own place. She hadn't been there for over a week. But now, as she eased herself to completely lie on the floor, she knew. She needed to be alone. She needed to process everything that had happened.

She couldn't face Carlton. Not now. This was her fucked-up battle, an inner war of sorts. She didn't want to see his face or deal with his reaction yet. And the last thing she could manage at that point was submission.

Her submission actually scared the fuck out of her. She'd submitted to her father her entire life, doing what he said, being who he wanted her to be. Well, that wasn't entirely true. She had never been the daughter he wanted. But she'd exerted a tremendous amount of energy faking she was someone she wasn't, for his sake.

And all that time she'd never known he'd actually hired her own cousins to fucking track her down and beat her up in a dark alley? *Fuck*! And he was still having them trail her around town to make sure she was toeing the line? Goddamn, that was fucked up.

Even more fucked up than she ever imagined.

Suddenly she winced. Holy shit. Her cousins were the ones following her. They were the ones who left the notes on her car. She'd been so stunned since running out of her parents' house, she hadn't stopped to realize her stalkers were in fact her cousins. Damn them. Fuck them. Fuck all of them. She heaved back new tears.

She needed to call the cops. But she couldn't bring herself to sit up yet.

It grew dark. She lay on the hardwood floor, her face pressed against the dark wood, the coolness a refuge that grounded her to the earth. The only thing she knew was the wood against her cheek. She spread her fingers on the slats, thinking perhaps she could also grip the floor with them and not disappear.

Her cell rang many times. She didn't move to answer it. It sat in her purse next to her body and she left it there. She didn't care who was calling. She wanted to talk to no one. She didn't have the energy to speak to Carlton yet, and she'd rather die than answer a call from her mother or father.

She had no idea how much time passed. It grew dark. Hours. Her face had dried, but it felt tight from the streaks of tears. She didn't even sleep. She just lay there almost dead inside.

She didn't flinch when a knock sounded at the door. She'd known it would happen eventually. She'd never entered past the foyer and she hadn't turned on a light, but anyone who came looking would know she was there by her car out front.

"Maggie? Are you in there?" Carlton. She'd know his voice anywhere, and he was the only person alive who called her by that nickname. "Maggie. Please. Open the door." He was persistent. She knew that about him. He wouldn't leave. And if she were honest with herself, she wouldn't love him as much as she had grown to if he were the kind of man who would give up on her.

But he wasn't. If she didn't open the door, he would break it down.

Pulling herself from the floor, she reached up and turned the handle enough to unlock the door and allow him to get through.

He pushed it open slowly. "Maggie?" He stepped inside, glancing around the dim room for a second before he spotted her on the floor. He pushed the door shut behind him as he gasped. "Maggie? What the hell? What happened? Are you all right?" While he fired all the right questions she'd known he would ask, he bent down, grabbed her shoulders and held her at arm's length to assess her for injury.

"Baby, talk to me. Are you hurt?"

She shook her head. Tears fell with renewed force, shocking her that there was enough moisture left in her body to produce them.

Carlton hauled her into his arms and lifted her off the ground. He cradled her against his body and carried her to the couch.

She cried harder at how caring he was, her tears mixed with her runny nose, soaking his T-shirt.

"Baby. Talk to me." He smoothed her hair back as he sat with her in his lap. He tipped her face up to meet his gaze, but she saw nothing through the haze of her tears.

"Maggie." His voice was sharper that time. He shook her shoulders a bit. "Do I need to call the police? Did someone attack you?"

She shook her head, perhaps too violently as she realized what a mess this was and how her situation must have appeared to him. "No. I mean, yes. Someone did attack me, but not today. Twelve years ago. We need to call the cops, but not yet. I need to pull myself together."

✦ ✦ ✦

HE FLINCHED. "I'M confused. Talk to me, baby." Whatever the hell had happened with her parents, it was bad. He'd never seen her like this before. Agonizingly distraught.

Even when she and Lori broke up, he'd never seen her this upset.

He'd been out of his mind when she hadn't returned home. He'd called her several times and then driven to her parents' house. When he didn't find her car, he didn't go to the door. Instead he drove to her apartment. He'd sat in his car for a full minute, hyperventilating, when he realized she had to be inside.

His fear of cars was irrational. He knew that. And he needed to get a grip on himself before he let his fear manifest as anger. It wasn't her fault he hated her driving around.

"Maggie, open up to me. This isn't fair. You scared the shit out of me. Do you know how worried I've been looking for you?"

She squirmed off his body with enough sudden energy to face him head-on. She stood next to the couch and pointed at him. "You? *You* were worried. Fuck you, Carlton. This is so not about you and your concern for my safety. This is about *me*." She jerked her finger to point at herself.

He opened his mouth, but then he sat there stunned, saying nothing.

She continued, backing up and then pacing around the

room. Stomping really. She dug her hands into her hair and pulled them through the long locks, yanking hard enough to wince. "My parents are fucking freaks, Carlton. I'm in a state of crisis here. So don't fucking talk to me about your concerns right now. I can't take it after what I've been through today."

"Okay," he managed to mumble.

Maggie paced the room for several minutes. He watched as she got her breathing under control and then finally turned to face him.

Carlton leaned forward, afraid to do anything else. "Talk to me, baby. What happened? Did you confront your parents?"

She lifted her gaze to meet his and took a deep breath. "I never even got a chance. My aunt and uncle were there. And their oldest son, Robbie."

"Okay."

"I went outside with my mom and aunt to sit on the porch. When it was time for lunch, my mom sent me in to give the men a head's up."

Carlton pursed his lips, fear climbing its way up his spine. He pressed his palms together and leaned his elbows on his knees.

Maggie picked at invisible lint on her shirt. "They were talking in my dad's study. I heard my name from the hall, so I stopped in my tracks and listened." She licked her lips. She didn't speak again, her gaze focused on something across the room Carlton was sure she didn't actually see.

She didn't move until a tear ran down her cheek, and she flinched and reached to wipe it away.

Bile rose in Carlton's throat. He forced himself to remain still and quiet. But it was a challenge. "Go on."

"It was my cousins."

"What was your cousins?"

"The ones who followed me and Leslie that night. The ones who beat us up and screamed those hateful words at us." She stood straighter. A fire burned in her eyes, fury Carlton hoped to never see in anyone's expression ever again in his life. "My own cousins fucking followed me and my girlfriend, beat us up and ran like the fucking bastards they are, leaving us to die.

"My father and my uncle fucking told them to do it." She yanked her gaze back to the floor as though facing him with this information was more than she could bear.

Carlton couldn't move. He sat stunned in his seat. And that was a good thing.

Who did something like that to their own child?

Maggie's head bolted back up. "Can you believe it? My fucking *father*." She was screaming again now. "That asshole and his brother fucking hired my cousins to rough me up to set me fucking *straight*."

Carlton swallowed. It seemed his heart stopped beating. He couldn't think of a thing he could possibly say at that moment. Rage burned in his entire body. If he moved, he would break something.

And he'd never heard so many cuss words coming from her mouth. But he'd also never imagined a time when they would be as necessary as they were. She'd dropped more F-bombs in two minutes than he'd ever heard from one sweet mouth. And still, she was totally in the right.

BECCA JAMESON

The rage that ran through him made his ears ring until he felt like he were in a bubble. He watched as Maggie sobbed, tears running down her face. He watched, but he couldn't move from his spot, nor could he hear a sound.

Who did something like that to a child? Their own *daughter?*

Carlton gripped his knees with both hands, hoping to keep himself from jumping off the couch, tearing through the door and making his way to Maggie's parents' house to fucking *kill* her sad excuse for a father.

He didn't though, and that's what mattered.

His gaze moved to Maggie, the woman he'd fallen in love with, the broken woman who'd been treated with such disrespect for so many years. Her head was tipped toward her feet and she wiped her eyes with the backs of her hands.

He said the first thing that came to mind. "We should call the police."

Margaret lifted her face. "Yeah, cause that's not all." Her shoulders slumped and she didn't meet his gaze. "They've still been following me." She turned to face the wall away from him.

"What?"

"Apparently my father still has them tailing me, everywhere. I knew it, but I didn't want you to freak out, so I didn't tell you."

"You knew your cousins were following you? Like recently?" He thought about the car that had driven by his house so slowly the other night and shivered. He gripped the arm of the couch with his fingers until they hurt.

She turned to face him. "I knew *someone* was following

262

me. I've already gone to the cops." Her voice was dead calm.

Carlton took a deep breath, staring at her. He wanted to jump up and scream, but that wouldn't help right now.

She continued while he sat silently, "They've been leaving nasty notes on my windshield while I was at work."

Now he stood, slowly. He walked past her, through the kitchen and out the back door. She had a small balcony, and he used every inch of it to pace back and forth, trying to get himself together before he screamed.

Minutes passed. He ran his hands through his hair until it hurt from pulling. His heart still pounded. He couldn't stop the flames that threatened to consume him. His face was so hot it burned.

The sliding door opened, and Maggie stepped out after a while. "I called the cops. They're on their way over." Her voice was still dead.

Carlton turned to face her. He opened his mouth, but she held up a hand. "Don't start. I'm not in the mood right now. I've been through hell. Either support me or leave. I'm exhausted. My world is fucking upside down. I don't need you to lecture me about fucking safety."

He took a deep breath and then let it out slowly. "You're right." He wanted to turn her over his lap and spank her sexy ass, but she couldn't handle that right now.

"I'm sorry I didn't tell you. You're a worrier. Way over the top. I wasn't really sure if someone was following me or if I was being paranoid. There was no way to know who left the notes, and I did go to the cops. There's nothing different you could have done but worry more."

*And fucking drive you everywhere.* Which was precisely what she didn't want, so he had to understand where she was coming from. He didn't have to like it, but he got it.

"Come back inside. I need to be able to hear the front door." Maggie backed through the sliding door, nodding behind her.

Carlton followed.

She led him to the living room and sat in a chair. Not the couch. A chair. Where he couldn't touch her. She curled her legs under her.

Carlton wanted to know what else happened. "What did your dad and uncle say when they found you standing there?"

She let out a long breath. "They didn't. I backed away and left the house without a word."

"You didn't face them?"

"Fuck no. Not going over there again in my life."

So her parents didn't even know what she'd found out. He leaned back against the couch. Great.

They sat in silence. He felt like he was walking on pins and needles with her. He couldn't say anything because if he did, she might go ballistic on him. Not that he could blame her.

He jumped when a knock sounded at the door, and then he stood and took two strides to get to the entrance before Maggie.

Two police officers stood outside.

Carlton let them in, and they spent the next half hour going over all the specific events of today, the last few weeks and twelve years ago. Neither cop thought there was much they would be able to do or prove. But they did suggest Maggie get an order of protection.

When they left, Carlton turned toward Maggie again. "Let's go home. You need sleep." He felt almost as wrung out as she looked.

She shook her head and jerked to attention. "No."

"No what?"

She stepped back. "No. I'm not going home with you, Carlton. I need to be alone. My life is a fucking mess. I need to deal with this on my own."

"You're my submissive, baby. I can't just leave you here to figure things out alone. That's not going to happen."

"See," she screamed, "that's just it. Am I? Am I even submissive? I've lived my entire life under my father's thumb. I submitted to him for years, just like my mother. That's disgusting, Carlton. I'm not a real submissive. I just learned how to appease my father. I never ever want to bow to anyone like that again."

"Maggie." He stepped forward, but stopped dead when he saw the glare she shot him.

"Don't. I can't talk about this anymore now. And I'm not going with you. I lost so many years of my life submitting to my father. I can't do it anymore. I'm done. I'm not a real sub, Carlton. Can't you see that? I'm a byproduct of my father's mission to save me from myself."

"That's not true, Maggie. The two things are not the same." He'd explained this to her before. Apparently she hadn't understood.

"Go." She pointed at the door. "Please, Carlton. Just go. Let me be alone. Don't come back. I can't stand the idea of anyone telling me what to do right now."

He opened his mouth again, but then shut it. If looks could kill... He had no choice. He needed to leave. This wasn't over, but Maggie was frantic, and the only way she was going to calm down was for him to leave her to grieve alone.

He trudged to the front door and opened it. When he turned back to glance at her, she was still staring him down with daggers. He started to tell her to lock the door, but thought better of it.

And then he did the hardest thing he'd ever done in his entire life. He left.

# Chapter Seventeen

MARGARET TOOK MONDAY off work. She hadn't slept and she couldn't bring herself to get out of bed. She knew she would have to face the world eventually, but for hours she just lay there staring at the ceiling.

She wondered if her cousins were outside even now, watching her apartment. She shivered from head to toe and pulled the covers up higher under her chin.

She couldn't face Carlton yet. It infuriated her to no end that his efforts toward safety had been well-founded. She wasn't crazy. People had been following her. And she'd been too pigheaded to tell him because of what she'd thought was his irrational concern over her safety. Apparently he'd been correct to worry.

Her phone rang several times. She never looked at it to see who called. She could imagine. Her mother. Her father. Carlton. Jason…

She wasn't too stupid to realize she would have to face her parents eventually. She'd left with no explanation. She would have to go back and give them a final piece of her mind in order to put that situation to bed once and for all.

Someone knocked at the door. Margaret groaned and glanced at the clock. Noon. She closed her eyes, willing the person to go away. She didn't have the energy to speak to anyone on that mental list, and if by chance the guest happened to be one of her cousins, there was a good chance she would shoot first and ask questions later. Jail sounded good right about then.

The knocking continued. She threw a pillow over her face to block out the insistent sound, but it never stopped, and all she managed to do was deprive herself of oxygen. Finally, she dragged herself to sitting and then pulled to a standing position. She felt as though she'd been beaten. In a way, she had.

She padded down the hall and tiptoed to the front door to peer out the peephole.

Jason.

A huge sigh escaped her lips. He was definitely the least of the evils. She decided to let him in, opening the door and stepping back enough to allow him entrance.

The inside of the house was exactly as she'd left it last night, a mess. She didn't give a fuck. "Jason."

He furrowed his brow. "You okay?"

"No?" She sighed again and shut the door.

Jason held up a drink carrier she hadn't seen in his other hand. "I brought coffee."

"Bless you." She made her way to the couch and curled up in one corner, pulling a throw over the loose T-shirt and shorts she'd worn to bed.

Jason took a spot next to her and wiggled a steaming cup from the cardboard carrier. "I figured you wouldn't have had any yet today. Or at least you'd need more." He smiled.

She took the cup from him and sipped the elixir. "I guess you spoke to Carlton."

"Yep."

"He told you everything?"

"More or less. He was pretty upset. I'm sure I missed a few of the details."

Margaret nodded. She leaned back and stared at the ceiling. "I think I need to distance myself. I've been going to Emergence for all the wrong reasons. I should move to another city. Start over. Reclaim my life."

"And you think that will cure you of your submissive tendencies?"

She jerked her gaze back to meet his.

Jason continued, "Listen. I know what you're thinking. I mean, I sort of understand where you're coming from, but what happened with your father has nothing to do with how you interact with Carlton or anyone else for that matter."

"How do you know? How do you know I'm not just acting the mousy submissive, kneeling at Carlton's feet because my father raised me to obey his every fucking command?"

"I don't." Jason shook his head. "I won't deny that your father influenced you. It's a matter of nature versus nurture. Did he cause you to be submissive? Or would you have been anyway? You'll never know. But the bottom line is, it doesn't matter."

"How do you figure? If I spend my life allowing some

Dom to order me around and control my every movement, how is that any different from what my father did?"

"Choice." He spoke that one word and stared at her.

"Huh?"

"You have free will, Margaret. You're an adult. You make your own choices now. When you were a kid, you had no free will. You had to do what your parents said or suffer the consequences. When you were a teenager, you were forced to continue feeling that lack of choice in order to bide your time and wait for the moment you could escape.

"Hell, even kidnap victims make similar decisions. They might pretend to agree with their captors for weeks on end, waiting for an opening so they can flee. As soon as their attackers get lax, they run.

"It sounds like that's how you lived under your father's roof for years, waiting, hoping, biding your time, playing his game until you could escape."

She nodded. He was so right.

"Well, you did. You aren't there now. You made it out. Did it shape you? Probably. But the type of submissive you are now is not the same. Now, you're the one with all the control. Do you think Carlton runs your life? Hell no. You run his. He has to wake up every day praying you'll still submit to him. All Doms do. As soon as you say *no*, it's over. All the power is yours."

God, why did he make so much sense?

"Giving freely of your power to a Dom is a choice you make because you like how it feels to be controlled. For you, it's sexual. For others, it's domestic or for pain or any number of reasons. But you're a sexual submissive, Margaret. It's freeing for you to let Carlton make choices for you. Right?"

"Yes." She moaned around the word. Damn him.

"That's all you. You have the power. Does Carlton force you to do anything you don't want to do?"

"No."

"See? And when you use your safe word, he stops, right?"

"Yes."

"Look, I'm not trying to talk you into anything. If you stay with Carlton, great. If you leave town and find another Dom, that's also your right. But I want you to think about your choices hard before you act. Your father has already won so many battles against you. He forced you to give up your girlfriend, your friends, your high school activities, a normal college life, and the list goes on. Don't let him win again. Take this bull by the horns and fight.

"I know you don't want to hear this, but Carlton's right. You need to go back over there and face your parents. Tell them who you are, and give *them* the final choice to shut you down. If they do, good riddance. Some people are far too toxic to keep around, even family."

"I know."

"I'll be happy to go with you if you want."

"Thanks, Jason. I'll think about it." She released the grip she had on the throw, completely unaware she'd been holding it so tight her knuckles hurt.

"Promise me you won't go over there alone."

"I won't."

"Don't let them win, Margaret. This is your life now. I've seen you with Carlton. You two are fantastic together. He loves you more than life itself. He would do anything for you. And I think you feel the same."

"I do."

"Well, then don't run out of town and give him up simply because you're afraid of your submission. It's who you are. Face it head-on. If you run, your father wins this round too. Talk to Carlton. Let him help you. You won't be disappointed."

✧   ✧   ✧

WHEN JASON LEFT, Margaret was more tired than she had been before he arrived. She crawled back into bed and slept for so many hours it was dark out when she awoke again. Her stomach rumbled. She hadn't eaten in almost two days. Not since breakfast with Carlton on Sunday.

She heaved her sorrowful self out of bed again and padded to the kitchen. The blessed freezer had a wonderful assortment of dinners to choose from, and she grabbed one without looking at the box, tossed it in the microwave and tapped her foot while she waited for it to heat.

When the timer went off, she peeled back the plastic surface and shoveled the pasta into her mouth so fast she was still starving when the tray was empty.

Easy fix. She repeated the steps again. This time, she managed to sit at the table and slow down the fork-to-mouth process to a reasonable speed.

As she sat back and took a deep breath, she thought for the first time in over twenty-four hours that she might possibly live.

She had to. Her father was a jackass. She needed to tell him and get on with her life. Every minute she spent moping around in her apartment was another minute he stole from her. Jason was right. She couldn't let him win. And until she confronted her parents, she would be living in limbo.

She stood from the table, deposited her fork in the sink and her trays in the trash and went in search of her phone.

The least she could do was text Carlton and let him know she was fine. Leaving him hanging was cruel. It wasn't his fault she was so fucked up. He'd only been trying to help.

She wasn't sure she could face him yet. She was too emotionally drained to endure another round with Carlton. She needed more time to sort through her thoughts before she made any decisions. But he at least deserved a text.

There were six texts from Carlton. The latest one had been from that morning before Jason came over. She figured Jason must have talked Carlton into letting her be after he'd visited. She quickly typed a message to him.

*Hey. Just want to let you know I'm fine.*

Two seconds later she had a response.

*Maggie. Thank God. I've been… Well, you know me…*

She smiled. *Lol I do. Don't worry so hard. I need time.*

She stared at the screen, knowing he wouldn't be finished. *I know. I'm here for you. Day or night. You know that, right?*

*Yes. And I appreciate it. Thank you.*

*I love you.*

She choked up when she read the last line, and a tear ran down her cheek. God, how she loved that man back. She set the phone aside and padded to the bathroom. A warm bath would help lessen the pounding in her head.

She moaned as she leaned back against the side of the tub as it filled, closing her eyes and letting the water wash over her.

Tomorrow she would face Carlton. Tonight she needed more sleep. She couldn't possibly go to her parents' house alone. It wouldn't be prudent, and she would need someone for moral support after she saw them.

Carlton was the only man for that job.

After her bath, she felt much better. Relaxed. The weight on her shoulders didn't seem as heavy. Carlton loved her. He did. It was real. She could trust him with her heart. With him by her side, she could face her demons and come out on the other side.

Was she submissive? Yes. Even after two days without Carlton, she missed the way he took care of her, the way he made her want...need...feel... She missed his commanding voice and his hands on her skin. He could draw out her deepest desires and turn her into a ball of sexual energy with a look. And she missed that. Craved it. She wanted to claim it back. If he would have her, she was his.

She fell asleep with a smile finally.

✧　✧　✧

ON TUESDAY, SHE woke up alert and rested and went back to work. She thought about Carlton all day, unable to concentrate on anything without his face popping into her mind, the way he smiled or smirked at her when she didn't do what she was told. The way he narrowed his gaze when he was about to let her come or come himself. She couldn't stand another night without him.

She texted him at three. *Can I come over tonight?*

His quick response wasn't surprising. *Of course. You don't have to ask. I'm here for you when you're ready.*

*Thank you. I'll be there after work then.*

*I'll make dinner,* he typed back.

She hesitated only a second and then added, *I love you.*

There was a long pause. She stared at the screen, worrying her lip.

*I love you too, baby. So much it hurts. Come home.*

Margaret's heart beat faster. *I'm already there.*

She left work early and went straight to his house, opening the garage door as though she lived there and had a right to do so. She took a deep breath and fortified herself to slip back into her submissive role.

She entered the house through the garage as usual, her head bowed. Carlton was in the kitchen, and whatever he was cooking smelled delicious. She knew he wasn't expecting her to assume any sort of role yet, but she wanted to move on with her life, and the best way to get that started was by submitting.

"Hey, baby."

Without comment, she set her purse on the counter by the door, kicked off her shoes and removed her clothes. She'd intentionally dressed to Carlton's specifications that morning—no panties and a Carlton-approved lace bra that did little to hide much of anything.

Carlton stepped up to her and tipped her head up to meet his gaze with a finger under her chin. "Baby, if you're not ready…"

"I am, Sir."

He held her gaze for a long time, his eyes boring into her, undoubtedly assessing her mental state. Finally, he smiled. "You're spectacular." He released her chin. He nodded toward the dining room table.

She knew she was meant to go kneel in her spot. And she did so without hesitation. As she assumed his preferred position, knees spread, hands behind her back, spine long, an overwhelming relaxation settled over her. The stress of the last several days had left her tense. Returning to work today had been a challenge.

She wasn't sure if Carlton understood, but she needed this. She needed normal. She needed to relinquish control and let him take the reins for the rest of the evening. It would relax her and rejuvenate her to repeat the process tomorrow.

She inhaled slowly as she watched him move about the kitchen. Italian. God, that man could cook.

By the time Carlton settled next to her with several platters of food, her stomach was growling.

He sat in his usual spot, but he swung his body to face her and began to feed her bites of the various foods he had prepared.

She moaned around each bite, glad he didn't comment on her noises. Apparently he wasn't a stickler about her dining enjoyment. His noise rules applied more aptly to *his* dining enjoyment, specifically when the feast was her.

When she was full, she waited for him to finish eating and clear away the dishes.

He took her hand and helped her to her feet before leading her down the hall to the bedroom. He left her standing in the center of the room and slowly circled her while he removed his shoes and then his shirt and then his jeans. He approached her from behind, snuggled up against her back and stuck his chin on her shoulder. He wrapped his arms around her center and crossed them under her breasts. His lips tickled her ear as he whispered, "Are you sure, baby? We don't have to do this if you're not ready."

"Yes, we do, Sir. I *need* this. It relaxes me."

Carlton lifted both hands to cup her breasts, and he grasped both nipples to pinch them tightly, tugging them outward.

She gasped, rising up on tiptoes and fisting her hands at her sides.

"This is what you call relaxed?"

"In the end, yes, Sir. The more you demand of me before you take me, the higher the bar is raised, the more relaxed I am in the end."

He twisted her nipples just enough to get her attention. His lips settled against her ear again. "I understand, Maggie. Perfectly. I just don't want you to push yourself to do anything you're not ready for."

"On the contrary, Sir, I'm ready for anything."

There was a pause as he released her nipples and soothed them with the pads of his thumbs. She knew he was thinking about her words. "Anything?"

"Yes," she said on a breath. "Please, Sir. Stop tiptoeing

around me. I hate it. I need normal. I need you inside me. I want to look in your eyes and see the same possessive gaze I saw before all this happened with my parents. I need to know you still see me the same way."

He squeezed her breasts and spoke into her ear again. "You are still you. And I still adore you. If you're sure you're ready, I'll take you to the peak, baby."

"Don't go easy on me."

"I don't intend to." He paused, his lips on her shoulder. "Mmm. I bet I know how to work out some of the stress."

"How's that, Sir?"

He set his finger on her lips. "Shh." He soothed a hand up to her neck and whispered so close she shivered with each word. "Kneel, baby."

She didn't hesitate. The second he released her, she complied.

He left her there for a while, rummaging around on the other side of the room before he returned.

She didn't dare glance up at him the entire time. She kept her head tipped toward the ground, her hands clasped behind her back.

When he stepped in front of her, he reached for her breast and clasped her nipple between his fingers so fast she gasped and swayed forward.

He didn't comment. Instead he worked the bud with his fingers for a minute and then clamped it without saying a word. She could see the tiny heart dangling from her nipple. He repeated the action on the other side.

When he was finished, he stepped back and didn't

move for a long time.

So long she grew self-conscious. He loved to look at her. How long would he stare before he continued?

He reached out and flicked the little hearts at one point, letting them swing against her breasts. The motion pulled on her nipples and made her more sensitive than she already was.

Finally, he spoke. "Follow me, Maggie."

She lifted one foot and worked to get her balance so she could stand without toppling over while keeping her hands behind her back. Her knees had grown stiff. She followed his retreating back down the hall to the dining room.

He pulled out a chair and sat, motioning for her to approach.

She expected him to have her kneel at his feet as usual, so he took her by surprise when he grabbed her by the waist and tugged her forward until she fell across his lap on her belly. Her arms flew out in front of her instinctively.

The breath whooshed from her lungs as he spread his legs so her breasts hung over one thigh and her pussy hung past the other thigh, exposed. She had no balance. Her feet didn't reach the ground.

But Carlton held her steady, rubbing her back and then her ass with a firm hand. He shoved her thighs apart, making her more off balance.

She winced as her breasts bounced, the clamps reaching toward the floor.

He held her steady. "What's your safe word, Maggie?"

"Red, Sir."

"I expect you to use it if this is too much." He squeezed

her ass cheek with his hand, almost too hard.

Her pussy clenched in response. "I will, Sir."

"I'm going to spank you." He switched cheeks. "You aren't allowed to come while I'm doing it. This isn't for sexual release. It's to help you release frustration. Do you understand?"

She did. She had no idea why, but she understood perfectly. And she wanted him to spank her. "Yes, Sir."

The first swat landed low, almost on her thighs, and although she wasn't meant to be aroused, she couldn't help the wetness that gathered between her legs or the moan that escaped her lips.

Carlton spanked her three more times in succession, not lightly. He smoothed his palm over the offended flesh then. "Your skin is so lovely all pink from my hand."

She fought to avoid squirming. If she moved, her clit would rub against his thigh.

"You okay, baby?"

"Yes, Sir."

"May I continue?"

"Yes, Sir."

He lifted his hand and slapped his cupped palm several more times, alternating between cheeks, working his way toward her thighs. And then he rubbed her skin again. The sting made her feel alive. Her entire body hummed from his touch. She was on fire, and she loved it. She'd been spanked before, many times, but never quite like this. Never by Carlton.

His voice soothed as he caressed her butt. "Baby, so sexy. Do you want more?"

"Yes, Sir." She did. She wanted the high she felt from giving her body over to his care. She wanted the endorphin rush she got from the spanking.

She moaned, her mind slipping into a perfect subspace as he rhythmically started another set of smacks. Even the sound of his hand striking her butt cheeks and thighs relaxed her and drove away some of the mental anguish she'd been fighting.

She didn't know how long he continued, but she knew every cell in her body craved his touch. Her breasts swayed, the clamps rocking back and forth to make her nipples hypersensitive.

Even though he'd specifically told her he wouldn't let her come, she felt her pussy tightening, threatening orgasm without his touch. She spread her legs farther than necessary and ground her clit against his jeans, each swat of his hand pressing her shaved sex into his leg.

Suddenly he stilled his hand on her ass and thrust his fingers into her pussy.

She climaxed so fast she didn't know what hit her. And then he rubbed her clit with several of his fingers…his entire hand, grinding against her pussy, spreading her wetness around and pressing on her clit. He rubbed harder and faster as one orgasm became two and then three, crashing over each other, each one more forceful than the last.

He didn't stop until she flinched. It took three intense orgasms before his touch became sensitive. And then he eased his fingers gradually away from her pussy.

She lay limp across his lap until he turned her around

and hauled her into his embrace, carefully keeping her butt to the outside so he didn't rub it against his jeans.

He lifted her, hugging her against his chest, and carried her away from the dining room.

She couldn't open her eyes. She knew her mouth hung open, but she couldn't speak. And her lips were so dry, but she couldn't bring herself to lick them. She heard water running, and still he held her against his chest like a child.

Margaret felt so loved and cherished and protected, she didn't bother to pay attention to what he was doing. She trusted him implicitly. He'd just given her the best high of her life, and now he was caring for her in true Carlton fashion.

And she let him.

She heard a splash and opened her eyes a slit to see him lowering both of them into the tub. He had all of his clothes on. She was naked. She smiled inwardly at his care, but her mouth wouldn't lift at the sides.

She noticed her nipples were bare. When had he removed the clamps? He must have done it during one of the building orgasms and she hadn't noticed.

The tub continued to fill. The water covered both of them—Carlton in his jeans and Margaret snuggled against him naked. He caressed her ass, taking the sting away. The water was cool. It felt wonderful on her tender flesh.

When he flipped off the water, he sat there holding her, rocking, his hands running all over her body. And he never stopped whispering in her ear. "I've got you, baby... So sexy... I'm so proud of you... You did so well..." On and on he murmured soft praises as she sank into his chest, relaxing every muscle in her body.

# Chapter Eighteen

"**Y**OU'RE SHAKING." HE set his hand on her thigh and squeezed. Even that simple touch sent her heart racing.

Margaret stared out the window of the SUV. She didn't respond or even glance at Carlton, but she did lay her much smaller hand on top of his and thread her fingers between his.

She had to get out of the car and go to the door. Sitting out front was only prolonging the inevitable. She wasn't about to introduce her parents to Carlton. Her life with him was none of their business. They didn't deserve that courtesy. But she did want him to wait right out front, making it obvious she was not alone. She was glad he'd insisted on coming along. For one thing, he was right—she was too shaky to drive. And she expected to be even shakier by the time she left the house. For another thing, facing her dad head-on wasn't remotely smart. She didn't think he would injure her himself, but she also didn't trust him. She would never feel safe around him again. Her own father.

They'd already been to the police station that morning

and met with Officer Brantly. As luck would have it, they had pulled prints off her car. Not shocking to find several prints from good old cousin Robbie. How fortunate that he was already in the system for other petty crimes. As soon as Margaret told Brantly what she'd overheard, he agreed she needed an order of protection.

Their next stop had been the courthouse. She wanted this over with. A restraining order against her father, her uncle and her cousins sat on the seat next to her. They would each be served with papers tomorrow.

She took a deep breath, held it and then exhaled slowly. "Give me an hour."

"I'll give you thirty minutes, Maggie. I told you that."

She nodded. There was no sense arguing with him. Besides, she doubted she needed a full thirty minutes.

She opened the door, jumped down to the curb and pushed the door closed gently. As though headed for the guillotine, she dragged herself to the front door. She knocked and then rubbed her palms on her jeans. She glanced at the street while she waited. Carlton smiled at her.

Finally, the door opened. "Margaret?" her mom asked.

Margaret turned to face her mother, watching the woman take in the black SUV and its driver at the curb.

"Come in. I was just baking." Her mother turned toward the kitchen and Margaret padded across the living room and around the corner, following. Her mother was nearly always in the kitchen. "Where's Dad?" Even though it was a Wednesday afternoon, she knew he was there. His car was in the driveway.

"David? Margaret's here." She turned toward Margaret, wiping her hands on her apron. "Can I get you something to drink? Coffee?"

Margaret shook her head. "No, I just came to talk to you and Dad for a minute. I don't have much time." *You probably won't want me to stay after you've heard what I have to say.*

Margaret flinched when her father entered the room. She didn't make eye contact with him as he took a seat at the table behind a steaming cup of coffee. "What's this all about, Margaret? First, you sneak out of the house during a family get-together without saying a word, and then you don't return your mother's calls, and now you call a family meeting?"

Margaret's mother scooted out the chair next to her husband and sat. Even the high, piercing squeak of the chair legs against the linoleum grated on Margaret's nerves in this house.

Margaret licked her lips, although her tongue was too dry to moisten them. *Time to get this over with.* She lifted her gaze to meet her father's head-on. "I know what you did."

"What are you talking about?"

"I know you and Uncle Rocky hired his kids to follow me that night." She stood taller, emboldened by the rush of words. The truth. "I know you asked them to knock some sense into me."

Margaret's mother gasped. She turned toward her husband. "David? What is she talking about?"

Margaret kept her gaze locked on her father, but she

watched her mother out of her peripheral vision. The woman's shock was genuine. So she hadn't known. Interesting.

"For all the good it did." Her father shrugged.

Margaret's mother shook her head. She grabbed her apron with both hands and wadded the material in her fists. "David? Please tell me this isn't true."

Her father ignored her mother. He kept his infuriating gaze locked on Margaret's. He wasn't even apologetic in his body language. The man didn't give a fuck that he'd been found out. "Were you eavesdropping on us? You always have been a sneaky brat."

Margaret fought not to let him get to her. She wasn't about to try to explain how her mother had sent her in to give him the fifteen-minute warning till dinner. That was a moot issue. "I could've died."

The bastard laughed. "Don't be so dramatic."

Margaret sucked in a breath. Even though she should have expected this reaction, it still shocked her. Her own father. Hell, even her mother had blinders on. "Wow. So this is funny. Okay. Well, here's the deal. I'm not the sweet, innocent, heterosexual daughter you'd hoped for. I never have been. And this is the way my God made me.

"Moving me to another city didn't change that. Sending me to a private Christian school didn't change that. Locking me up for two years, essentially grounded, also didn't change that. Nothing is going to change the fact that I'm bisexual. Not you. Not Uncle Rocky. Not Robbie, Ross or Petey, the most fucked-up cousins a person could possibly have. Not your church. Not your counselor. I am who I am. I also know you still have those thugs following me, and they've been leaving me threatening notes. I got a restraining order this morning against you, Uncle Rocky and his sons. Don't come near me. Don't send anyone near me. I'll call the police if I so much as suspect one of you drives by my house."

Margaret's mother stared at her only child in disbelief, her eyes wide, her mouth hanging open in shock.

"I'm not going to sit here and listen to this. Get out of my house. Don't come back. Clearly, the devil has a hold of your soul." Her father shoved his chair back and stood as he spoke. The second he was finished, he turned and left the room, taking long strides to escape Margaret's presence.

Margaret directed her attention to her mother. "I won't put up with it anymore, Mom. I'm done. I'm tired. You have my cell phone. I won't change the number. If you ever want to reach me, that ball's in your court."

Without waiting for her mother to shut her mouth, Margaret turned and left the room. She walked straight out the front door without glancing back over her shoulder. She knew she hadn't given her mother a chance to speak, but she also realized there was no way the woman could possibly process everything Margaret had said in one sitting and make a coherent response. Her mother would need to ponder what she'd learned for a long time. If she chose to contact Margaret at some point down the line, that would have to be her decision.

Margaret was done.

She reached the passenger door of the Land Rover at a near jog. Seconds later, she was inside the car, buckling her seatbelt before she turned to Carlton and gave a half smile. "Go."

"That was fast." Carlton pulled away from the curb as she'd requested. "How did it go?"

"As expected. I don't think I'll be hearing from my father again in this lifetime." She turned to stare out the window, watching the houses go by.

"I'm sorry, baby. And your mother?" His voice was soft, soothing. He set a hand on her thigh and squeezed.

Margaret shrugged. "Time will tell." The weight of her confrontation bore down on her, pressing her into the seat. She bit her bottom lip, but there was no way to keep the tears from escaping the corners of her eyes. Tears she'd held at bay for twelve years. Perhaps even longer. She mourned for the loss of something she never really had. She knew that. But it didn't lessen the pain.

Margaret didn't meet Carlton's gaze on the drive home. In fact, she appreciated the space he allowed her. He didn't say another word. He didn't move his hand, but he kept it still on her thigh, grounding her. Keeping her from floating away.

Thank God it was Friday morning and she'd taken the day off. She had almost three days to pull herself back together before she needed to go to work. When he reached the house, she dragged herself inside as though she weighed a ton.

Carlton set his hands on her shoulders as they entered the kitchen. "Why don't you take a nap, baby?"

*Excellent idea.*

"I love you." He set his forehead against hers and drew

her closer to his body.

"I love you too." She smiled up at him, feeling her shoulders sag in relief.

"Go." He nodded toward the hall and released her.

She padded to the master bedroom, took off her shoes, wiggled out of her jeans and slid between the sheets wearing her T-shirt and bra.

# Epilogue

"WHICH ONE IS IT?"

"That one." Carlton pointed to the green house on the right with the brown shutters. He pulled the Land Rover to a stop next to the curb and turned off the ignition. "Ready?"

"I don't know." She stared out the window, unsure.

"Want me to wait here?"

She turned toward him. "Of course not. Why would you do that?"

He lifted his brows and smiled. "You deserve some time alone to get reacquainted. I thought—"

She shook her head. "No." She squeezed his hand. "I want you with me. We're a unit."

"Okay, baby." He took her chin in his hand and kissed her soundly. "I don't know what you're so worried about. It's going to be fine."

"I know. It's just been so long…" She looked back out the window.

He released her hand and she heard him exit the car. She watched as he rounded the hood, opened her door and helped her to the ground.

"Do I look okay?"

"You look fabulous."

She smoothed the material of her sweater and wiped her palms on her best jeans, a nervous habit. She wasn't wearing panties under the denim, but at least she wasn't dressed in a skirt. She needed some sort of protection today to ease her nerves. "Let's go."

Carlton took her hand in his and led her to the front door. He nodded for her to knock, and she did, although her hand felt like lead when she lifted it.

"I'll get it," a voice said from the other side of the door. A moment later, the door opened and a tall blond woman stood at the threshold, a huge smile on her face and the cutest baby in her grasp.

Margaret lowered her gaze from the woman to the baby. She smiled at the little girl, an exact clone of her mother, who was clearly not biologically this woman.

"Can I help you?"

Margaret lifted her gaze. "I'm an old friend of Leslie's from grade school and later high school. Her mom gave me this address."

"Oh. Well, come in." She opened the door wider without asking another question. "Les, someone's here to see you," she yelled over her shoulder. She turned her attention back to Margaret and Carlton as she shut the door. "Please sit down. If you can find a spot." She giggled. "Sorry about the mess. We have our hands full lately."

The living room was warm and inviting, and littered with toys of every shape and size. A small boy, older than the girl, sat on the floor, zooming a truck around his body in circles while he made tiny motor noises with his puckered lips. His blond hair lay in disarray across his forehead.

The blond woman, obviously the boy's biological mother, worked her way through the toys and shoved several off the couch. "There," she declared. "Please, sit. I'm sure Les will just be a second." She lowered herself into a rocker next to the couch and settled the baby against her chest, soothing the child with a hand on her back.

Margaret fought back tears as she and Carlton perched on the couch. Leslie was happy. She had a great life. She was clearly married to a wonderful woman and enjoying the entire package.

The woman rolled her eyes to the ceiling. "I'm so sorry. I haven't introduced myself. I'm Carrie." She tucked her chin to the baby and kissed her forehead. "And this is Maggie."

Margaret nearly choked. She grabbed Carlton's hand and squeezed, swaying into him. A tear slipped from her eye unbidden. Shit. She hadn't wanted to cry. She'd told herself over and over she wouldn't cry. But this sweet, unknowing Carrie had blindsided her.

"Oh." Carrie's eyes grew wide. "God." She stopped rocking. "You're Margaret."

Margaret nodded. She wiped her tear with the back of her hand.

Carrie's smile widened. "So nice to meet you. Les will be so happy."

At that moment, footsteps sounded in the hall. "Who is

it, Carrie?"

And then she was there, standing in the entrance to the room, looking better than ever. Her hair was longer. Her hips were rounder from childbirth. She looked fantastic. She grabbed the doorframe and leaned into it, never taking her gaze off Margaret. "Oh my God. Margaret. I can't believe it."

Margaret smiled. *Please, God, let her forgive me.* She finally cleared her throat and said the first thing that came to mind. "Leslie, I'm so sorry." She swallowed back emotion. "I've thought about you every single day of my life. I've wanted to find you and apologize for twelve years."

Leslie released the door to slip farther into the room. She made her way toward Carrie and perched on the arm of the chair Carrie occupied, setting a hand on the woman's shoulder. Maybe for moral support or maybe to make a statement. "Apologize for what, Margaret? You didn't do anything wrong."

Margaret sniffled. "I felt horrible that my parents whisked me away and I never even knew if you were alive." She choked on a sob, losing the battle to control her emotions.

Carlton wrapped his huge arm around her and held her tight. He squeezed her shoulder in support.

Margaret took a deep breath and continued. "I was fifteen years old. I should have fought them harder. Said something. Come to find you. I was only in the next town. A half hour away. I could have hitched a ride or walked even. God, Leslie. You look so happy."

Leslie smiled. She leaned into Carrie and kissed the

baby Carrie held. "I am. And you?"

"I am now." Margaret took Carlton's hand and squeezed it. "It's been a long time coming, but I'm healing."

"Your parents never came around?"

Margaret shook her head. "Took me twelve years to confront them and sever that vile relationship."

"God. That's awful."

"It's worse. My father and my uncle hired my cousins to attack us. I just found out a few weeks ago."

"Oh my God. Margaret. I'm so sorry."

"I'm so sorry it was my own family who attacked us. I'm still stunned. And you were hurt by my own flesh and blood."

"Margaret. It wasn't your fault. You shouldn't carry that sort of guilt. You aren't responsible for their actions."

Margaret gave her a wan smile.

"How are you doing with all this? It must be difficult. Especially if you just found out."

"I'm learning to live with it." She glanced at Carlton. "I have the most supportive boyfriend I could ask for." She turned back toward Leslie. "You were very hard to track down."

Leslie chuckled. "Yeah, my parents moved me also. So, see, you wouldn't have been able to find me even if you'd looked for me back then. Not only did we move a few months after you, but they changed my last name. They were extremely paranoid about us, not knowing who attacked us. How did you find me?"

Margaret smiled even bigger. "Your mom, actually.

When I learned my cousins had been the ones to attack us, a few months ago, the police contacted the precinct where our first case had been filed. There's no way to go back and apprehend my cousins after all these years. Some sort of statute of limitations, but the police had all the information about your name and address change so they could contact your parents in the event there were any developments in the case.

"I gave them my information and asked them to pass it to your mom."

Leslie beamed. "I'm so glad. She never said a word."

"Yeah, when she called me the other day, she gave me your address and said she would let me surprise you. I've never been so nervous. Your mom was always so nice. I miss her."

"I'm sure she'd love to see you. Both my parents are a huge help to us. They live a few blocks away. They help out tremendously with the kids. I'm so blessed."

"You are. I can see that." Margaret looked around, taking in the love scattered all over the room. "I wanted to see you. Know if you were okay."

"I'm better than okay. I'm perfect."

Even Carrie had a few tears.

Then Leslie confronted the elephant. "So, you're with a man?"

Margaret chuckled. "Oh, yeah. Sorry. This is Carlton. And yes. I'm with a man. We've been together three months. He's my first…man, that is."

"I always thought you were an either-or kind of gal." Leslie grinned. She looked at Carlton. "Nice to meet you.

You seem to love Margaret."

"With all my heart." He squeezed her closer and kissed the top of her head. Anyone would be able to see how he felt about her. He wore it on his face.

Leslie turned back to Margaret. "I'm so glad you found your way. And I'm so glad you found me. I've always wondered about you. I had no idea where to start looking. I tried several times when I was young, but didn't have the resources back then to do a thorough search. I've thought about finding you on social media, but I didn't want to upset your life by possibly dragging up memories you might have preferred to leave buried."

Carrie stood, easing the now-sleeping baby into Leslie's arms. "Can I get anyone anything to drink?"

Leslie took her wife's spot in the rocker and held the baby tight.

"We're fine," Margaret said. She moved to stand. "I don't want to disrupt your day. I just wanted to see…"

Leslie nodded. "I'm so glad, hon. So very glad. How far away do you live?"

"Not far. Half an hour."

"Let's get together then. It's hard with the kids these days, but my parents love an opportunity to babysit."

"That would be wonderful." Margaret's heart filled. Her friend was safe, happy and whole. Maybe she'd gone through some of the same stresses as Margaret over the years, but she'd come out in one piece on the right side.

Leslie stood. She walked Margaret to the door.

Carlton opened it.

Before Margaret stepped outside, Leslie reached for her

hand with her one free one and pulled her close. She hugged her tight, the baby squished between them. "Thank you," Leslie murmured.

Margaret nodded into her childhood friend. She couldn't speak again without bawling, so she turned and left the house, shutting the door behind her.

Carlton led her to the car, never releasing her hand. He helped her inside and then quickly rounded the front to climb in beside her. "You okay, baby?"

"Perfect." She leaned back into the seat as he started the engine and drove away. She let her eyes slide shut. "So perfect."

"Yes, you are, Maggie. Yes, you are." He took her hand as he drove. "It was chaotic there."

"Yes. But warm and inviting and...like a home. I felt the love as though it were vibrant in the air."

"It was. I felt it too." He squeezed her hand. "So many toys. I had no idea babies needed so much stuff."

Margaret giggled. She slid her gaze to him and watched his profile as he drove. "Was it that bad?"

"Nah. It was...kinda nice. Made me think."

She sucked in a breath. They'd never discussed kids in any fashion. Not other people's and certainly not their own.

"You want that kind of mess in our house one day?" He glanced at her.

"Umm." She didn't know what to say. Was he suggesting they have a baby?

"I mean, I'm fine either way, if you don't want kids. I'll live."

*He'll live? He'll live?*

"I'm just saying, if you do, I would be open to the idea."

Margaret fought back tears again for the tenth time that day.

He smiled at her, a quick glance and a wink. "I mean, you're already moody most of the time. How much worse could it be if you were pregnant?"

Her ears were ringing. Her chest pounded. And damn him. He kept driving. As though they weren't discussing the most important thing in her life. Their lives. "Carlton Fisher, pull this car over right now."

He chuckled, but he did as she said. And then he turned to face her. "What, baby?"

"Don't *what, baby* me. You can't nonchalantly tell a woman you'd be willing to have a baby with her and keep driving." She sat up straight and then moved so fast he wouldn't even know what hit him. She scrambled over the console and planted herself straddling his lap.

She took his face in both her hands and held it. "Did you mean it? You'd do that for me?"

"No." He grinned. "But I'd do that for us. I'm not going to be one of those absent fathers who waves on the way in the house and goes to his study to work all night. If that's what you were hoping, you'll need to find a different Dom."

She slapped his chest as he teased her. "Carlton. You can't just say shit like that. This is important."

He sobered and set his hands on top of hers. "Yes, it is, baby. And yes, I would like to have a baby with you. I've thought about it for a while. Seeing those sweet kids of your friend's and how happy they were made me go all mushy inside. And I don't do mushy."

"You've thought about it for a while?" Her pussy clenched. Damn him for making her horny with such a serious topic.

He shrugged. "A month or so."

"You've been thinking about having a baby for a month or so, and you didn't think to tell me this?" She pushed back an inch, but he wrapped his arms around her and hauled her closer instead.

"Well, I hadn't worked up the courage to get the first step in that equation covered yet, so it wouldn't have been prudent of me to charge that far ahead."

"Carlton, what the hell are you talking about? You're speaking in riddles. As far as I know, the first step is sex. We have that every day. If you wanted to have a baby, you would have needed to speak to me about not using birth control."

He shook his head. And then he jostled her on his lap, lifting her right thigh off his leg and bucking his hips up to reach into his front pocket.

Perplexed by his weird behavior, she watched as he pulled something from his jeans and twisted it in his hand until he held it between two fingers right in front of her face. "This first step."

Margaret couldn't breathe. She stared at the giant, glaring diamond ring in shock, afraid to reach out and touch it for fear it was an apparition.

"Will you marry me, Margaret Donovan?"

"Fuck." She couldn't even answer his question right. Stunned.

"That's not the answer I was hoping for, baby." He chuckled. "And you've cussed twice since we left Leslie's. Your ass is going to be sore for days. As soon as we get home, I'm going to make sure of that. Now, answer my damn question."

She lifted her gaze from the sparkling ring to his face. Emotion overflowed, threatening to take her under and drown her. Could a person drown in happy tears?

She nodded.

"I need a little more than that, baby. Maggie, will you marry me?"

"Yes, Sir. I will marry you." She squealed.

Carlton took her left hand and slid the ring into place.

It fit perfectly. She held it up in front of her face to see if it was real. "Oh my God." And then she hugged him to her, never ever wanting to release him.

"So about that birth control," he mumbled into her neck, nibbling a path to her ear.

"Stop it. I can't take more in one day. My chest is going to burst. I'm so damn happy." She lifted off him to meet his gaze. "Do you know how happy I am?"

"Nope. But you can show me. Later. On your knees. Your sweet ass burning and pink from all the cussing."

"Gladly, Sir."


*Two weeks later…*

CARLTON COULDN'T STOP smiling. He glanced at Margaret every few minutes where she sat perched at the bar in

Emergence, chatting with Jason and lifting her hand every few minutes to show off her ring, more for herself than for anyone else.

She'd told him she needed to remind herself often because she couldn't believe the luck she'd found.

He was working the front door tonight. Even with his woman all sexy as shit, sitting at the bar, giggling in a tone he could hear all the way to the door over the din of the club, he still hadn't learned to delegate very well. He loved his job, and he was good at it. Very little happened inside Emergence that he didn't know about, allow or condone. And he intended to keep it that way. Emergence had an excellent reputation for a reason, and he liked to think he had something to do with it.

Nevertheless, it was getting late. A tap on his shoulder had him leaning back to see who was there. One of his employees smirked at him and shook his head. "You're like a lovesick puppy. Go be with your woman. I've got this."

"You sure?" He didn't even care about the puppy remark.

"Go, man. If that were my woman, there's no way I'd be arguing with the staff about wrapping her in my arms."

Carlton narrowed his gaze at the man.

The guy laughed and rolled his eyes. "*If*, dude. Don't get all worked up. She's not mine, and I wouldn't dream of touching her. Go." He nodded toward the bar.

Carlton turned and left the guy standing there without saying another word or even thinking about the front door.

He wrapped his arms around Maggie from behind, hoping to surprise her. "Hey, baby," he whispered in her ear.

She didn't flinch. "I can sense you coming, you know. You can't sneak up on me." She smiled up at him, her eyes twinkling with happiness.

"I'm glad you can sense me *coming*, baby. That's a relief. Saves me from having to announce my orgasms."

"Ha ha." She wrapped her hands around his arm just below her breasts.

He slipped his fingers under the opening in her dress to fondle her nipple. "Are they sensitive yet?" he asked her, licking her ear. He emphasized his words by squeezing her breast, his entire palm circling the globe.

"What?" She giggled again.

God, he loved that sound. She had started making it a lot lately. A whole lot. More in the last two weeks than in the previous year and a half since he'd met her.

She squirmed and rolled her eyes up at him. "It's been like a week since I stopped taking birth control. It doesn't happen that fast. What's your rush? First you yank me to Vegas before I can catch my breath from the blinding ring you put on my finger, and then you start choosing baby names before any semen has had a chance to partner up with an egg. I think you've lost your mind."

"Hey, when I have a good thing, I want to make sure I keep it."

She straightened her face. "You don't have to do any-thing to keep me, Carlton. I'm here for the long haul. Ring or no ring. Last name or no last name. Baby or no baby. I'm the happiest woman alive. You don't need to do a damn thing to keep me that way."

He lifted an eyebrow and pinched her nipple again. "Did you just cuss at me, baby?"

She rolled her eyes again. "I might have, Sir."

"Do you like your ass pink?" He slid his free hand from under her breasts to down between her thighs, pushing her dress out of his way to reach her pussy. He stroked a finger through her folds, making her hitch her breath. He loved that sound. He also loved the way she lifted her sweet ass off the stool as he thrust into her.

He leaned closer and held her tighter. "Stay still, baby. You suck at learning this lesson."

She let her head fall back against his chest and her next words were breathy, ragged. "You're so distracting."

"That's my intention. That and having sex with you multiple times a day until your nipples hurt and your breasts get heavy carrying my child."

"You've been reading too many baby books." She moaned on the end of that sentence when he added a second finger to the first and dragged them both across her G-spot. "Can't we just go back to your office?"

"No, we cannot go back to my office," he mocked in a close approximation of her whiny voice. "First of all, you forget who's in charge here. And second of all..." He pressed his thumb against her clit. "...I want you to come right here for me first. Quietly. And without moving." He kissed her temple and then angled his head to take her lips briefly. "Think you can do that?"

"History would suggest otherwise." She moaned again, her head rolling on his shoulder.

Carlton pulled his hand out of her and released her

breast. Except for her leaning against his chest, he didn't touch her. He held his hands out in front of her.

"No, honey. Please..." She reached for his hands as though she were strong enough to force him to complete the deed.

"You want my cock inside you?"

"Yes," she answered breathlessly.

"Yes? That's it? Just yes?"

"Yes, Sir. Please, Sir. I need you. Please. I can't stand it."

"Hmm. What are you willing to do to get my cock?"

"Anything, Carlton. Please." She grabbed his wrists, tugging to no avail.

"Look at me."

She leaned her face back again and met his gaze with lowered lids.

"You'll sit here until you come without making a sound or moving a muscle. I don't care if it takes all night or halfway into next week. I don't care if you have five hundred noisy, wiggly orgasms before you master the task. Until you can manage that simple request, I won't let you move. Understand?"

She nodded, her eyes huge, her mouth hanging open.

"You believe me?"

"Yes, Sir."

She should. He'd never backed down on a threat. "You do that. You find a way to come to my specifications on this bar stool, baby, and I'll fuck you so hard in my office you won't be able to see. Got it?"

She nodded.

"And don't tempt me to spank you by letting out a string of cuss words. I know you like to be spanked."

Carlton stuck his hands back into the same places he'd had them a minute ago, one wrapped around her gorgeous tit, the other pressing into the sweet pussy she hid between her thighs.

He stroked her skin and then pinched and pulled on her nipple and her clit simultaneously.

She hitched in a breath, but otherwise didn't move. Her eyes rolled back in her head and she finally closed them. He let her have that, knowing it would help her concentrate if she didn't have to look at the people around them and wonder if they all "knew".

Not that it mattered. It was a BDSM club, but all the more reason to practice here. He wanted her to be able to come for him anywhere at any time. But she wasn't anywhere close to letting that happen yet.

But here in Emergence? There was no better, safer place for her to let herself go.

"That's it, baby. So good. So wet. So fucking hot." He tugged on her clit between his fingers and then smoothed them over the surface and rubbed.

She mewled, but not loud enough for anyone but him to hear.

"I'm going to slide inside you now. Brace yourself." He followed his words with a thrust of his fingers.

She held her face steady, scrunching up her nose, but otherwise not moving her body.

He stroked slow and easy, molding her breast and cupping her hot pussy. "Spread your legs wider, baby.

Nobody's looking. They all just think we're whispering to each other at the bar."

She complied, pulling her knees farther apart.

"That's it, baby. So submissive. Do you know how hard you make me when you obey me?"

She didn't answer.

He chuckled into her neck. "Very fucking hard."

She flinched when he hit her G-spot again.

"Easy." He grazed his fingers over the spot, praising her. "Still. You can do it. I know you can. Let the orgasm build. Don't fight it. Let it rush out of you. Just concentrate on your pussy and the pressure building in your belly." He stroked some more, knowing the signs she was getting close.

She fought, gritting her teeth together.

He was so proud. "That's my girl. So sexy. Are you close, baby?"

She didn't answer that question either.

He knew she couldn't. "So obedient. So submissive. I love you so much, baby." He thrust deeper. Nothing existed around him. He had no idea if the stools next to her were occupied or not. He didn't care. All he could see was his Maggie and the look of raw passion on her face. She might be able to come without moving her body or moaning her release finally, but she was fooling no one with her expression. Her entire face was lit up with unadulterated need.

He thrust harder, deeper, watching for signs she was about to come.

When her breath hitched, he knew it was time.

"So close. I'm so proud of you. I know you can do it. Come, baby. Come for me. Now."

Except for the smallest stiffening of her torso, the only thing Carlton could feel was the gripping pulse of Maggie's pussy around his fingers. He kept stroking her until the tremors subsided and he knew she was coming down.

And then he kissed her, taking her lips in a long, slow, sexy melting of mouths. He plundered every inch of her mouth, wanting to climb inside her and fuse their bodies together as one so she'd never be separated from him. Safe. Protected. Loved.

Finally, he released her lips.

She smiled at him, her eyes hazy with lust. "Did I pass? Will you please fuck me now?"

"Baby, I was going to fuck you no matter what. How long do you think I could have resisted?"

Her eyes widened. "You're cruel." She swatted at him, making contact with his arm.

"It worked, didn't it? Did you not just have the most glorious orgasm?"

She shook her head in dismay. "You're so cocky, Sir."

"Yes, baby. I'm cocky. Now please take my cock back to the office and let me fill your pussy with it." He lifted her off the stool and took her hand.

"What if I want to suck you off instead, Sir?"

He shook his head. "Not gonna happen. Maybe after I see those two pink lines on that pregnancy test, but not before."

"What's the hurry?"

He knew what she meant. He shrugged as he pulled her

into the back hallway and shut out the noises of the club. He pressed her into the door and took her face in his hands. "I'm not getting any younger, baby. And when I put my mind to something, I tend to go for it until I get what I want."

She pinkened, her skin flushing. "I'm glad I'm on that list."

"You're so totally on that list, baby." He kissed her again.

"And you're sure about this? You don't think we're rushing it?"

He paused and met her gaze. "Are *you* sure?"

"Never wanted anything so badly in my life. Now that I have you, I want to fast-forward to the perfect picture frame."

He stared at her, an idea forming in his mind. And then he quickly pulled her down the hall until they were secured in his office behind the locked door.

"What?" she asked. "What did I say?"

"I was just thinking I don't have enough pictures of you."

She shook her head. "Not this again. You took some of my nipples that day you put the clamps on for the first time."

"Yeah, well, now I need some more. Lower. To mark the day I got you pregnant." He pulled her dress over her head easily, leaving her awesome naked body open to his perusal.

"Lower?" she hedged, backing up a step.

"Yep. Lower." He backed her into the couch. "Sit.

Spread your legs. Hold them open for me."

She shivered as she obeyed him, grasping her knees from behind with her hands and holding her pussy open to his view. "Are you sure about this?"

"Very." He pulled his phone from his pocket. He stared at her for a moment first. "Do you know how sexy you are? Your pussy is swollen and red from your orgasm." He flipped to the camera and snapped several shots of her wanton pose before she could think about it further.

She moaned.

"Ah, you liked that." He set the phone down and climbed between her legs.

"If you tell anyone, I'll deny it."

He chuckled, taking her thighs and holding them open wider. He leaned in and kissed her pussy reverently. "Mmm. You smell so good. I want to eat you so bad."

She squirmed at his teasing.

"But I'm not going to." He stood and made quick work of losing his clothes. "I want to take you with my cock this time. And then, when you're full of my semen, I want you to lie there and hold it in while I wrap up things at my desk. Okay?"

"Yes, Sir."

"I have a good feeling about this."

"Me too, Sir." She stared up at him.

He knew two things. She wasn't referring to his ability to impregnate her tonight. Her good feeling was much deeper than that.

And secondly, they were both right.

# AUTHOR'S NOTE

Thanks for taking the time to explore my BDSM world. I hope you enjoyed this fourth book in the Emergence series. If haven't read the first three books in the series, I've included the links for the rest of the series: *Bound to be Taken, Bound to be Tamed,* and *Bound to be Tested.*

If you enjoyed my BDSM series and would like to try more of my BDSM, check out my Claiming Her series, *The Rules.*

## *The Rules* (Claiming Her, Book One)

*He has his rules. But she has some of her own...*

Amelia Kensington is ready to climb the corporate ladder. She finished her MBA and landed her dream job in downtown Atlanta. She has to work her way from the bottom up, but she's more than willing. Until she meets the owner of the company. In less than five minutes, her new boss manages to flip her world upside down with his panty-dampening mannerisms and shockingly good looks.

Cade Alexander can't believe his good fortune. The stunningly beautiful woman recently hired as one of his company's assistants is not only sexy as hell, but the perfect submissive. She doesn't know this yet, but he intends to show her. And he isn't a patient man. He means to lure her into his world with all haste. As a Dom, Cade has his rules. But the woman of his dreams isn't a pushover. She has her own rules.

Blending an average middle-class woman with the upper echelon isn't an easy feat. Cade's world may prove to be more than Amelia can tolerate. Some complications are insurmountable. Others are unforgivable...

*Bound to be Taken* (Emergence, Book One)

*She's theirs for a weekend. Will they be hers for a lifetime?*
Stephanie Parkins doesn't date—ever.

After years of watching her mother's antics, men are off her menu. But the truth is, now she needs one, and fast. Proving she's approachable is the only way her bosses will promote her to a position that requires her to work directly with the public.

Restaurateurs Aiden Collins and Dane Whitman need a date—now.

They're perfectly happy as a twosome, but without a woman on their arms, admission to this weekend's fetish party will be denied. For a while now they've had their eye on the sexy beauty from the tenth floor—even though she buries herself under a frumpy wardrobe. What better time to bring her out of her shell and add the third they've been craving?

When the three quite literally collide in the elevator, a miracle happens: she agrees to their proposal. And Stephanie turns out to be the submissive of Dane and Aiden's dreams. But as she slips deeper under their thumbs, she could be more than either man bargains for.

*Bound to be Tamed* (Emergence, Book Two)

*She's agreed to meet their demands…but can they meet her halfway?*

Stephanie Parkins has decided to take a chance.

After a whirlwind week under the tutelage of two hot Doms who make her feel more than she's ever experienced, she's taking up the ultimate exercise in trust: quitting her job to put herself completely in their capable hands. Even when it pushes her way beyond her comfort zone.

Aiden Collins and Dane Whitman have fallen hard and fast.

Their unexpected submissive presents them with a challenge of their own: to train her to embrace her new lifestyle in an atmosphere of security and safety. Even when it means hiding a shocking secret until the right moment presents itself.

Her Doms push, and sometimes Stephanie pushes back, with deliciously wicked consequences. But just as her red-hot learning curve reaches its peak, secrets from her past come to searing light. Threatening to send her running back to familiar territory—alone.

*Bound to be Tested* (Emergence, Book Three)

*The whip never leaves a mark. Love…that's another story.*

Lori Polluck has reshaped her kink from bottom to top.

In the two years since her Dom disappeared without a trace, she's transformed herself from perfect submissive to successful Domme. Her relationship with her submissive, Margaret, is…comfortable. Life is good. Until her past strides into Emergence, commandeers her scene, and turns her heart inside out.

Jude Cavanaugh can't change his past, but he can definitely take charge of his future.

A mission he can never reveal took him away from Lori, he thought for good. But a twist of fate has brought him back to his life, his town, his club. He plans to reclaim it all—including his woman. Sure, she's with someone else. Sure she's switched in every possible way. But the instant they touch, it's clear Lori is still his to control. And she doesn't like it one damned bit.

The road ahead will be rocky. Especially since Lori will just have to take it on faith that he won't skip out again. Because when nightmares turn real, they'll both need to show ultimate trust to survive.

# BOOKS BY BECCA JAMESON

**Wolf Masters Series**
Kara's Wolves
Lindsey's Wolves
Jessica's Wolves
Alyssa's Wolves
Tessa's Wolf
Rebecca's Wolves
Melinda's Wolves
Laurie's Wolves
Amanda's Wolves
Sharon's Wolves

**Arcadian Bears Series**
Grizzly Mountain (Coming April 11, 2017)
Grizzly Beginning (Coming Spring, 2017)

**The Fight Club Series**
Come
Perv
Need
Hers
Want
Lust

**The Underground Series**
Force
Clinch
Guard
Submit
Thrust
Torque
Saving Sofia

**Spring Training Series**
Catching Zia
Catching Lily
Catching Ava

**Claiming Her Series**
The Rules
The Game
The Prize

**Emergence Series**
Bound to be Taken
Bound to be Tamed
Bound to be Tested
Bound to be Tempted

**Durham Wolves Series**
Rescue in the Smokies
Fire in the Smokies
Freedom in the Smokies

**Wolf Gatherings Series**
Tarnished
Dominated
Completed
Redeemed
Abandoned
Betrayed

**The Art of Kink Series**
Pose
Paint
Sculpt

**Stand Alone Books**
Blind with Love
Guarding the Truth
Out of the Smoke
Abducting His Mate
Three's a Cruise
Wolf Trinity
Frostbitten

# ABOUT THE AUTHOR

Becca Jameson is the best-selling author of the Wolf Masters series and The Fight Club series. She lives in Atlanta, Georgia, with her husband and two kids. With over 50 books written, she has dabbled in a variety of genres, ranging from paranormal to BDSM. When she isn't writing, she can be found jogging with her dog, scrapbooking, or cooking. She doesn't sleep much, and she loves to talk to fans, so feel free to contact her through e-mail, Facebook, or her website.

...where Alphas dominate...

Email:
Beccajameson4@aol.com

Facebook:
facebook.com/becca.jameson.18

website:
beccajameson.com

twitter:
twitter.com/beccajameson

Newsletter:
beccajameson.com/newsletter-sign-up

Made in the USA
San Bernardino, CA
14 July 2019